SHIFTING SHADOWS

An Adam Alba Mystery

Book Two

JOSEPH ONESTA

Shifting Shadows

Joseph Onesta

Copyright © 2025 Joseph A Onesta

ISBN: 979-8-9872548-5-1

Library of Congress Control Number:

Pittsburgh, Pennsylvania

Integrity HPI

All Rights Reserved.

You Should Know!

The people, places, and events in this book are pure fiction and are a product of my early morning imaginings and a few too many cups of coffee. Any resemblance to real people, places, or events is completely coincidental (though if you think you recognize someone, feel free to keep it to yourself and feel special).

Of course, like any writer, I borrow flavors from life. I know two gay men who wrangle a pair of high-energy golden retrievers. They know who they are. Pittsburgh is my hometown, and yes, it's real—unapologetically so. Broken Arrow, Oklahoma, is also a real place. I've never been there, but I liked the name and sent Adam there in *Long Shadows*. It looks lovely online, especially the Ray Harral Nature Park. I hope to visit it someday.

And then there's the Mother of Sorrows Church. It was real until the Diocese of Pittsburgh sold it off and combined congregations. I grew up in that community. Just like Adam, I did time as an altar boy and a Boy Scout, the whole shebang. And yes, we really did sell pizza on Fridays. Like Adam's grandmother, my mother worked in the church's pizza kitchen for years.

So, while this story is fictional, it's seasoned with memory, curiosity, and a fond nod to the past. Hope you enjoy the ride.

Shifting Shadows

An Adam Alba Mystery

www.adamalbamysteries.com

Joseph Onesta

www.josephonesta.com

One

After his early workout, Adam returned to his room at the cheapest motel he could find. At first, it seemed like a bargain. From the outside and in the lobby, though dated, it was nice enough. The rooms seemed clean—until he decided to move the upholstered chair and look under the bed.

He grabbed a pair of socks and underwear from his duffel bag—so carefully packed that he didn't need to unpack it to find what he wanted. In the garish light of the bathroom, he kicked off his sneakers and stripped down, started the water flowing, and slipped into the torrent of hot water.

Plunging his head under the showerhead, he mentally followed the cascade of hot water as it traced over his toned, muscular body. At thirty-five, he kept fit using a rigorous series of wrestling drills and calisthenics to maintain his flexibility, agility, and strength. Moving slightly, he let the water massage his neck and shoulders, still sensitive from a recent fall.

There were two reasons he stayed in that questionable motel. It was the only affordable place within reasonable walking distance of his new job tending bar in the Creekstone Hotel. The other was simple. No bedbugs: he had checked thoroughly. Bedbugs would have been a deal breaker. He had just one more night there. Adam couldn't wait to leave.

Steam filled the bathroom and clung to the mirror above the sink as he soaped up his body and then rinsed off. He was thinking about moving into the townhouse he chose. It was the first time Adam had ever taken a lease on a space that wasn't furnished or shared.

The townhouse was bigger than Adam needed or wanted—two bedrooms and two and a half baths that would mostly sit empty. All he really needed was a bedroom and a bathroom. Still, it was cheaper than the motel, and it was close enough to work and affordable enough if he was careful. He figured once he got his footing, he'd take on a second job—not just to pad his wallet but to keep the shadows at bay.

Adam's sense of shadow, a fishbowl feeling of being observed, had nipped at his heels and, at times, crept up to his neck and shoulders, and had dogged him ever since the accident that ended his college career some sixteen years earlier.

After the accident, what had once been important no longer mattered at all, and some insignificant events had a portentous aura. Sometimes the shadow felt faint and barely noticeable. Other times it was dark and menacing. The shadow feeling would never completely go away. He accepted it as part of himself.

Adam braced himself and flipped the lever, switching to only cold water. At first, it felt shocking, but then as he pushed through, he could sense the wellness in his body, the familiar confidence and strength that he would carry throughout the day.

He moved often, chasing new places, new people, new challenges. It was all to keep him busy, to keep him from looking too long into the shadow that trailed him. It was as if he were a fugitive. For years, he tried to blur it with alcohol and reckless dares. Anything once was more than a motto; it was a lifestyle.

In time, he understood that numbing the shadow only gave it more room to grow. It would become larger and darker. Sobriety never made it disappear, but it gave him new tools to face it: his renewed fierce focus on wrestling drills, the discipline of focused calisthenics, and the quiet order of jigsaw puzzles, worked face down, demanding all his attention. And when these weren't enough, he packed up and moved again, chasing the distraction of newness.

The yearlong lease was more commitment than he had made since his sobriety. Adam wasn't about to waste time or money furnishing a place as big as that townhouse. A few essentials would do. He'd ease into it, necessities at first, picking up what he needed from thrift stores, and buying a bike to make his commute easier. When it came time to move on, as he knew it would, he'd just leave it all behind, sell it, give it away, or donate it.

The town, Broken Arrow, struck a bell for him. He had visited once, long enough to notice how it hovered between two worlds: the close congestion of a city, his last had been New Orleans, and the vast rurality of Ur. He wasn't sure yet if a sprawling suburb would be a good thing in the long run, but for now, it was perfect.

When Adam arrived at the coffee and sandwich shop halfway between his motel and the Creekstone hotel where he worked, the line to order was already snaking through the place. He helped himself to coffee from the refill station, settled into a seat, and raised his cup toward the counter to show he wasn't skipping out. The girl behind the register, recognizing him from his many visits over the past few weeks, gave him an easy wink.

He claimed a spot by sitting down on the booth side of a small two-person table with an empty chair across from him. He had plenty of time to wait. He didn't have to be at work for hours. Next to him sat a woman who was probably in her sixties. Her hennaed hair was cut in a bob that some might say was too young for her. She was engrossed in the tail end of a paperback novel. Adam noticed that one of her

3

sleeves was siphoning up melted butter from the plate of a half-eaten cinnamon roll.

"Excuse me, ma'am."

Her eyes darted to him. He pointed at her sleeve.

She looked down. "Shit!" She rolled her eyes, grabbing a paper napkin from a small stack she had on the table. She dabbed at the stain. "Thank you." She shrugged her shoulders. "It's worth it. These are the best cinnamon rolls in town. I go out of my way to come here."

"Maybe I'll try one after lunch. I'm just waiting till that line goes down a bit."

"Would you like the rest of this one? I didn't bite it. I cut it with a knife. I never finish them. Too much sugar. I'm diabetic, you see."

She was wonderfully friendly, pleasant, a kind of shining person.

"Why not take it home for later?" Adam smiled at her.

She laughed. "Oh, honey, it would never make it home. Take it. It's yours." She placed the plate with the cinnamon roll on his table.

Seeing that he didn't have much of a choice, he thanked her and asked her about the book she was reading.

"Do you like murder mysteries?" she asked.

He didn't want to say that there had been more than enough murder in his life in the last two years. Or that he wasn't much interested in cheesy murder mysteries.

"I like puzzles," he shrugged his shoulders.

"That's all they are anyway," she waxed on. "Oh, they aren't what they used to be. Some of them are just silly; others are too dark. This one engaged me despite the gruesome corpse on the first page. I hate that." She wrinkled her nose and shook her head. "Nope, for me, part of the fun is the setup, the characters, the environment, and trying to figure out how it all adds up and fits together."

It was remarkably similar to how Adam felt about jigsaw puzzles. At that moment, he liked her even more.

"I'm Stevie, by the way." She extended her hand.

Adam took her hand. "Stevie…like Stevie Nicks?"

She seemed flattered. Her hand was warm, and her handshake firmer than he expected.

"I'm—" He was about to tell her when she held up a hand with a ring on each finger, including the thumb.

"No, wait. Let me try." She closed her eyes, still moving her upheld fingers as if she were searching for something. "I'm getting an A. Is it Allen?"

"No."

"Albert, then."

"No. I'm Adam. Adam Alba." He expected her to say something like she knew it, but she didn't.

What she said was, "Adam Alba, huh! Lots of As." She appeared to consider. She spoke aloud to herself. "Well, Stevie, close but no prize this time." She beamed a smile.

"You did get the A, though," he encouraged her. He found her delightful.

"That's the easy part." Stevie reached for her purse and started digging through it. Finding a pen, she opened her book and inscribed the first page. *To Adam.* She underlined the A in Adam. *May all life's mysteries be as easy to solve as the one in this book.* She signed it. *Stella Vera Tramonto.* She placed the book on his table. "You take this, too. I've finished with it."

Adam watched her slide out of her seat. He felt uplifted. He opened the book and read the inscription, half expecting to see her phone number. Stella Vera, Stevie, he thought. Her last name meant *sunset* in Italian, and Stella Vera meant *true star*.

As she left the café, his mind flashed back to a memory. He was eight or nine and was walking with his grandfather up a blacktop road that wound around a hill. At the top of the hill, Adam was enthralled by the view of the city, but his grandfather sat down looking in the opposite direction toward the southwest.

He called for Adam to sit next to him. Wrapping his arm around his grandson, he pointed out the clouds brushed by the wind against a multicolored backdrop, everything seeming to point to the last edge of sun dipping behind the horizon. It was dramatic and beautiful. They watched the sunset as occasional breezes tossed their hair and ruffled their shirts.

Together they walked home along the dark blacktop road, moving from one lamppost circle of light to the next.

Adam breathed deeply and cut a piece of the cinnamon roll.

The Creekstone Hotel, a modest mid-range establishment that catered mostly to businesspeople and consultants with mid-level expense accounts, was busy and booked solid Sunday through Thursday. Deeply discounted rooms on Friday and Saturday nights kept the hotel running.

On weekends, the complimentary cook-to-order breakfast offered by the restaurant became a simple continental buffet in one of the conference rooms. The lounge stayed open in name only, staffed by inexperienced part-timers who served draft and bottled beer and the occasional shot, for which they had to use a jigger to measure accurately.

Adam's experience behind a bar had earned him the coveted Sunday through Thursday evening schedule, which meant a busier lounge, more patrons and better tips. The downside was that most patrons were hotel guests who charged their drinks and also their tips to their rooms. Cash tips were few, so Adam had to wait until he got paid to get his tips.

Adam arrived for work early enough to cool down in the lobby and freshen up in the men's room. He splashed water on his face and, undoing the buttons of his shirt, he used a gentle body spray just in case. The scent reminded him of his Nonno, his grandfather.

It was Thursday, and Adam was finishing his second week at the Creekstone. After he finished his shift at midnight, he'd have two free days to get settled into the townhouse.

At the sight of Adam walking into the lounge, Hector Garcia, a foreign college student from Venezuela who worked split schedules at the Creekstone, moving from front desk to lounge when needed, grabbed his backpack, shook hands with Adam and darted out to get to his evening class in Tulsa.

The lounge occupied a cozy corner of the lobby floor of the hotel. Enclosed by smoked glass walls, the lighting was subdued, indirect, and calming. Unlike the restaurant where customer turnover was key, the lounge cultivated patrons who lingered. The longer they lingered, the more they drank.

The lounge had only one patron, sitting in a back booth, clicking away at a laptop. After making sure he had everything he needed, Adam set about cleaning, tidying the bar, getting ice from the machine in back and checking the stock of well liquor and bottled beer. The Creekstone didn't hire barbacks.

Ready for the evening crowd, Adam tied up a trash bag and carried it out to the dumpsters behind the hotel. He pulled at the heavy metal door that blocked off the dumpster enclosure. It was hot to the touch and creaked in protest when he tugged it open.

He walked into the enclosure, lifted the cover of the dumpster and dropped the bag inside. Out of the corner of his eye, he glimpsed a woman's shoe peeking out from behind the dumpster. Thinking it was trash, he tried to pick it up and discovered that it was still occupied.

Posed awkwardly behind the right-hand dumpster, slumped back against the grimy cement wall of the enclosure, haloed by dried urine stains, was a woman he knew as Candy. Her eyes were slightly open as if she were about to fall asleep. She stared vacantly at something off to her left. The color had drained from her skin and settled in her hands, which lay at her sides, and in her legs, which were separated slightly in a less than ladylike pose. She wore a skirted business suit, a blouse with a high ruffled collar, and shoes with modest heels.

His heart sank into his gut. He could feel his own energy drain. She looked like a life-size doll, propped against the wall. Adam could see she was dead. Leaning cautiously behind the dumpster, he felt for a pulse at her neck just to be sure. Despite the heat radiating off the cement, she felt unnaturally cool and clammy. Cautiously, he backed away and out of the enclosure.

An all-too-familiar feeling of being watched crept up behind him and occupied him. The menace of that shadow feeling ran up his spine and triggered a quivering contraction in the muscles of his neck. They seemed to stiffen and then solidify. For a moment, he just stood there trying to pull himself together. He blinked. Unconsciously, he touched the cleft in his chin.

He knew he needed to do something but couldn't think what. She was beyond help; that was obvious. He blinked again slowly and looked back at the shoe sticking out from behind the dumpster. She was still there.

Adam could feel his guts harden, gaining weight as they did. Multiple emotions eddied and swirled inside him: anger, resignation, and just a bit of what some might call envy in the often-used but little-understood construction of "Why me?"

Candy was a regular patron of the hotel lounge. Adam supposed she was local because few people stayed at the Creekstone for more than a few days at most. She was nice, polite, and, as she had confided in him, sober. At first, he thought she frequented the lounge as proof of her decision to be free of alcohol. But all too quickly, he realized that she had other reasons for being in the lounge.

He never charged her for the seltzer and lime pseudo cocktail she sipped through a plastic swizzle stick. She tipped him well, and she had been good for business.

He felt sick. His heart raced, and a lump of nausea clogged his throat. He walked far enough away to breathe. It was summer. It was hot. The sun was pushing its way west, but the day wasn't cooling off.

He looked up at the windows of the hotel. Perhaps there actually was someone looking down on him. More than likely, it was all in his head. It didn't matter. It still felt the same.

He knew he had to report Candy's body to the police. At the thought of it, his first response was selfish. *I'll be in this up to my neck... again!* He closed his eyes for a moment, trying to clear his head. He used his cell phone to call Jenna, the food and beverage manager, his manager. She had just left for the day.

She answered. She was talking through the dashboard of her snazzy brand-new red Miata. The sound of traffic all around her. He could tell she had the top down.

"Jenna, this is Adam."

"T'sup, Adam?"

"You need to come back."

"Why?" she snapped.

"I just found a body out back." He could hear the screeching of brakes and the sounding of horns. He hoped he hadn't caused her to have an accident.

"Yeah, well, fuck you!" she shouted. "Sorry, not you, Adam. What a fucking asshole! Say that again. I don't think I heard you right." Jenna was a woman of extremes. She was beautiful, with a perfect body, sophisticated and elegant, and she could stand in stilettos for hours, but when she was off duty, she was a different person—brash, rough, and kickass. Adam liked both sides of her.

"I said I just found a dead body out back." He raised the volume of his voice, hoping that it would help.

"Holy fuck! Where?" There was a little more curiosity in her voice, but she still sounded pissed off.

"Behind the dumpster. There's no one in the lounge, and I'll have to wait here."

There was a moment of silence, as if she were deciding which Jenna would be proper in the situation. In the end, a little of both. "Anybody we know?"

"Candy." Anyone who ever worked the evening shift in the lounge knew Candy.

She paused again, took a deep breath, and sighed loudly. "Oh fuck, I'm turning around." Was it disappointment, anger, or resignation in her voice? "I'll call Cody Biggs. He's the manager on duty. Have you called the cops?"

"As soon as we hang up. I called you first."

She hung up without another word.

Adam dialed 911. He reported finding the body.

"Is she breathing?" the operator asked.

"No, she's dead. She's not breathing. She is cold and there is no pulse."

She instructed Adam not to touch anything but to wait there for the police. She meant to keep him on the phone but when the duty manager exited the back door of the Creekstone, without thinking, he hung up on her.

Cody Biggs looked nothing like a man named Cody Biggs. Adam recognized him only because Jenna had pointed him out on the day she offered him the job. Biggs cut a striking image. In his early twenties, Adam figured he was a kid who just graduated with a degree in hotel and restaurant management, or someone's nephew, or both. He had a slight build and a tanned, smooth face that looked like it still was carrying some baby fat. His straight frosted hair swept around his head like a bully had tried to flush him headfirst down the toilet.

"You're Adam?" Biggs asked as he approached. "The new mixologist, right?"

"Yes, sir." The sir was automatic. The kid was a manager after all. "I'm really just a bartender," Adam admitted truthfully, and he hoped Biggs knew the difference.

Biggs nodded. "I'm Cody Biggs. What's going on?"

As Adam described finding the body, he watched the color behind Biggs' tanned skin drain away, only to be replaced with a queasy expression on his face. The sight of him calmed Adam down. Someone needed to be clear-minded, and this manager was not going to be helpful.

"Would you like to see for yourself?" Adam asked, though he already knew the answer.

Biggs' eyes bulged. "I don't want to see it. I never saw a dead body before," Biggs admitted. "What are we supposed to do?"

Adam felt like correcting him. Candy was a she, not an it. "I already reported it, and I have to stay here until the police get here."

"I guess I should stay here, too?" He really had no idea what to do.

Adam decided to be kind to him. "You're welcome to do so. Fair warning, though. If you stay, they'll show you the body. You won't have much of a choice. They'll ask if you know her and a lot more questions. You wanna go through that?"

He paled again. "No."

"Then may I suggest you find someone to pour drinks until Jenna gets here. They're going to keep me for a while, and there may be patrons in the lounge. You'll probably still have to answer questions, but at least not in the presence of the body."

Adam watched him think. The sound of a police siren cut through the air and was getting louder.

"Good thinking," he said and fled back inside.

Seconds later, a patrol car angled into the area behind the hotel. The light on the roof of the car continued to flash as the officers got out. The driver got out first. He was thin, wiry, and energetic. The other officer, a middle-aged man with more around his waist and less on top of his head, followed more slowly. The younger cop called as he approached. "In the dumpsters?"

Adam nodded. The older man greeted Adam. "Mr. Alba?"

"Yes. Adam Alba." He offered his hand.

"Sergeant Riley, you might want to see this." The younger officer called from the front of the dumpster enclosure.

The older officer nodded to him and excused himself from Adam. "Just a second, Mr. Alba. I'll be right back."

They both took inventory of the scene. Riley, the older officer, was clearly the senior partner. He might have lost some of the enthusiasm of the younger one, but had replaced it with composure. "Tape off the crime scene, Terry. Nice and wide. Block the alley. Then radio in the details. We'll need the ME and a CSU."

Returning to Adam, he led him some distance away while Terry followed orders.

"Were you the first one to find her?"

"As far as I know." Adam glanced at the name on the older officer's uniform. "Officer Riley."

"How long ago?"

"Five or ten minutes ago. I called it in right away." Adam looked absently at his watch. It was almost quarter to five.

"How did you know she was dead and not merely injured?"

Was that a trick question? Adam searched for a way to answer without sounding like a smart-ass. Police officers didn't often take well to smart-asses, and this one had the power to ruin Adam's life for the next twenty-four to forty-eight hours. The Pittsburgher in him would have wanted to say something like, "Call it a hunch. The same reason you didn't rush in there to perform CPR." Instead, he shrugged his shoulders and answered calmly. "She looked dead. I tried to feel for a pulse, but there was none, and she was cool."

"Tell me exactly what happened."

"I was taking out some trash when I noticed a shoe. I thought it was trash, so I tried to pick it up, but she was still wearing it. I tried to be careful to feel for a pulse."

Riley tilted his head toward the dumpster enclosure. "There's a chain and padlock on those doors. Were they locked?"

"No. They were closed but not locked." He looked over at the doors. He had left them open.

The younger officer was stringing crime scene tape around the dumpster area.

"Did you touch anything else?"

"Not today. Just the door, the dumpster top, and her shoe." Adam answered. "I braced myself on the back wall to lean in to feel for a pulse." Adam looked back at the enclosure.

"Do you know her?"

"I recognize her. I've only been in town a couple weeks."

"Do you know her name?" He took a small notebook out of his pocket.

"Candy."

"Candy," he wrote. "That's short for?" he asked.

"Not sure. I only know her as Candy."

His eyes met Adam's. "How do you know her?"

"I don't *know* her. I *recognize* her." He emphasized the distinction. "She was a regular in the lounge."

"How regular?"

"She's been in every night that I've worked here. That's only two weeks but... still."

The young officer finished with the tape, and the radio in the car sounded. He ran back to the car.

"Was she a guest of the hotel?"

14

"I don't think so, but I don't really know for sure." Adam wanted to be clear.

"Did she charge things to her room or pay with a credit card?"

Adam felt himself getting agitated. If she had charged her drinks to her room, he would have known that she was a guest. Adam couldn't figure out if Riley was slow or just trying to trip him up. He reckoned it was the latter. "Not while I was on duty, sir." He repeated the reason for his ignorance. "Like I said, I've worked here only two weeks. When I was on duty, she never paid at all."

"You mean other people bought her drinks?"

"Sometimes, but she only drank seltzer with a lime wedge. I don't charge patrons for a glass of water."

Terry, the young officer, loped past them. To Riley, he said, "ME is on the way."

The older cop nodded. Then to Adam. "You were saying?"

Adam had finished speaking, but decided to add, "She tipped me in cash."

"Let me get this straight." The officer was looking skeptical and, at the same time, was catching on. "She was a regular in the bar. She didn't drink. And she tipped you—in cash."

"You got it."

"Did she meet friends?"

"I don't know whether she knew anyone or planned to meet them. She *made* friends easily enough. She was very sociable." Adam was trying to be discreet, and the officer sensed it. He cut to the quick.

"She was a hooker?"

"I never saw money change hands."

"Mr. Alba. Let's be frank here. It will help us to know the context of what has happened."

Adam looked him in the eye. "Okay. I really don't *know*, but that's what it looked like to me."

"You didn't feel the need to report this?"

"Report what to whom? I wasn't going to follow her around to see what she was doing."

"A manager or a supervisor might be a start."

Adam wanted to clam up. Jenna knew of Candy, and she likely knew what Candy was about. But they had never discussed her. Jenna wasn't stupid, but Adam didn't know what Jenna did or did not know.

"This hotel caters to businesspeople, mostly men who are here for a night or two. There are very few women who come into the lounge." He shrugged his shoulders. "Candy was popular. I'm only guessing she was a hooker. If she was, she was discreet. She never caused a fuss. Never openly flirted with anyone. She wasn't bouncing on anyone's lap. She didn't even dress like a hooker. She wore business suits."

"Okay, Mr. Alba. You seem like an observant guy. Why don't you tell me what you *observed* about her interactions in the lounge? It might help."

Adam smiled at that and composed his thoughts. "She came in regularly, between seven and seven-thirty each night."

Riley looked surprised. "She's early today."

"I suppose someone might wear the same clothes two days in a row." Adam shrugged.

"These are the same clothes she had on last night?" Riley started writing something in his notebook.

"She always dressed in business suits, skirt and jacket, but I remember that blouse, the little ruffles around the collar. A high collar. No flash. No cleavage. All class."

"I see. Did she ever come on to you?"

"No. But to be accurate, I don't think she ever *came on* to anyone. If anything, they came on to her."

"Did she tip you last night?"

"Yep. Twenty bucks." The image of the fan-folded twenty-dollar tip lying on the bar mat flashed in his mind.

"Small price to pay for free drinks," Riley said.

Adam wondered about the editorializing. His tone seemed to have some suggestions of malfeasance behind it. He chose, however, to ignore it, waiting for Riley to continue.

"You've worked here for two weeks. Where was your last job?"

Now Adam felt his defenses rise and his shadow creep up his spine. He wanted to say it was irrelevant or that it was none of his fucking business, but he knew if he overreacted, he might spend time in a holding cell. Rubbing his chin, he breathed deeply and said, "I spent the last couple months in a small town called Ur. Before that, I tended bar in New Orleans."

"So, you move around a lot."

Adam held his tongue and casually shrugged his shoulders.

"Anything else you can tell me about this woman?"

Adam wanted to just end it there, but knew that the more he could say, the more questions they would have. But he didn't want Candy to end up just being another dead hooker to the police. He ran a tongue under his lower lip. "She was incredibly careful. She never took a drink from anyone's hand but mine. If a patron wanted to buy her a drink, no matter what they asked for, I'd make her seltzer with lime and hand it to her myself."

"Why did you do that?"

"Gallantry, I suppose. Lots of women are cautious about accepting drinks from strangers. I'm sure you've heard about Rohypnol. The first night I worked here, she sat at the bar, introduced herself, told me she was sober and had to be careful about what she drank. She asked me to never give her alcohol of any kind."

"That seems an unusual thing to do, doesn't it? A little too much information, don't you think?"

"Not to me. People talk to bartenders, especially if the bar isn't busy."

Candy had the air of someone who had successfully begun pulling her life together and was keeping momentum the best she could. Adam knew that feeling, had experienced it himself, and recognized it in her. He suspected she had somehow recognized it in him as well. He'd be her ally. He respected her. It was as if, despite their never having met, they had recognized the kindred spirit in one another. When she entrusted him with the information about her sobriety, he wasn't surprised. It was as if he had known it all along.

Riley editorialized again. "A sober drunk hanging out in a bar. Will wonders never cease?"

A classy black jaguar parked just outside the police tape. Adam imagined the Jaguar belonged to a medical examiner or coroner. The younger officer called to Riley, and the older raised a finger to wait.

Out of a corner of his eye, Adam noticed a news van stop in the middle of the alleyway. He turned his head toward them. A cameraman and a reporter climbed out. The reporter, a small woman with wavy blonde hair, walked toward the cordoned-off area.

The senior officer followed Adam's gaze and, seeing the approaching reporter, muttered, "What fresh hell is this? Damned police scanners." He left Adam and headed toward the reporter. Adam watched as he gestured to her to stop.

Riley began speaking with the reporter, and Adam noticed the man with the camera aimed it at the officer. They were going to get their footage no matter what. Adam wanted no part of it. He figured that not wanting to be on the news was sufficient justification to leave the scene. Riley had all the information he needed to find him if he had further questions.

As he stepped away, Adam tried to be discreet without appearing stealthy. Sensing the back door to the hotel was a little too conspicuous and going that way ran the risk of his being stopped, he quietly backed up and stepped behind the enclosure. If someone came after him, he could always say he thought the interview was over.

The young officer, Terry, hadn't cordoned off the area behind the enclosure. As he passed behind it, Adam was tempted to lurk for a brief moment. He could hear the ME mumbling either into a recorder or his cell phone, making notes. Between ME jargon and the low volume of his voice, Adam couldn't discern what he was saying.

As he moved toward the corner of the building, his body felt stiff and on edge. Unconsciously, he watched his step, his eyes scanning the ground. His gaze landed on something that looked like one of those pen-style injectors diabetics discreetly used in restaurants. It lay alongside the back wall of the enclosure.

He froze. The gears of his mind cranked. It took him a full minute to process and decide what to do. It could have been completely unrelated. It might have just been a bit of loose trash. Then again, it could have been important. It could have been evidence. Adam knew he had to tell them.

He retraced his steps, and his movement caught Terry's attention. Adam signaled.

"I think there's something you should see."

Terry's eyebrows raised. Adam led him to the syringe. "I haven't touched it. It may be nothing, but it might be something. I just wanted to point it out to you."

"Sarge!" Terry called.

Two

Adam's mind played a montage of images of Candy in the lounge, snippets of conversation with him or overheard with others and the friendly acknowledgment of his understanding as she slid a sizable cash tip onto the bar mat, winking as she left. These memories interlaced and flashed around that now central image of Candy, propped against that filthy wall, haloed by the stains on the cement blocks of the dumpster enclosure.

Propped, that was the right word. Her position didn't look natural. It wasn't as if she had snuck behind the dumpster for a moment of solitude and just passed away. Given how meticulously she dressed, he couldn't imagine her going anywhere near those dumpsters. Somebody either made her go there or put her there, and Adam thought the latter more likely.

When he saw the syringe and pointed it out to the police, for a second he wondered if her death was drug-related until he heard the ME narrate into his recorder that the syringe was for insulin. Then he wondered if Candy had been diabetic.

Without any hope of sneaking away, whether it was because he felt that he was somehow getting in the way or he just wanted to leave, Adam caught the attention of Riley.

"I'm heading back to work unless you need me for something specific. I'll be in the lounge until midnight, and you have all my contact information." Adam presented his case for leaving.

Riley just nodded in response. Adam knew it wasn't an endorsement or even permission. He left all the same.

As Adam rounded the back corner of the hotel, the pressure of an assumed but unseen gaze was replaced with a wave of heat. The parking lot dotted with rental cars was to his right, and the western wall of the hotel, pulsating with heat, rose three stories to his left. This side of the hotel was well-maintained but plain and functional. There was a side entrance to the building, but it required a room key to open. It led through a corridor of first-floor rooms.

Between the direct rays of the sun and the heat radiating off the wall of the hotel, it felt like stepping into an oven. He'd been outside in the sun now for more than an hour. It wouldn't do to go back to the lounge dripping with sweat.

He increased his pace, winding around the front corner of the hotel and making a beeline for the shaded portico where taxis and airport van services dropped off and picked up hotel guests.

A group of airline crew members, prim in their uniforms, stood just inside the automatic sliding doors, each with a hand on an extended luggage handle. Several airlines used the Creekstone for overnighting flight crews, but seeing them in the afternoon was rare. He passed through the group.

In the lobby, the hotel kept a large glass water dispenser filled with water laced with citrus slices and ice cubes. He filled a plastic glass and downed it, sensing the cold liquid spread through his torso like branches of a tree. He filled another glass and drank it down again. He watched the flight crew file out of the lobby into an airport van.

Before going back to the lounge for the second time that day, he first ducked into the restroom to freshen up. By six o'clock, his constant five o'clock shadow looked like a cultivated two-day beard. It suited his strong jaw, cleft chin, and dimples when he smiled.

Adam still turned heads. Eight years of his youth wasted on hard living hadn't erased the gifts of his southern Italian heritage; his dark hair, an athlete's frame, and captivating blue eyes. As a teen, he had luxuriated in positive attention. More than his looks, other kids, their parents, his teachers, everyone, thought of him as the nicest young man. He had a knack for making people feel seen and valued. He fit in everywhere.

After his accident, he sank into a hedonistic vortex, trading charm for the comfort of a drink, and companionship for a place to stay, sometimes for a few days, sometimes a month or two. Sometimes it was just for the night. He knew he wasn't himself. He'd used people without apology, burning through eight years chasing the relief of numbness.

Eventually, he realized that he wasn't really surviving but merely treading water, not swimming to shore, not getting anywhere, just day by day growing more tired, more cynical and less the man he wanted to be.

Having learned his lessons, he never judged anyone who was still clawing their way out of that kind of life. He couldn't. He respected them. Sometimes folks had to do whatever they had to do to put their lives back together. He'd been there. He well remembered how hard it was to free himself from the quicksand of despair.

He used the forced air hand dryer to make sure his face, hands, and armpits were dry. He examined himself in the mirror, adjusted his clothing, and combed his hair with his fingers. Reasonably satisfied with his appearance, he headed toward the lounge.

His mind automatically returned to finding Candy. He consciously interrupted the thought, replacing it with Stevie Tramonto, the woman who loved cinnamon rolls and murder mysteries. It lightened his mood, not completely, but enough.

The lounge was next to the restaurant and occupied a corner of the lobby enclosed in smoky glass with subdued lighting. The bar itself had only five stools for lone riders. Most patrons opted for one of the small tables. A few more secluded booths were toward the back.

Jenna stood back at a slight distance from the bar rail; her hands clasped in front of her. She never leaned, never really seemed to relax at work. She stood erect, poised, and posed. She could have been a girl from finishing school, balancing a book on top of her head. When she sat down, it was with an uncommon degree of elegance. She was beautiful, with light brown, almost blonde hair, wonderfully proportioned, a sharp dresser, and a crack food and beverage manager.

When she saw Adam, she threw a smile that turned into a grimace. He understood her completely. She was glad he was back. She wanted to leave. She imagined how he must have felt finding Candy's body. She worried that it would freak him out entirely and cause him to quit. He was an asset that she didn't want to lose.

"How was it?" she asked as he slid past her.

"Pretty grim. I imagine there will be more questions. It's an unexplained and unattended death. There will be an investigation."

She took a deep breath. "Are you okay, Adam?"

"Yeah. It's sad, though. She seemed like a nice person." His voice was low, hushed, like it would be in a funeral home.

Jenna nodded. "You have to respect someone like Candy. Life can't have been easy for her."

"Respect is a good word," he said. "I'd use it, too… respect." He wondered how much Jenna knew about Candy, other than she was a lounge regular. After finding Candy's body, he didn't want to encourage the conversation, not now, not yet. All he wanted to do was get on with his job.

Thankfully, Jenna didn't ask for details, not about the body or the cops. "Still, she said, "I hate to admit it, but better you than me. I don't know if I could have held my composure. Are you sure you're going to be alright?" she asked.

"Yeah, no problem." He sounded more dismissive than he intended, but it got the reaction he wanted.

As she left, she stopped, turned around, looked him in the eye and said, "Call me if you need anything." Her voice was more compassionate than he expected. There was yet another side to Jenna. He smiled at her.

The shift kept him busy. By seven-thirty, the lounge was packed, and there was a steady sequence of patrons buying rounds at the bar. The time went quickly. Thursdays were often busy. Most of the hotel guests would be checking out in the morning. For many consultants and traveling businesspeople, Thursday evening was the new Friday night, the night to relax and let your hair down. He thought of Candy. He missed her.

Shortly after seven-thirty, a customer caught Adam's attention. Standing at the bar, androgynous—short hair, stocky build, and features that could belong to either a woman dressing like a man or a man with softened edges. In these days of pronoun preferences, Adam wasn't sure how to address the patron.

"Good evening. What can I get for you?"

"Do you have Diet Coke?" Their speech was clipped and sounded deliberately masculine.

"Yes," he offered.

"I'll have a Diet Coke then, please."

Adam served up the drink. The patron paid in cash, leaving a sizable tip. The patron went to a far table and sat down with their back to the wall.

Every now and then, when there was a free moment, Adam glanced at the patron. Though he didn't normally do table service, his curiosity got the better of him. Twice he brought a fresh glass of Diet Coke, asking if he could get the patron anything else. Both times the offer was refused.

Only a few customers remained at the last call. Adam busied himself preparing to close. He collected and washed glasses, wiped down the bar, straightened the top-shelf liquors, and restocked the cooler and the well. When it came to taking out the trash, he could feel his heart beating in his chest. As he approached the back door, he noticed a remnant of torn police tape. *They must be done out there*, he thought.

He pushed the door open and stepped out into the night. A bright floodlight now illuminated the area. He couldn't remember if it had been there before. It cast a harsh light. He looked up at the guest room windows. Blades of light cut through closed curtains in a couple of them, but most were dark.

The enclosure doors were wide open, and new dumpsters had replaced the old ones. He wondered if the crime scene techs were spending the night going through the hotel's trash. He dropped the bag of trash into a new dumpster and went back to the lounge with the image of Candy, slumping against the wall, burning in his memory.

When Adam got back to the lounge, it was empty of patrons. A ghostly feeling came over him as he picked up a fan-folded twenty-dollar bill from the bar.

Three

When Adam finished his workout, he took time to sit cross-legged, eyes closed, and focused his attention on his breathing. He watched it deepen and slow. He was conscious of the slowing of his heart rate and the tensing and relaxing of his muscles. He had a long day ahead of him, and he wanted to be in the right mindset.

His brief meditation was interrupted by the approach of a dog, panting. He could hear the voice of the owner calling her. "Lacey, Lacey, no!" The dog sniffed Adam's legs, and Adam opened his eyes. She was a large golden retriever; one of a pair he recognized from the park.

"It's okay. She's friendly. Lacey, come back here," he heard the voice call. Her owner was running along, another golden retriever running with him. "I'm so sorry. The leash just slipped out of my hand."

Adam grabbed the leash and stood up. "No problem," Adam said. "I've seen you or the other guy walking these two every morning. They look like a handful." He handed the leash over to Lacey's owner.

"That's Will. I'm Jason. These two forever puppies are Cagney and..."

"Lacey," Adam finished the pair. "Like the TV show. I'm Adam." He handed the leash over to Jason.

"Nice to meet you, Adam. I'd shake your hand, but I've been picking up, well..."

The dogs were tangling their leashes around Adam's legs. He laughed, reached down, and petted both dogs. He watched them continue on their way before returning to the motel.

Adam checked out early on Friday morning. His duffel packed tight, his rucksack over his shoulder, it felt good to be out of that room and on the move. He'd have one last stop at the coffee shop before he moved.

He decided to splurge on an Uber from the coffee shop to his new apartment complex. Adam would have otherwise enjoyed the walk. It was still cool enough, but he had a long list of things he needed to do. He would pick up the key to his place and drop off his things before heading out to the thrift and discount stores that he had mapped out. The Uber decision gave him time for a cup of coffee, probably his last cup at his favorite coffee shop.

He had two lists on his phone: *must-haves* and *would-likes*. The *must-haves* were simple enough and could fit into his rucksack. They were mostly things for the kitchen and bathroom. He could sleep on the floor until the *would-likes* could be found. Most of those he would need to rent a truck or a van to get home, unless, of course, delivery was reasonably priced.

The enticing aroma of freshly baked bread, rolls, and pastries enveloped him as he pulled open the glass door of the coffee shop. The line to order almost reached the front door. He had to be careful to maneuver his bags so that he didn't clip anyone as he passed through the crowd.

Adam quickly scanned the tables for somewhere to place his bags while he got a cup of coffee. A multi-ringed hand, bangles jingling on her wrist, caught his attention and beckoned him. Stevie Tramonto sat at the same table she had the day before, her face beaming with delight.

He set his duffel on the floor and balanced the rucksack on the chair across the table next to her. "What a pleasant surprise!" His smile was genuine enough to reveal the beginnings of crow's feet at the corners of his eyes. "Let me get my coffee. I'll be right back."

Adam was glad to see her. He had thought of her several times the day before. The memory of her easy, pleasant demeanor had been an effective counterbalance to finding Candy's body. *Sometimes,* he thought, *you need to remind yourself that the world is not as ugly as it appears.*

She nodded and called after him. "Don't buy a cinnamon roll. You can take this half off my hands."

Again, she had lifted his spirits. Adam felt connected to her, as if he had known her before. That feeling of connection was rare for him. Despite the efforts of family, friends, and even some strangers, Adam often felt alone.

His only permanent ties were his sister and grandfather back in Pittsburgh as well as his nephew, Jake, who was traveling through the country in a van with his friend, Julian, on a gap-year adventure. He enjoyed their YouTube channel, *Jake and Julian's Big Adventure*. They were the only recurring characters in his life, and they were far away because he was always somewhere else.

There were moments when people surprised him. Rosie, the owner of the Pioneer's Rest back in Ur, had sat all night in a chair on his first night in the hospital and had been both attentive and generous during his recovery. He smiled to himself as he thought of her and Henry sitting with him, and Bax, the police sergeant, visiting him daily.

Most people were friends of circumstance. Such ties are as important as they are temporary. The sense of the temporary nature of life had become part of the way he experienced the world ever since his accident. Stevie was different. She seemed to be a missing piece in the puzzle of his life.

Setting his coffee down, he moved his rucksack and sat with her.

"Is today laundry day?" She eyed his duffel bag. "Or are you on the lam?"

Adam furrowed his brow. "On the what?"

"On the lam. It means running away, like a fugitive from the law or something. Oh, my stars, that would be exciting! A fugitive in the coffee shop."

"Nothing that romantic. I'm moving into a new apartment today.'

She wrinkled her nose. "Why didn't you just leave these things in the car?"

He shrugged. "I don't have one. Anyway, this is all my stuff."

She froze. "You're joking."

"He shook his head. "I don't need much."

She accepted the statement on face value. They chatted amiably while Adam indulged in half of her cinnamon roll and scheduled his Uber ride. When the Uber driver was minutes away, not wanting the visit to end, Adam suggested they exchange numbers.

Stevie didn't hesitate. "I was going to insist. Adam, you are my newest old friend. I hope you don't mind."

"Not at all, Stevie. I like that. My newest old friend."

As he walked away, Stevie called after him. "Enjoy your new roommates."

Turning around, he looked at her. "I don't have roommates."

She seemed confused. "Oh, really? Huh! I guess I'm wrong again." She winked.

Adam spent hours in thrift stores carefully fitting essential purchases into his rucksack. A secondhand bike in surprisingly good condition made getting around easier, even with the now heavy rucksack on his back. A discount furniture store had sold him a few pieces of furniture—a bed, a nightstand, a couple of lamps, a table, and a chair. He planned on renting a truck later that day or the following day to pick them up.

Adam was sincerely hungry. It was just after one, and the parking lot of the Moonstone diner was full. It had been almost two months since he last patronized the establishment in the company of Sergeant William Baxter, hoping to extract some information from the ex-con cook, Elf, who was working his way through Bible school.

The server was the same. Her name was Brooke. She was a matronly-proportioned woman with a pile of blonde hair on the top of her head. She recognized him. "Only have the counter at the moment, honey." Then she turned her head toward the service window. "Elf, your friend is back."

Brooke was a warm and gregarious person. She wasn't as flirty as Rosie had been back in Ur, but the occasional teasing remark could be heard when she was at a table of regulars. With her strong memory and ease of conversation, she would have made a good therapist. Adam had little doubt that she probably served that function for some of their regular customers.

The backwards baseball cap behind the service window rose, and a pair of eyes peered over the sill. Elvin Lawrence Flemming was probably standing on his tiptoes to see into the main dining room. His initials spelled Elf, and the nickname suited him. He was short, thin, and pixyish. He was about thirty, but until you got close, he looked like he was half his age. His brows raised as their eyes met, and Adam threw him a quick wink in reply. Though Adam could only see his eyes, they smiled back at him.

Adam took the stool farthest along the counter, next to a small booth where a man sat wrapping cutlery with paper napkins in little bundles. He wedged his rucksack next to the back of the booth, standing it on end and steadied it with his leg. The thrift store pot and pan he had bought clanged slightly on the two plates and the mismatched pieces of cutlery he needed for his kitchen. He had wrapped the plates and cups in towels and bed linens when he packed the bag, but they must have shifted as he pedaled to the diner. He hoped nothing had broken.

It was almost two in the afternoon, and the smells wafting from the grill and fryer were enticing. Adam's stomach growled in answer to the call.

"Do you know what you want, or do you want to look at the menu?" She smiled and pointed at the menu that was wedged between a napkin holder and a bottle of Heinz ketchup.

"A cheeseburger and fries," he said.

"Onions? Pickles?" she asked.

"The works," Adam said.

"And to drink?"

"Coffee and water."

She scribbled his order onto her pad, ripped off the page, and slid it onto the stainless-steel ring where orders were displayed. As she poured his coffee, Brook said, "Elf says he'd like to eat with you if you can wait for him for about fifteen minutes."

"That would be great. Happy to wait for him." Adam had liked Elf from their first meeting back in Ur. In their few interactions, Elf had proved himself to be a genuine soul and a man of integrity as strong as his faith.

As he waited, he sipped his coffee. The sound of idle chatter, occasional laughter, and the chalk-on-blackboard sound of cutlery on ceramic plates nearly drowned out the 1950s music. New to the diner since his last visit were little tabletop jukebox selectors where patrons could choose the music they wanted to hear.

The day was going well. In just two thrift stores he got all his necessities, apart from things like soap and shampoo. There was a grocery store close to his complex where he could easily get those things, especially now that he had a bike. What a find! He had expected he'd have to buy a brand-new bike, but the one he found at the thrift store was in perfect condition. Whoever donated it either never used it or had it serviced before giving it away.

Elf backed his way through the swinging kitchen door, carrying two plates. A former heroin addict and dealer, among other things, he found Jesus in prison, and, in Adam's estimation, his experience was both real and life-changing. He set Adam's plate in front of him and slid onto the stool next to him.

"Good to see you, bro." His face was bright, and he wore the familiar smell of the kitchen like a cologne.

"It's my pleasure, Elf. How've you been?"

Elf tilted his head to one side and then the other with an audible crack to his neck. "Oh, you know. Same old, same old. I should be asking you the same. Tom told me what happened." Tom was a student in the same Bible school as Elf and the son of the church deacon whose death Adam had witnessed during a stopover in Ur.

Adam looked down at his plate and sighed. "I'm doing alright. They took good care of me in Ur. They didn't have to do that. It was pretty amazing, but I never really intended to stay there. I just got caught up in that whole mess." He bit into his burger. "This is good."

"Thanks." Elf raked a fry through a pool of ketchup and popped it into his mouth. "I heard it was the pervert. I keep thinking if I had only said more… Dude, I'm so sorry."

"You were scared," Adam said. "I experienced that creepy guy myself, though my memory of it isn't the best. Dude, I don't blame you at all. He was and is truly a fucked-up individual. You and me, we're cool." Adam thumped his chest with his fist. He used almost the same words that Elf had said to him a couple of months earlier.

"Are you here now or are you still headed to…" Elf's eyes darted as he searched his memory, "…was it Phoenix?"

"Flagstaff," Adam corrected him. "When Baxter and I came here to see you, something just clicked. I liked the name of the place, and the open space felt like a relief after the claustrophobia of the French Quarter. But unlike Ur, it didn't feel lonely or empty. I guess I like being around enough people to feel… anonymous, or at least inconspicuous." Adam paused, searching for the right words. "Anyway, I'm here for a while."

"Are you looking for a job?" Elf's eyes flickered toward the man wrapping cutlery on the other side of Adam.

"Not now. Maybe later. I'm tending bar in the lounge at the Creekstone Hotel. I just took an apartment and may be looking later for a second job. I just need to get settled first."

Elf nodded.

"Have you been back to Ur since...?" Adam said, changing the subject.

Elf shook his head. "I don't want to set foot in that town."

"Still worried about the other guy?"

Six weeks earlier, Elf had mentioned two people in Ur who had known him in his past. One was a sexual sadist, the other politically powerful. One of the two would be in prison or a mental institution for the rest of his life. Adam had only a guess at who the politically powerful one was.

Elf sipped his sweet tea. "Not anymore. He's got too much to lose messing with me now. Especially since he knows I could wreck his political ambitions with just a whisper. It's just better to keep my distance, at least until I'm off parole. I have another six months."

"Six months is nothing. Congratulations. I'll bet you're counting the days."

Elf nodded.

Adam looked down at his plate and sighed, remembering the aftermath in Ur—the small town that had sheltered him after witnessing Deacon Delgado's violent end and how Elf's simple, straightforward advice had helped him through an exceedingly difficult situation.

He said, "Tom's brother Ben really connected with you over video games. I know he was looking forward to playing with you again."

Elf smiled. "I know. I like that kid. We play online a couple of times a week. It amazes me what he's willing to say while he and I are on some quest together. It's like my first experience in pastoral counseling. He's in grief, and there's no other guy for him to look up to now. He has Tom, of course, but Tom isn't ready for that—not yet."

Adam marveled at the surety, the strength of character, and the honest wisdom that was coming so casually out of Elf's mouth. *He's going to be an amazing pastor,* Adam thought. All he could say was, "That's really nice of you."

"Don't get me wrong. I enjoy playing the game with him. He just needs a guy who is more experienced in life to ask questions or test ideas. No reflection on Tom. I have ten years and a lifetime of experience over Tom."

Adam contemplated while chewing his burger and washing it down with a sip of black coffee. He wasn't sure he wanted to broach the subject. He had heard comments back in Ur during his recovery from severe neck trauma, but he knew nothing about how Elf was managing.

"And how about Grace?" Adam asked with extreme caution. When Adam first met Grace, she had spoken enthusiastically about her relationship with Elf. It sounded like she intended to marry him.

Elf took a deep breath and bought time with another bite of his burger. "Okay, I guess. Not good at first. She dropped out of school and went back to Ur." He paused. "She broke up with me." He pressed his lips together. "It was probably for the best."

"I'm sorry. Why for the best?"

"I really couldn't help her with what she was going through. I couldn't be there for her. Her mother didn't like me, and that made things harder for Grace. Grace had to do a lot of quick growing up in the last couple of months, and there's a lot more to come." He paused, taking another deep breath, then slowly admitted, "It was probably in the cards anyway. The differences in our ages, I suppose."

"She seemed really in love with you."

Elf set down his burger as if the question had put him off his food. "I imagine she thought so, too." He sighed thoughtfully. "Me, I wasn't so sure. She's a sweet girl, but she didn't have filters. She'd just say things. She wanted to be a pastor's wife. I want to pastor a church. That much worked. Married ministers have a better chance of getting hired than single guys, but not if their wives just say whatever crosses their minds and makes people uncomfortable."

Adam was confused. "You need a wife to get a job?"

Elf let out a small laugh. "Oh, I'll get a job as an assistant pastor or a youth pastor in some tough neighborhood. That's where I'll meet a good Christian woman who has a past of her own and the discretion to go with it. We'll get married and, eventually, I'll have my own congregation. It's just easier if she's there from the start, already sharing the ministry. I hate to admit it, but it helps if she's pretty and can sing, too. The church gets two for the price of one."

He interrupted himself and turned his face toward Adam. "Don't get me wrong. That's *not* why I was dating Grace. I was genuinely attracted to her at first. She was nice, pretty, and knows the Bible well." He paused again, looking at his plate. "I just think she was a little further along in our relationship than I was."

Having grown up Roman Catholic, where priests are celibate and assigned to churches, and pastors are appointed by the bishop, Adam had never thought of pastors as being more stable if they were married. "This is fascinating, Elf. I just had no idea that churches hired pastors, and the process sounds pretty cynical."

"It is in some ways, but I'm not afraid of the truth, and that's the truth. Married guys look more responsible, more stable, and more trustworthy. They might not be, but they look that way. Listen, if you are going to stay in town, we'll have plenty of time for you to extract my cynicism. It feels good to be able to talk about these things openly." He sipped his tea. "Let me change the subject. Where are you staying?"

A party of three had vacated the booth behind them. Before Elf could get up to bus the table, Brooke tapped his shoulder. "Just enjoy your lunch, sweetie. I got this." He thanked her and grinned at Adam. "She's so nice."

"Just signed a lease in the apartment complex about a mile that way." Adam pointed. "It's huge. Apart from the kitchen, bath, and bedroom, I won't use any of it."

"Oh my gosh. Why did you do that?"

Adam dropped his head. "It's still less than half the price I was paying for the cheapest motel I could find that was within decent walking distance from my job."

"Do you need furniture for your apartment? I can probably make an announcement at church. Nothing will match, but people are always willing to help."

"I just bought some basic stuff down the street at the discount furniture store. I don't need much and probably have enough." Adam pointed in the opposite direction. "Just a bed and a table. I'm going to rent a truck to pick it all up later today or tomorrow."

Elf thought for half a minute. "How much are you going to pay to rent a truck?"

"About a hundred bucks."

"And you're going to do the moving all by yourself?"

"I guess so. It's not a lot of stuff. I just can't carry it on foot… or on my bike." He paused. "I could always call the Mormons and see if the missionaries are available. But I can really handle it myself."

"Mormon missionaries will help you move?"

"Yeah. They'll do lots of things if you ask and if they can. They won't take money, but you can buy them lunch. And of course, you'll learn all about Joseph Smith and how Jesus came to preach to the Indians and how some lost tribe of Israel landed in America." He shook his head to clear it. "It's been a while since I heard the story, but it was fascinating."

"That's... interesting," Elf said from behind a furrowed brow. Then he seemed to land on an idea. Holding up a finger in a wait-a-minute gesture, he pulled out his cellphone. Adam watched his thumb flick and tap at the screen. Elf waited. "Hey, it's me. What time are you leaving?" Pause. "Do you want to earn fifty bucks?" Pause. "Today. Now." Pause. "Pick us up at the Moonstone. I get off..." he looked at his watch "...in an hour." Pause. "Yeah, I'll just come back to get my car after." Pause. "We need your truck to move some furniture." Pause. "It's a surprise."

"What did you just do?" Adam smiled, half knowing.

"I just saved you fifty bucks. He has a truck and needs the money."

"Who?

"Tom Delgado. His mom gave him his dad's truck. He goes back to Ur every weekend. He always needs gas money."

"And what's the surprise?"

Elf chuckled while munching his last fry. "You, of course." He slid off the stool. "I'll just go and help set up the kitchen for dinner before we go."

Adam's cell phone rang. He pulled it out of his jeans pocket. It was Jenna. He swiped the screen. "This is Adam."

"Hey Adam, do you want to work this afternoon and tomorrow? Hector just got picked up by ICE."

Adam was shocked. "What?" Hector was the Venezuelan college student who worked part-time at the front desk and weekends in the lounge. Fridays and Saturdays were so slow that he could study while he worked. The hotel didn't care. It was a minimum wage job with little chance of tips, but perfect for a guy like Hector. He was friendly, nice-looking, and still needed a jigger to get the shot measure right but on the weekends, it was mostly draft and bottled beer.

"He got picked up by ICE," she repeated. "Can you believe it?"

"ICE? What the hell? He was in college. He had a student visa and permission to work, didn't he?"

"Yes." Jenna lowered her voice. "It's political bullshit. All of a sudden, Venezuelans are enemies of the state despite their visas. Fucking federal government bullshit. Half the kitchen staff went home sick out of fear. Biggs says housekeeping is in chaos." Her voice came back to volume. "Can you do it? It would really help me out."

Adam sighed. He wanted to help, but with all he had to do, he needed at least the day. "Jenna, tomorrow is okay, but I'm in the middle of moving today. I got way too much to do."

She suppressed an expletive. "I'll have to do it myself today. Tomorrow at eleven, okay? I know it's a long shift, but you get two meals from the restaurant, anything you want, no limit. I won't be here, so get the keys at the front desk."

"Will do," Adam assured her.

"Wait—before you go. Have you spoken to Detective Harjo yet?" Jenna asked.

"Detective? No."

She lowered her voice. "Listen, the shit is hitting the fan. They asked for the surveillance footage from the back lot. Biggs gave them a list of guests whose windows looked out on the alley. Harjo sounds tough. He asked about you. I gave him your number. He'll be calling you."

Adam's heart stuttered. He knew it was going to happen, but hoped it wouldn't be so quickly. How much of his day off would be lost in an interrogation? "He should already have my number. I gave it to the police yesterday. But depending on what he wants, I might not be able to cover tomorrow."

"Why?" She seemed surprised by the statement.

"Jenna, I found her body. I'm on the list until they take me off it."

"List? What list?"

"I'm an automatic suspect. They'll call me a person of interest, but it almost means the same thing. If he wants me to go into the station, I might not have a choice."

Silence. "Damn! I'll have to call him. I was supposed to go into the station. He'll have to come here if he wants me to talk to him today."

"What's his name again?

"Harjo. Joe Harjo. Want his number?"

"No. He'll get me when he wants me. Thanks for the heads-up."

A detective meant that the investigation into Candy's death was escalating—that the crime wasn't a simple one to solve. *I'm in the thick of it... again.* Adam thought. He once again felt the eerie feeling he got when he saw that fan-folded tip lying on the bar last night, just the way Candy used to do.

Four

Tom Delgado took Adam's offer of a handshake and pulled him into a hug. It wasn't unwelcome, just a surprise that reminded Adam of the kind of affection he would expect from his cousins. When he stepped away from Adam, Tom's eyes were moist, and he followed the hug up with a firm handshake, and for a second, they just looked at one another.

"Good to see you, Tom. Thanks for coming to help me out." Adam's voice was deep and calming.

Tom just nodded, smiled, and looked away as if he were embarrassed by his emotion. He was looking better than he had in Ur. Despite his athletic build, he had been looking pale and deflated. Now his vigor seemed replenished, and he was full of energy.

Elf started giving Tom instructions about what they were about to do. The three of them climbed into the cab of the pickup. Elf slid into the tiny excuse of a back seat behind Tom. He recognized the discount store Adam had described and gave Tom directions as they drove. Adam sat in the passenger seat.

"How's the church gardening seminar?" Adam asked. He recalled that Grace had emphasized the importance of Tom attending the special summer course when he was thinking about staying home for the summer.

Tom shot a confused look toward Adam. "Huh?"

Elf snickered. "He means church planting."

Adam enjoyed the laughter at his expense. It was good to be around laughter. Though they had met only two months earlier, he felt like he was with friends. He was beginning to see real potential in having ready-made friends in his new surroundings.

Tom's answer was considered. "It's not exactly what I expected. It's more intense. It's all about how to start a new church congregation from scratch in a new place, and there's more to it than just finding a location and putting up a sign. There's real strategy behind it, and it doesn't always work."

Elf chimed in. "I wish I could be there, but I couldn't afford to take the time off for the seminar schedule. Tom fills me in, and I'm reading the material they give him. I doubt I'll ever be a church planter, but you never know."

"You mean you can just go somewhere and start a church? If just anybody can do that, it sounds like the way to start a cult." Adam turned to look at Elf.

Elf took on the tone of an instructor. "Fair assumption. It happens. I suppose there are people who start new religions. Most cults, however, come from congregational splits. It starts with some disagreement over doctrine or a challenge to the pastor. Congregation members take sides, causing the church to divide. It happens all the time. Not every split ends up creating a cult, but some do."

"How did you know about the seminar?" Tom pulled into the parking lot of the discount furniture store.

"That day we were having lunch, and you were thinking about staying home for the summer." Adam was relieved that the short answer had been enough.

It took less than ten minutes to load up Adam's purchases in the truck.

"Is this all you got?" Tom seemed disconcerted.

Adam shrugged. "It's all I need." Adam didn't know what else to say. "I guess I'm weird."

As they drove to Adam's new apartment, his cell phone alerted him to a text. He fished the phone out of his pocket and touched the sensor to light up the screen. The number was Baxter's. Adam read: "What the hell is going on? Call me when you get the chance. Harjo is a stand-up guy."

Harjo, Adam remembered, was the name of the detective Jenna had mentioned. Adam felt his pulse quicken. How did Baxter know that Adam was involved in anything at all? Did Harjo talk to Baxter, or did Baxter somehow find out about the investigation? Adam hadn't heard from Harjo yet, but figured it would happen soon. He couldn't shake the dread of another interrogation coiling in his stomach. How long would it be before Harjo got to him, and how would it happen? Would he just show up? Would he send someone to arrest him?

"What is a stand-up guy?" Adam asked.

"What?" Tom said.

"What does stand-up guy mean?"

They both seemed to be searching for words.

Elf said, "Honest, trustworthy, straightforward, and not to be messed with." Elf leaned over and glanced at the screen of Adam's phone.

Tom said, "Strong, someone you can depend on to do what is right and won't back down."

Elf continued. "You. You're a stand-up guy. Who is Harjo?"

Adam didn't want to say who he was because there would be a lot of questions. He really didn't want to talk about finding Candy's body. At the mere thought of Candy, the image of her pale body, her blank stare surfaced in his mind. Adam blinked hard, trying to banish the vision, but its shadow lingered.

"Never met him. Must be someone Sergeant Baxter knows. I guess Baxter thinks I'm going to meet him." It wasn't a lie, exactly.

Pulling into the parking lot of the apartment complex, Tom said, "If Mr. Baxter says he's a stand-up guy, he's a stand-up guy."

"My building is the farthest one in the back." The complex had five buildings, each with five townhouse-style apartments. "My unit is the last one in the building on the end," Adam said.

Tom wound his way through parking lots until Adam said, "It's this one. Those two spaces under the carport are mine."

Tom pulled into one of the spaces. Tom looked at him. You have two parking spaces? How big is this place?" He cut the engine.

"They only had two- and three-bedroom units available," Adam admitted.

"This is all the furniture you bought?" Tom asked.

They each took something easy to carry as Adam led them into the apartment. The front door opened to a long hallway. Stairs to the left, an empty living room to the right and behind that a kitchen with a back door to a courtyard.

"This is huge," Tom said when they walked through the front door. "I think it's bigger than my house in Ur."

"It's a lot of space," Adam confessed.

They set the things they were carrying down in the living room.

"I need a restroom," Elf said.

"That door under the stairs is a powder room, but I don't know if there is paper there."

"Don't need it," Elf said, opening the door.

"Mind if I look upstairs?" Tom asked.

Adam's phone rang. Answering it, he signaled for Tom to explore all he wanted. He looked at his phone. The caller ID read "Broken Arrow Police." After confirming that he was Adam Alba, he listened.

"Hello, this is Detective Harjo from the Broken Arrow Police Department. First, I want to thank you again for your cooperation yesterday. I know this has been difficult. To help us fully understand what happened, we'd appreciate it if you could come into the station to provide a formal statement about finding the victim and..." He paused. "Any background information you might be able to provide. We can arrange a time that's convenient for you. Would you be available to come in today?"

Adam was shocked at how softly he had phrased his request. He would have expected something more curt, more direct, that didn't sound like an invitation. Something like, *You need to come into the station.*

Elf exited the powder room. "No paper. You need some. Should we take you to a store after we finish unloading?"

Adam held up his phone and mouthed the word "Harjo."

Elf silently asked where Tom was. Adam pointed up.

Adam looked at his watch. "Certainly, sir. I'd be glad to do that. It will have to be a bit later. I'm in the middle of moving at the moment, so there are a few things I need to do before coming in. Would 5:30 or 6 be too late?"

"That's fine. We'll expect you here at the station between..."

Adam cut him off. "Wait, sorry. I don't know where you are or how to get there. I'm not from here. If you give me the address, I can bike over."

"You're moving into…"

Adam could hear him leafing through pages.

He read off the address of Adam's apartment. "Is that correct?"

"Yes, that's right."

"I know the place well. I'll send an officer to pick you up at 5:30."

"That's fine. I'll be here." He slipped his phone into his pocket and climbed the stairs. He heard Elf and Tom talking in the front bedroom, their voices echoing off the bare walls.

"This place is huge," Elf said.

"And nice," Tom added.

"Are you thinking what I'm thinking?" Elf said.

"It couldn't hurt to ask," Tom countered.

"Ask what?" Adam walked into the room.

Elf and Tom looked at one another and nodded.

"Could I ask how much you are paying in rent?" Elf was the practical one.

Adam told them.

"Utilities?" It was Elf again.

"I pay for electricity, cable, and internet. Everything else is included."

They seemed to communicate telepathically. Tom nodded, and Elf broached the question. "It's okay if you say no, but would you like roommates?"

"Yeah, if you know anyone. I mean, the place is empty. I'd have to meet them, of course."

"You already have," Elf ventured. "Tom and I could share this room. If we each pay a third, that's really manageable for both of us. This is a much nicer place than both of us have right now, and we've been talking about moving in together anyway."

Since leaving university, Adam had never completely stopped living like a student. He once shared a house in LA with a bunch of aspiring actors. People came and went, and the house just seemed to perpetuate itself. There was always someone who needed a place to stay, and the house always needed another person to help with the rent. But he had no history with anyone he lived with.

In his drinking days, he might couch surf for months with friends and friends of friends and people so strung out, they didn't notice. Sometimes a woman would take him home and wouldn't want him to leave. That was always good for a couple of weeks or even months, but eventually things got complicated, and the arrangement got in the way of his drinking.

This would be the first time in his adult life that he chose to live with people he knew. In that moment, he realized something about himself. He envied his nephew traveling around the States in a kitted-out van with his best friend. *What would it be like to be so connected and trusting with someone?*

"It sounds like a great idea," Adam said.

Tom relaxed his shoulders.

Elf asked, "Are you sure? Don't you have questions for us?"

Adam shook his head. "I can't think of anything to ask."

Their faces grew lighter and lighter.

"This is amazing," Elf said.

"Thank you, Jesus," Tom said. "And you too, of course, Adam. Thank you."

Adam continued. "You won't be paying a third of the rent each, but a quarter. I pay half, you two pay the other half. I have one bedroom; you guys have the other. That's fair."

Elf began to object, but saw the look of relief on Tom's face. Looking sincerely into Adam's eyes, he simply said, "Thank you."

In a matter of a few minutes, everything in the back of Tom Delgado's truck was in the apartment, and almost all of it was in Adam's room.

An hour in a Walmart supercenter was more than enough time for Adam to get what he needed for a functioning apartment. Most of what he bought was from the grocery side of the store, but he ventured throughout, picking up a bicycle lock, a small desk lamp, and a jigsaw puzzle. He even had time to copy the keys to the apartment for Elf and Tom. The only time wasted came from a glitch in the self-checkout when one of the products he wanted to buy would not scan.

As Adam slid into the passenger seat of Elf's Honda, he handed the keys to Elf. "You guys move in whenever you want, okay?"

Elf blushed. "Actually, I threw a few things into the trunk, if you don't mind."

Adam said, "Anytime."

By five-fifteen, showered, shaved and neatly dressed, Adam stood looking out through the peephole in his front door. A meeting with a detective meant interrogation, no matter what they called it. He could feel his stomach churn, fearing hours of repeated questions. He went out and sat down on the steps to his front door.

The front of the building faced east and was now well shaded and cool. Still, he felt overly warm and chalked it up to the stress of meeting the detective. He pulled out his phone and tried to distract himself by scheduling an internet installation online. He had barely opened the website when his phone rang.

He swiped the screen and spoke into the phone. "Hey, Bax."

"How are you, Adam?"

"Just moved into my apartment. Waiting for the escort for an audience with the stand-up Joe Harjo." He leaned back against the black wrought iron railing. It still held heat from the day and felt warm against his back. "News on that front. I'm going to have roommates. Elf and Tom Delgado helped me move in and are going to share the apartment."

"That's cool. Tom's mother will be glad to hear that. She worries about him."

Adam looked at his watch. "He should be in Ur soon."

"Okay, enough of the small talk. What the hell is happening? I got a call from Joe Harjo. DuPuis sent him to me. What have you got yourself into that he looked you up in the system?"

"Didn't he tell you?"

"He said you were a person of interest in a homicide case."

"Bax, it's nuts. I was taking trash out where I work and found a body. I called- 911. Officers and a medical examiner came. The officer in charge asked me a bunch of questions. I answered them. I know finding the body marks me to some extent, but I don't know what else I can tell them. Harjo wants to see me."

Adam could hear Bax breathing on the other end of the line. "You still there, Bax?"

He interrupted Baxter's train of thought, and he could hear it in his voice when Baxter answered. "I wish I could give you more advice. Like I said in my text, Harjo is a stand-up guy. We met at a training seminar. One thing, though…"

"What's that?"

"He's a detective—much more training in interrogation than I have. Keep your statement straightforward, honest. If you feel threatened, stay calm, quiet, and think before you answer. If it sounds like he has more of a case against you than you know is possible, don't rise to the bait."

Adam almost said that he knew that already, but he also knew that Baxter had his best interests at heart. It was nice having someone, particularly a police officer, assume his innocence. He felt like he had that assurance from both Baxter and DuPuis.

"Bax, gotta go. My ride is here."

A cruiser pulled to a stop at the end of the short walkway to his front door. A young, uniformed officer jumped out of the car and galloped toward Adam. "Mr. Alba, I'm …"

"Terry…sorry, I don't know your last name, Officer, but I remember the name Riley used."

Terry stopped and straightened. "Yes, sir. It's Gamble. Terrance Gamble."

Silently, Adam wondered if Harjo had chosen to send someone so earnest to put him at ease or to see if he'd slip up when he felt most unguarded. But his guard rose again when Officer Gamble opened one of the back doors to the cruiser for him.

Five

Detective Joe Harjo rose from his seat when Officer Gamble ushered Adam into his office. He smiled and greeted Adam with a firm handshake. Harjo was a barrel of a man who looked to be in his late fifties. He was dressed in plain clothes: a pair of tan gabardine slacks that matched the sport coat hung over the back of his chair. He wore a pastel-colored short-sleeved button-down shirt open at the collar, revealing a white T-shirt underneath. His black, short-cropped hair showed grey at the temples. The setting sun, angling through the window, highlighted his copper skin. The chair he offered Adam was padded and comfortable.

Gamble sat down on a hard chair in the corner. Adam could still see him out of the corner of his eye, but to include him in the conversation, he'd have to turn and look at him. He questioned whether the rookie was observing the interview to learn or to witness his statement. He suspected it was a little of both.

Adam tried to remember all the good things Elf and Tom had said about what it meant to be a stand-up guy, but the one quality that stood out was that you shouldn't mess with one. He felt unsure whether the safety he experienced was genuine or deceptive. His sense of shadow and wary caution grew inside him. It was as if he were both participating in and observing the interview.

Harjo's tone was softer than he expected. On the phone, his voice had been polite and purposeful. Now he spoke softly, almost soothingly.

"Thank you, Mr. Alba, for coming in. I appreciate your help."

"Glad to help if I can. I don't know much. Like I said on the phone, I've only been in town a short while, but I'll tell you what I know."

"Well, sir, we couldn't ask for more." He repositioned himself at his desk and shifted a few pages from a file folder on an old-fashioned desk blotter. "I need coffee. You want a cup of coffee?" He stood up and stepped from behind his desk.

"Is it good coffee?" Adam asked, pretending to hide a gentle grin. If this guy was trying to make him feel comfortable, he'd let him think it was working.

Harjo sent him a sideways glance. "Been around a few police department coffeepots, have you?"

Adam shifted his eyebrows. He shrugged his shoulders helplessly.

Harjo loosened. "Yeah, it's good coffee, fresh too. We got one of those pod things. How do you take it?"

"Black," Adam answered.

"Man after my own heart." He left the office.

Adam turned to look at Gamble. "I'm surprised he didn't send you."

Gamble shrugged his shoulders. "He's like that."

"Where's your partner? Riley... isn't it?" Adam made small talk.

"He's off. I'm working overtime," Gamble said pleasantly.

Adam was aware that the real conversation hadn't started yet. Adam looked around the room, casually scanning for cameras, but didn't see any.

He leaned his elbow on the arm of the chair and rubbed his eyes. He could hear the gurgle of the coffee maker in a room down the hallway. He could feel Gamble's eyes on him, but for all the young man's enthusiasm, he said nothing. Adam moved his forefinger to the cleft in his chin and gently pressed. It helped him relax. Harjo returned, carrying two branded ceramic mugs.

"Is this swag or do you want to make sure no one steals the cups?" Adam joked.

"Funny." Harjo laughed. "Swag. We had a community relations consultant in. We got a shitload of them to give out at community events. That one is yours if you want it. Hell, take six. You just moved into a new apartment," he said, sitting back down. The swivel chair squeaked under his weight. He chuckled again. "My wife has already seen them in thrift stores and rummage sales."

Adam noticed the foam on the top of the coffee and sipped. It reminded him of his grandmother's coffee that she made with a stovetop espresso maker. Surprised, he said, "This is good. It comes out like this?"

"Yeah, it's a different kind. What's it called, Terry?"

"Nes-press-o." He sounded out the word carefully separating the syllables. "We send the pods back to be recycled," he added.

"Fancy," Harjo said. "I told you it was good." He took a deep breath and focused on the file on his desk. "Okay, Mr. Alba, let's get down to business. I'm sure you don't want to be here long."

"As long as it takes. I want to help." He meant that, but he was also relieved that it sounded like he'd be going home and wouldn't be held at the station.

Harjo nodded. "I'm going to record our conversation. I just want to ensure accuracy."

"That's okay. I expected it." He wasn't being cynical but honest. He knew that anyone who found a body would automatically be a suspect, even an unlikely one."

Harjo pressed a button on a tiny black box on his desk and ran through a standard procedure for starting the recording, stating the date and the time, and obtaining Adam's permission. Adam noticed that he hadn't read him his rights.

"Mr. Alba. I have Officer Riley's report here." He fondled a piece of paper on his desk. "It seems pretty straightforward, but in your own words, just tell me what happened yesterday. I'm sure I may have more questions, but I'll try to avoid interrupting you too often. Start with your arrival at work and be as detailed as you can."

Adam did as he asked. He recounted his movements from the time he arrived at the Creekstone until he walked back into the lounge to take over for his shift. Adam noticed him making a few notes in the margins of what he imagined was a copy of Riley's report. Keeping his word, Harjo didn't interrupt him until he finished.

"I do have a few questions. First, in your statement, you said you did not know any information to identify Candy, no credit card transactions, no mention of a last name or any other identification information. I'd like you to think again, even the smallest, most insignificant morsel of information can help us."

Adam considered, then shook his head. "There is nothing. She did carry a purse, a fairly large one. There may have been something useful inside."

Harjo said, "No purse has been found. We looked. If something does come to mind or if you hear anything, please let us know."

Adam agreed.

"Okay, now, who is Hector? You mentioned he was in the lounge when you arrived."

"He's a college student who works, or rather worked, part-time at the hotel—mostly front desk and a little in the lounge."

"Worked? Past tense?"

Adam nodded. "According to Jenna, the manager, Hector was picked up by ICE. He is a foreign student on a visa."

Harjo wrote that down. "Do you know his last name?"

"I think it was Garcia hyphen something, but Jenna will know for sure. He said he was from Venezuela."

"Anything different or abnormal about the way Hector looked or acted when you arrived?"

Adam slowly shook his head, thinking. "No. Hector just took his cash tips, grabbed his knapsack, and left. He has... had... evening classes in Tulsa."

"How long after you arrived did he leave?"

"Just a few minutes."

"Can you put a timestamp on when you took out the trash?"

"It was about twenty after four. It's usually about then."

"Usually? You mean you take out the trash every day at the same time?"

"Sure. I follow a routine to get ready for a shift. Mostly checking, restocking, and cleaning. We don't have a barback, so I do most of it at the beginning of a shift while it's still slow."

"Is there always trash to take out?" Harjo seemed more interested in Adam's routine than in what he knew about Candy.

"I always empty it, no matter what. Overflowing trash behind the bar makes it tough if it gets busy."

"When are the busiest times?"

Adam wasn't sure where he was going with these questions. "Between six and eight or nine. It slows down after that."

Harjo ran his finger down a page on his desk. "I understand the victim was a regular patron, and she arrived with consistency."

"Between seven and seven-thirty every night but my first shift. She was early that day, and it was quiet enough to talk."

Harjo was silent for a long pause. "What do you remember of that conversation?"

Adam nodded. It was familiar ground and felt safer. "I told it all to Riley. She asked me to never serve her alcohol because she was in recovery. I am too, so I understood. Like we say in the program, 'One is too many and a thousand is never enough.'"

"When did you figure out that she was a prostitute?"

Adam hesitated. "That is an interesting question. It started that first night. She would be talking to someone, and then she would leave, and then the guy would leave, or vice versa. She'd be back usually within half an hour." Adam sensed he was getting too comfortable with the conversation. He shifted and sat up in his chair. "To be honest, I still don't know for sure that she wanted to be paid, though it is a reasonable assumption. I also had the idea that quickies were her entire repertoire. She was never gone for a long time."

"So, you observed her carefully?" Harjo said.

Adam hesitated. "Because of her confidence, I guess I felt a little protective of her."

"Did she have any regular clients?" Harjo asked.

"None that I could name. Maybe she had repeat clients, but most people in the lounge were hotel guests. They'd be around for a couple days. I haven't been around long enough to be aware of any regulars other than Candy."

"Let's back up a bit, Mr. Alba. When was the last time you saw her alive?"

"That's easy; last call Wednesday night. She usually stayed until last call. There weren't many patrons left at that time. Once I serve last call drinks, I start cleaning up. I didn't see her leave, but she left me a tip on the bar."

"How did you know the tip was hers?"

"She always folded it like a fan," Adam said.

"Did she leave with anyone?"

"I didn't see her leave. The lounge pretty much cleared out. There were two guys finishing their drinks. They left before midnight," Adam said.

"What time is last call?" Harjo asked.

"Eleven-thirty."

"Bear with me, Mr. Alba. Please describe your movements between last call on Wednesday night and your arriving for work on Thursday."

Adam offered a wry smile. "So, I am a suspect."

"Mr. Alba, it's fair to say that everyone is a suspect until evidence rules them out. I'm a detective, and part of my job is ruling out every suspect but one. Help me to do that."

Adam took a deep breath and leaned back in the chair. "I cleaned the lounge and restocked the bar for the next shift. I clocked out about twelve-fifteen. The exact time would be in the hotel records. Then I walked back to my motel."

Harjo looked at his notes. "You *walked* back to your motel?"

"Yes. I didn't have a bike yet."

"What time did you leave the Creekstone?"

He's after a timeline, Adam thought. "Just after clocking out. I got back to the motel about ten after one, and before you ask, I saw no one. It was dark. Cars passed me, of course. I didn't go into the motel office. I went straight to my room. Showered and went to bed… alone."

Harjo had an amused look. "Go on."

"I got up around six and went out to the little park near the motel to exercise. There were people there. One guy with two golden retrievers watched me for a while. I do wrestling drills. Some people find them… I don't know… entertaining, interesting, fascinating. I guess it looks funny."

"Did you speak with him? Know his name?

Adam shook his head. "Not then. I met him this morning. I recognized the dogs, though. Sometimes a different guy walks them. I've never talked to him. When I finished my exercises, I went back, showered, got dressed for work, and left the motel about ten-thirty."

"That seems early for work. Where did you go then?" He glanced at Gamble.

"I stopped at a coffee shop in a strip mall about halfway to work."

"I know it. Great baked goods," Harjo said.

Adam wasn't sure, but he thought he heard Terry Gamble's stomach gurgle. Adam described meeting Stevie Tramonto. Knowing Harjo would want to verify that meeting, "I have her number if you want it."

"She gave you her number?" Harjo tilted his head.

"Not then. I saw her there again today. She's really a nice lady. We exchanged numbers."

Harjo took down the number.

"After she left, I spent a couple hours in the coffee shop making lists of stuff I needed for the new place and looking up and mapping out thrift stores for today's move. The Wi-Fi is better there than the internet at the motel. I had lunch there. I left the coffee shop about two-thirty. The counter girl recognizes me there. Not by name. Take my picture if you are going to verify my story."

Harjo nodded. "That's a good idea."

Adam wasn't sure if he was genuinely commenting or if there was a slightly patronizing tone. "We can take a selfie together if you'd like," Adam offered facetiously. He was astonished when Harjo and Gamble both agreed.

"We'll do that after we're finished," Harjo muttered. "We're almost done here." He looked at his notes. "Two-thirty, you say. That still leaves you a lot of time to walk to the Creekstone."

"It's a little over three miles, and the weather is pretty hot. I took it slow because I didn't want to show up for work all sweaty. I walked into the Creekstone lobby at about three forty-five."

"I don't suppose you met anyone else along the way," Harjo said, sounding hopeful.

Adam shook his head and then remembered the recording. "No. Broken Arrow doesn't seem like a place with a lot of pedestrians."

Harjo leaned back, his seat creaking under his weight. "This concludes the interview with Adam Alba." He looked at his watch and read out the date and time. He pressed a button on the small device, picked it up and tossed it to Gamble. "Terry, please get a transcript of this for the record. And let's take those selfies."

Three cell phones and three surreal selfies later, Harjo said, "I'm going to take you home, Mr. Alba. If you wouldn't mind waiting here for a few minutes." He walked toward the door.

Harjo's car was a Jeep Wrangler Unlimited, a cross between a family car and a Jeep. It was black and looked as powerful as its owner. Harjo tried to make small talk. Adam was polite but didn't offer more than answers to his questions.

"My wife asked me to pick up dinner on the way home. Do you mind if we make a brief detour? Do you like Popeyes?"

"It's okay. I'll get something too. The guy who owns that chain has real restaurants called Copelands in New Orleans, and the food is amazing—pricey but good food."

"You don't say," Harjo said.

They pulled into a Popeyes drive-through.

They ordered and pulled forward. "I have it on reasonable authority that you are a man who can be trusted," Harjo said.

Adam thought, *There is something about being shoulder to shoulder and not face-to-face.* Adam kept his eyes on the dashboard. After a short pause, he ventured, "Was it Baxter or DuPuis?"

Harjo paused and then admitted, "Both. I had Gamble run a background check on you. DuPuis' report came up. Your boss, Jenna, mentioned you recently moved from Ur and cases like the one in Ur are talked about. I heard the FBI and DEA were involved."

Adam nodded. "Yep."

"So I called the sheriff, and he put me on to Sergeant Baxter."

"How can I help you, Detective?" Adam was getting wary of this off-the-record conversation.

"The thing that bothers me about cases like this one is people like Miss Candy either have no context or a dark one. No family or friends that ever report them missing, or the people they know are on drugs, or don't trust the police. If they don't have a criminal record, we may never even identify them."

"And they become just another dead hooker," Adam muttered.

"Exactly." Harjo exhaled.

"What do you want me to do, or how can I help you?" Adam was curious. Would he get an actual assignment like the one Baxter once gave him?

"Look me in the eye and answer one more question."

They moved up a car length, and Adam turned toward Harjo, looking him straight in the eye. "Did you know Candy before she walked into the lounge your first night at the Creekstone?"

"Never saw or heard of her in my life," Adam said plainly.

Harjo's expression was difficult to interpret. Finally, he said, "I believe you."

They pulled up to the payment window. Adam reached for his wallet, but Harjo held up his hand. "Not necessary. I'll put your portion in for reimbursement. We had you with us through the dinner hour."

Harjo paid, and the line moved forward to a separate window to get the food. He took a deep breath and stopped before turning onto the main road. He continued. "Mr. Alba, I have something else to say and I wouldn't say it except for the information I've received from both Baxter and DuPuis."

Adam braced himself, not knowing what to expect.

Harjo continued. "You asked me if you were still a suspect. On the record, yes, because you haven't been eliminated. Off the record, no.

But like I said in the interview, I don't have evidence to eliminate anyone at this point. We may get that evidence, and I sincerely hope we do." Harjo's eyes met Adam's in the rearview mirror, serious and piercing. "But neither can I eliminate you as a possible *victim*."

"I don't understand." Adam finally let the words escape. Momentarily stunned by Harjo's suggestion that he had been or would be considered a possible victim, his silence emphasized the impact of the suggestion. Eventually, he formed words, but the tone in his voice sounded angry. That wasn't what he intended but that's the way it came out.

Harjo debated how much he should say. The last thing he wanted was to frighten Adam into hypervigilance. "It's just a hypothesis. Sergeant Baxter suggested it." Harjo pulled out of the Popeyes lot onto the main road.

"Baxter?" Adam turned his head toward Harjo. Adam wondered how much Baxter might insert himself into Harjo's investigation.

"It's going to sound far-fetched," Harjo admitted.

Adam rolled his eyes, thinking, *What part of my last two years hasn't been far-fetched?*

"Considering your experience in Ur, an unexplained death within a couple of weeks of your moving to Broken Arrow is one hell of a coincidence."

Adam shifted in his seat. The take-out bags crinkled in his lap. "Are you suggesting that someone attacked Candy to get at me? That doesn't make sense."

There was a long pause. "Mr. Alba, there are several ways of considering it. I don't want to whittle it down to simple explanations. We simply don't know. There are too many possibilities, and this is just one of them. But if someone wanted to get at you, it would be easy for them to know when and where. Sergeant Baxter pointed out that it happened in Ur."

Adam rolled his eyes again. "Have you ever been to Ur? A stranger just stands out, and people notice. It's not like here. This is a much bigger place, and strangers aren't so uncommon."

Harjo appeared to be listening carefully. His head moved in subtle agreement as he drove. "Mr. Alba, you yourself described how regular your work routine is and your manager…"

"Jenna," Adam added.

Harjo continued. "Yes, Jenna said almost the same thing. It's possible that someone wanted you to find that body."

"Why? What reason would anyone want that?" Adam's mind was filled with untethered thoughts. The hypothesis really did sound incredible.

"For one, it would put you in the position you are right now. It could be someone from your past or someone who thinks you know something you don't. They might want to frighten you, to scare you off, even to get you to leave your job," Harjo said.

"Somebody would do that to get my job?"

Harjo sighed. "I didn't say that, but motives can be complicated things." Harjo almost went into detail but stopped himself. It was possible that the Creekstone had an unknown backroom narrative. "I don't mean to frighten you. Whether this angle on the case proves to be anything or nothing, it wouldn't hurt you to vary your routine a little for your own safety."

Adam could feel his shadow creeping up his spine. "I still don't see how attacking Candy could be aimed at me. If I'm so predictable, why not just attack me?"

Harjo nodded. "That's a valid question. I don't have an answer. But ask yourself this. If Candy spent the night in that dumpster enclosure, why were you the first person to discover her body after four in the afternoon? That is incredible planning."

"That would be impossible to arrange or control," Adam insisted.

"It certainly wouldn't be easy," Harjo admitted. "But not impossible. We're working on a number of theories. Once we positively identify Candy, we may proceed in an entirely different direction, but right now, I have to consider two possible victims. You are one of them."

Adam knew that Harjo was sharing more information than was normal. Perhaps it was because of Baxter. He had to admit his finding Candy's body wasn't logical unless she had been placed there in broad daylight. Kitchen and housekeeping staff used those dumpsters as well.

"Perhaps someone did see her but didn't want to get involved or didn't know what to do?" Adam suggested. "I mean, people are afraid now. Jenna said half the kitchen staff called off work because of what happened to Hector. Maybe they would be afraid to talk to the police."

"Mr. Alba, it's a possibility we are looking into," Harjo admitted.

Adam said, "Well, Detective, honestly, I don't envy you your job. I think you are a stand-up guy." Adam used the moniker that Baxter had used to describe him. Harjo gave him a sideward glance. Adam thought he noticed a slight smile.

It was dark when Harjo pulled up in front of Adam's apartment. The porch lights of all the units were lit. Adam suspected it happened on a timer. Streetlights dotted the parking lot with dim circles of light, and insects buzzed around and slapped into the globes.

"My apartment is the last in this building," Adam pointed out.

Harjo stopped in front of his unit. "Mr. Alba. Thanks again for your help. Here's my card. The number on the front is the station. You have my cell number on your phone. I'll be in touch. I may have more questions once we move further along in the case. If you think of anything that might be important in the meantime, please call me."

Adam opened the passenger-side door and slid out, putting Harjo's dinner onto his vacated seat. "Glad to help, Detective. Thanks for the lift home." He held up his Popeyes bag. "And thanks for dinner."

Six

Adam slid his key into the lock on his front door. Before he turned it, his mind glazed over for a second, and his heart skipped a beat. His off-the-record talk with Harjo in the car had unnerved him. He thought of the ghostly effect of the fan-folded tip on the bar the previous night. *Should he have mentioned it to Harjo? Was it a warning? A clue? A message from beyond?* He told himself he was just being silly, but he was still alert as he turned the lock and pushed open the door.

The inside was in utter darkness. He felt for a switch to the right but found only a smooth wall. It was his first time in the new place at night, and he hadn't thought to look for the light switch before. Even with the door wide open, the porch light was no help. If anything, the glare made the blackness darker and more ominous.

He set his Popeyes bag down on the floor and used his phone's flashlight. He found the switch behind the door. Flipping it, Adam squinted against the harsh brightness as light flooded the hallway. In the soft, filtered light through the living room window, he could see that Elf had left several boxes in the living room.

"Elf?" he called out, hoping Elf was around, perhaps up in the room he would share with Tom. Silence. Adam closed the front door behind him and walked down the hallway back to the kitchen. This time, a light switch was where he thought it should be.

Placing his bag on the breakfast bar, he was aware of the echoes of his movements, the crackle of the plastic bag, his steps on the tile floor, even the sound of his own clothing rustling as he moved. He could feel the emptiness of the space. He unwrapped his food. He hadn't eaten anything since the burger and fries at the Moonstone, and he was starving. The refrigerator kicked on, and that too sounded loud in the room.

There were no barstools for him to sit down. He didn't want to take the food up into his room, so he stood at the counter and unwrapped his dinner. There was always something both comforting and satisfying about fried chicken. The sides, mashed potatoes, and coleslaw were disappointing, so he ate the chicken and the biscuit.

He wrapped up the remnants of his takeout dinner and realized that apart from barstools, he also needed a trash bin. Popeyes had supplied a generous stack of paper napkins. After cleaning his hands, he left the rest on the counter, placed the bundled trash into the sink and climbed the stairs to his room.

His plan was to finish setting up his room and spend a while on the jigsaw puzzle he bought. More than a distraction, jigsaw puzzles were a kind of meditation for him. He pieced them together face down, relying only on the shapes to find pieces to fit. While his eyes focused, his brain often processed events of the day or explored thoughts about things that bothered him, a time without distraction.

As he began to put the bed frame together, something stirred inside him, a kind of memory from his youth. The contrast between the austerity of his Nonno's workshop, the small gardening shed he kept out back, and the exceptionally comfortable home his Nonna had kept. Adam had always admired his grandfather's uncomplicated needs and, until this moment, hadn't realized that his Nonno's simplicity was only made possible by Nonna's generous, loving housekeeping.

He smiled to himself, his mind touring their house the way he remembered it. Since Nonna passed, Nonno hadn't changed much, but the upkeep was too much for him. Adam's sister Cathy did what she could for him, but year by year, he used less and less of the house. He depended on her. She cleaned for him, shopped for him, and picked up his prescriptions at the Giant Eagle. She drove him to the senior center and took him to all his doctor's appointments.

Though Nonno was a decent cook, he lacked motivation and energy to do much of it himself. Though she complained about him sitting in the kitchen, hers or his, telling her how to cook, Adam knew it was valuable time with him, and he felt jealous of it. Even thinking about it, his eyes moistened.

In their most recent conversation, Cathy told Adam about taking Nonno to the Strip District to buy cheese, olives, and cured meats. Adam remembered every inch of the Pennsylvania Macaroni store: the rough floorboards, the shelves of imported foods, the amazing sections, and a third of the store where cheeses, olives, and cured meats were portioned out to order and wrapped in bundles.

The Strip was a former warehouse district where immigrants like his grandparents went for real food at real discounts. Over the years, it became a fashionable foodie heaven and a place to buy souvenirs and Steeler merchandise.

In that empty apartment, Adam's mind filled and reveled in memories. He thought of his grandmother's coffeepot, the stovetop espresso maker, and how good the coffee was at the police station. He used his phone to search for the coffee machine. He was astonished at the price of the Nespresso machines and the cost of the pods needed to make coffee—convenient but coffee-shop expensive. Instead, he searched for one like his grandmother's and ordered it—the first delivery to his new home.

He eyed the puzzle wanting to sit down and begin sorting the pieces. First things first, he bounded downstairs to get his laundry. He hung towels in the bathroom, folded his clothes and placed them on the shelf in his closet, and added hangers to his shopping list.

He made his bed using only a fitted and top sheet. The linens were thrift store mismatches, but that didn't bother him. They were all pure cotton, and that was what mattered. Adam hated synthetic fiber bed linens. That had been another strike against the motel he had checked out of that morning.

He sat down on the edge of the simple queen-size bed and thought about how much had happened in the span of a single day. His mind raced from one milestone moment to the next. Now he was here. In his own place.

Reaching for his cell phone, he snapped a selfie and sent it to his sister with his new address. Then, an afterthought made him smile. He sent the same picture and message to Baxter and Rosie back in Ur and his new old friend Stevie in Broken Arrow.

He waffled between starting his puzzle and just crawling into bed. Both appealed to him equally. But there was one thing he needed to do before either.

The smell of Popeyes chicken lingered in the kitchen when he went down to empty the dryer. He imagined that by morning, the smell would be less than pleasant. He had intended to take the smelly trash that still had the fake mashed potatoes and coleslaw out to the bin in the morning.

Telling himself he needed to do it now, he went downstairs, grabbed the bag and checked for his keys, went out the back door, crossed a patch of lawn wet from a sprinkler system, and across the road that wound its way through the complex. There were three dumpster areas for tenants to dispose of their trash. The closest one was behind the building next to his own.

Eerily illuminated by a streetlight above, the sight of the enclosure made Adam slow down. He felt like he was walking through waist-deep water. He could feel his heart pumping in his chest and his skin going cold. How many times in one day would that shadow feeling deepen? He watched himself walk the short distance to the dumpster.

The dumpster was angled so part of it extended outside the enclosure. He immediately wondered if there was something behind it. As he approached, the smell of garbage was even stronger than it had been at the Creekstone. He could feel his muscles tightening and his caution rising further.

He told himself he was being silly. He warned himself that if he didn't deal with his emotions, he might end up with a stupid phobia about dumpsters. Still, the image of Candy behind the dumpster at the Creekstone was seared into his mind like a ghostly image after a flash of bright light.

He shoved his bag of trash through the partially open lid propped up by trash. Something alive inside the dumpster moved. Adam's heart skipped a beat. He jumped back, and an opossum scurried out of the open dumpster and climbed onto the top of the enclosure wall. It stopped, turned on its rat like tail, and stared Adam down. It stood its ground, unwilling to abandon its scavenged meal.

For a moment, they just looked at one another, then Adam began slowly backing away.

"I brought you some mashed potatoes and coleslaw." He spoke to the creature, trying to break the eerie spell. But, instead, the sound of Harjo's voice intruded. *"Two possible victims."*

Adam left the hallway light on in case Elf came back. Sitting down at the table in his room, illuminated by his new desk lamp, Adam unsheathed his puzzle. Even at a thousand pieces, the dimension of the puzzle fit nicely on his tabletop. Handful by handful, Adam sorted through the pieces. He placed the edge pieces face down on the table; the other pieces ended up in the lid of the box.

Once he thought he had all the edge pieces, his eyes began what had grown to be an automatic process of matching shapes, and Adam fell into the concentrated trance of the puzzle. Disjointed ideas and images floated through his thoughts in the background.

Before he realized it, two hours had passed. A yawn told him how long the day had been. He surveyed his work. He was missing a piece of the puzzle edge. Still, there was enough of the edge completed to move forward. He'd find that missing piece eventually.

Remembering he needed to work the next day, and he needed to start at eleven instead of four, he switched off the desk lamp, dropped his clothes on the floor, and crawled into bed.

It was just after dawn when Adam stepped out of his back door. From his bedroom window, he could see that the grassy area he had traversed the previous evening was generous enough for him to do his wrestling drills.

He had taken up doing drills early in the morning. There was a park near his old motel that proved to be open and spacious enough for him to add moves back into his program. Almost all the moves were back, but he was still cautious about certain tumbles.

Adam's neck was nearly back to normal, but there were times when a quick turn of the head would cause him discomfort, and the muscles would tighten up. Slowly but surely, he'd get fully back in condition.

One of the advantages of the complex was a central community pool attached to a workout room with cardio and resistance equipment.

He made a mental note to tell Elf and Tom that they'd have to register and sign a waiver if they wanted to use it. He thought Tom might go for it—former state judo champ, still teaching when he could. Guys like that, Adam knew firsthand, needed a way to sweat out the static in their heads. As his Nonno would say, to release the tension out of an overwound spring inside. If Tom didn't push himself, maybe he'd just stagnate. Maybe Adam would need to push him a little. Like a coach. Or a friend.

Elf was a different story. He had the build of some of the scrappiest guys Adam had ever wrestled, but Elf couldn't believe it. He remembered the smirk on Elf's face the first time Adam said so, like he couldn't picture himself fighting anyone.

Still, Elf took judo lessons with Tom. That counted for something. Adam wondered if he could get him to try the gym, not for muscle, but for confidence. God knew he remembered how long it took to believe in his own strength again.

Considering how the manager of the apartment complex had warmed to him, he guessed that she wouldn't fuss over his having two roommates. His lease allowed for one. If there were an added fee, he'd just quietly pay it.

The grass was still damp with dew when he started, but it quickly dried. His clothes took a little longer, but eventually his perspiration replaced the dew. It felt good to push himself far enough to work up a real sweat.

Adam now sat cross-legged on the lawn, feeling the warmth of the sun and the slight cooling of an occasional breeze. The patch of grass was nestled between two buildings. When surrounded by windows, his sense of being observed crept up. He told himself that it was Saturday morning and most working people would still be in bed. "Get used to it, Adam," he whispered to himself. "You can't expect privacy here."

In truth, he couldn't expect privacy anywhere he did those drills unless he had a secluded, indoor space. Baxter had said that at least one person had commented on watching him do his exercises.

In Broken Arrow, there were the dog walkers, Jason and his friend. They sometimes stopped to watch him. Adam assumed they were a couple, but didn't know for sure. One or the other of them had walked by with the retrievers every time he was exercising in the park next to the motel. He might not have noticed them, but the retrievers were fully grown and still acted like puppies, tugging and straining at their leashes.

Adam froze. Had they been simply walking the dogs? Or, like Harjo suggested, might they have been watching him? His eyes scanned the windows and then the grounds just to check if someone was being as blatant as those two guys in the park. Technically, he saw no one except a tabby cat, sitting on its haunches, tail wrapped around its legs. It seemed to stare him down like the opossum had the previous evening. The cat blinked slowly a couple of times and then casually walked off, tail raised. *Probably to report on the new weirdo in town to its owner or perhaps the opossum,* Adam thought to himself. He watched the cat pass through the wrought iron fence surrounding the pool and disappear.

In a smooth move worthy of a wrestling drill, he stood up, brushed himself off and went to shower, shave, and dress for work.

Seven

Adam pedaled his way to the Creekstone. The ride was pleasant and easy. Broken Arrow was mostly flat, and there were sidewalks the whole way, even in front of empty lots. As a kid in hilly Pittsburgh, he never minded having to laboriously pedal his way to the top of a hill because of the reward of the speed of sailing down the other side. From his apartment to the Creekstone, he hadn't even broken a sweat.

He arrived half an hour early, still time to check out the breakfast buffet. Apart from coffee, nothing interested him. As he filled his cup, he anticipated getting the stovetop espresso maker he had ordered. He imagined coming in from his workout and leisurely enjoying a cup of coffee over his puzzle.

He asked for the key to the lounge at the front desk and asked them to advise security that the bike chained to one of the trees in the west parking lot was his and that he'd be working until after midnight.

The lounge was perfectly quiet. Jenna, the manager who worked Hector's shift on Friday, had left the place spotless, but she hadn't restocked anything. Much of that work was heavy, and he imagined her in her stilettos carrying small buckets of ice or a few bottles of beer as she needed them.

Adam began restocking everything, and at eleven, he unlocked the doors and turned on the soft lighting. There were no customers. He didn't expect many. If Hector had time to study, he would have time to waste.

A server from the restaurant sauntered into the lounge. She carried a menu and her order book. "Jenna said you get two meals today. I'm here to take your orders. We'll send them over to you." She was short and sturdily built. Her uniform fit a bit too snugly. Her brown hair was pulled tightly back in a bun. She was pretty in a plain sort of way. Makeup wouldn't have suited her. She seemed to have difficulty looking him in the eye.

Adam glanced at her name badge. "Hi, Alice. It's nice to meet you. My name is Adam." He offered her his hand.

Instead of shaking hands, she gave him the menu. Her eyes flickered at him, and then she looked away. "I'm Alice. Nice to meet you, too." She was nervous talking to him. It reminded him of the women he took advantage of when he was drinking. A little attention from a good-looking guy and she'd do whatever he wanted. Her shyness caused him to feel a flash of guilt and shame.

"Nice picture," she said.

"Huh?" Adam glanced at her, then followed her gaze. He hadn't noticed that his own photo now hung where the old bartender's used to be, framed in the mahogany molding above the backlit shelves of top-shelf liquor.

He walked over to it to get a better look. It was an edited copy of the photograph that Jenna had taken of him with her phone on his first day. The background was intentionally blurred, probably because patrons could be seen behind him.

"Wow! I hadn't noticed that Jenna changed the picture."

"It's a great photo of you." She blushed.

"It isn't bad. I wonder if Jenna still has it in her phone. I'll ask her." He was thinking his sister would like it. She always liked to see where he was and what he was doing.

"That's Candy behind you, isn't it?" Alice said. "You were the one to find her, weren't you?"

Adam looked more intently at the out-of-focus patrons behind him. He spoke slowly. "I think you are right. Did you know her well?"

Alice shook her head. "Not well. They sat in my section a few times."

"They?" He was curious.

"She'd come for dinner sometimes with her brother and her friend. They liked my section. Big tippers," she added. "Cash, and left it folded like a fan."

"Alice, did you talk to the police?"

She shook her head. "I wasn't here when they came. Everybody is talking about it." She found the courage to look at Adam directly. "She was nice. Her brother looked young. I'll bet he's taking the news hard."

"Alice, it could be important for you to talk to the police," Adam insisted.

"I don't really know anything," she shrugged.

"When were they last in your section?" Adam asked.

She thought. "Maybe last Monday. Listen, I got to get back. Do you know what you want?"

Adam placed his order, and since it was on Jenna, he treated himself to a T-bone steak for dinner. As Alice walked out of the lounge, he searched his call history for Harjo's cell number and described his talk with Alice.

The day was excruciatingly slow. His lunch was delivered and eaten before he noticed any activity at all. He had no idea how many guests were in the hotel. Either they were in their rooms or out for the day. He took the opportunity to dust the top-shelf bottles and clean the mirror behind the glass shelves.

The only lobby activity he saw was a few people going into or leaving the restaurant. Even the two people scheduled to work at the front desk spent most of their time in the back. Harjo had replied to Adam's text with a thumbs-up. Whether he had already planned to question her or was quick off the mark, Adam didn't know.

Harjo arrived with a uniformed officer in tow. It wasn't Terry Gamble but a lanky guy who was so tall, he had to special order his uniforms. Harjo sent a glance and a nod as he passed the lounge.

By three o'clock, Adam had sold one bottled beer to a man waiting for his wife and thoroughly cleaned the lounge. He sat down in the booth with the best view of the lounge entrance, pulled out his cell phone and watched several installments of his nephew Jake's travel vlog. Jake and his friend Julian were touring the country in a converted van, camping and making random stops in odd places. They had earned over five thousand subscribers in under two months.

When Harjo walked through the door to the lounge, Adam stood up, offered them something to drink and invited them to sit. They accepted the seat but not the drinks. The tall, uniformed officer excused himself to visit the restroom, and Adam sat down with Harjo.

"Thanks for the tip, Mr. Alba," Harjo said. "I knew we were missing a few people. I would have sent a uniform to take a statement, but your text convinced me to come myself."

"Alice seemed to know more about Candy than anyone else," Adam said.

"She knew more than she thought she did." Harjo sat back, considered, and then forged ahead. "Can you tell me about your experience in New Orleans?"

Adam was stunned. Slowly, he said, "There's a detailed report. I was exonerated. Detective DuPuis—"

Harjo interrupted him. "Mr. Alba, I've read the report. I've had a lengthy discussion with Batist DuPuis. I'd like to hear more about it from your perspective."

Adam sat back and considered. "Why, what's that have to do with this?" His defenses were rising, and Harjo sensed it.

"Mr. Alba, if I were accusing you of anything, I'd be advising you of your rights. I'm just exploring a hypothesis, one that I think needs to be considered."

Adam had heard that logic before. They were interrupted by the return of the tall, uniformed officer.

"Are you sure I can't get you something to drink, Officer…" Adam looked at his name badge… "Lake? Perhaps a soft drink?"

"No, thank you. I'm fine," Officer Lake said as he slid into the booth.

"Please, Mr. Alba," Harjo said calmly. "A few details in this investigation have come up, and I think your experience in New Orleans may or may not be relevant. As I said, I'm exploring a hypothesis."

"It'll take a while," Adam warned, "and if there are customers, I'll have to tend to them." They listened intently. As he was coming to the conclusion, he said, "Through most of it, DuPuis was a real dick, and I don't mean the abbreviation for detective. He came around in the end, but it wasn't easy for him to admit he was wrong. Now, I think he's a hero."

They looked at one another. "Mr. Alba, what you did was very risky."

"I know it, and I knew it then, but if DuPuis had been less of a dick, I wouldn't have had to do it. He just wouldn't listen, or better said, he couldn't hear what was being said. He ignored what he heard and discounted the people who said it. I couldn't let that go."

"That's why he speaks so highly of you, Mr. Alba. Please, if you ever think I or any of my crew are acting like dicks, I trust you will tell me."

Lake glanced suspiciously at his superior, but he quickly checked himself. Harjo noticed. Putting his hand on Lake's shoulder. "Yes, Lake, I want to know if you are ever acting like a dick."

As Harjo and Lake stood up to go, three guys walked into the lounge. It was just before five, and Adam excused himself to serve his customers.

Adam's dinner arrived, and while he was eating, his phone rang.

"Adam, Jenna here."

"Jenna, it's been dead here all day." He flinched at his own bad choice of words. "Should I call it a day? I've cleaned the place top to bottom."

"No, I forgot to tell you. The lounge has been booked for a bachelor party. There's a sign on a stand in my office that says the lounge is closed for a private event. Shit, I should have warned you. I'm so sorry. "

Adam took a deep breath and tried to hide his frustration. "No worries. Just tell me what I need to do."

Put the sign out at eight o'clock. It's a cash bar until the sign is out. After that, it all goes on the best man's tab. He's your go-to, but you can call me if you need advice. Ring well drinks, draft beer, and fountain only on this code. Got a pencil?"

"Yep." He jotted the number down.

"Cash bar for top-shelf liqueurs. Catering will bring in food about 8:30."

"How many people am I expecting?"

"The best man said about twenty. His name is Hamish McFadden. He'll introduce himself to you. Big guy with a red beard. He's huge, like six-six and huge muscles."

"Jenna, these guys are going to trash the place." Adam's imagination filled the room with drunk men, spilling drinks, throwing up, and starting fights.

"We got a cleaning deposit. But Hamish promises to keep them in check. You don't have to clean up. A crew will come in after close."

"Regular time?"

"Yep, last call eleven-thirty. Doors locked at midnight. Oh, Adam, listen. If someone seems a little too drunk, like liability-level drunk, ask to see his room key and let Hamish know. Someone will take him to his room. Most of these guys are from out of town, and the wedding guests have a block of rooms."

"What if he doesn't have a key?"

"Cut him off and let Hamish know. I'm telling you, Hamish is a real bruiser. He'll take care of it. Adam, I'm really sorry for not warning you. After the police were at us yesterday, I've been busy pulling reports. I got a request for another one just a while ago. They want the z-reports for the restaurant for the last seven days."

"What's a z-report?" Adam had never heard the phrase.

"It's everything. Every order. Every server. Every table. Every receipt. Every cash and credit card transaction. I'm fucked. Got to go." She hung up.

"If *you're* fucked, what am I?" Adam whispered to himself.

In preparation, Adam checked the fountain canisters and draft kegs, overstocked on imported beer, and made sure there was room for the catering table without having to move seats or customer tables.

It was going to be an even longer day than he had planned. Stevie Tramonto came to mind, and he immediately felt himself relax. He took out his phone, found her number, and invited her to join him for breakfast at the Moonstone diner at 10 a.m. He tagged a map in his text in case she didn't know the Moonstone.

The first kilt arrived at seven-fifteen. It was a cliché, but Adam thought of Hamish McFadden as a "mountain of a man." Jenna had called him a bruiser. He could have easily been a bouncer at the roughest club in town. Six foot four or five, he probably weighed 275 pounds of lean muscle. He was polite and, Adam thought, aware of but a little self-conscious of his intimidating stature—the kind of guy who could use it when he needed it but didn't abuse it.

His deep baritone voice was intentionally softened. He assured Adam that his "mates" were decently behaved, respectful lads, but he added, "Lads are lads." Adam wasn't sure what that meant, but he accepted Hamish's assurance that if any got out of line, he'd take care of them. His blue eyes twinkled like he had already had a few beers under his belt.

He handed Adam a platinum credit card and a room key folder. "Starting right now, any cash bar drinks go on this card. No limit. I'll pick that up and sign off on it at the end of the night."

Adam took the card and slipped it into the cash register drawer.

The guests arrived in groups of three or four. Adam thought he recognized several of them. People came and went in the lounge, but the Scottish accent made them distinctive.

Six of them were in kilts. There were twenty others, mostly family of the groom and a few men from the bride's side. They were enough to keep Adam busy with refills. When the groom arrived, he too wore a kilt. Hamish introduced him to applause. His sincere but brief speech revealed he, too, was from Scotland. Adam half expected bagpipes.

The food—wings, ribs, and nachos—was gone almost as quickly as it arrived, and the drinking did not stop.

Adam hadn't been in a room with so much testosterone since his last wrestling weigh-in. Apart from what Hamish assured him was just "laddy banter," there wasn't much rowdiness. By eleven o'clock, the only ones left were from abroad. They settled down and continued to drink until last call.

The only American to remain was one of the groomsmen. He looked familiar to Adam, but he couldn't place him. He sauntered toward the bar, his eyes fixed on Adam.

"You don't recognize me, do you?" He smiled coyly at Adam.

"I've been trying to place you. Please don't be offended; a lot has happened in my life recently."

The kilted man tried to look into his eyes. "The Balustrade."

Adam looked at him carefully, his mind tracing his time at the Balustrade, the gay bar where he worked in the French Quarter. The groomsman waited.

The look on Adam's face shifted. He was back behind the bar in the Balustrade. The image of that exaggerated creature sitting at his usual table with his usual friends, several men at least twice his age. Adam remembered the way he fluttered among them, the center of their attention, all the while sending furtive glances in Adam's direction. Adam had nicknamed him the Butterfly. He had never approached the bar in the Balustrade. His friends always bought his drinks for him.

Adam paused as he let the memory sink in. "I can make a Negroni for you if you'd like," Adam said, feeling his heart beating in his chest. He had always thought that the Butterfly was creepy. The way he flitted, landing on a forearm, a hand, or shoulder, sometimes boldly enough to send them an empty embrace, seemed teasing—an act—as if he had some power over them, but was pretending otherwise. It all struck Adam as unnatural.

Out of the corner of his eye, Adam noticed Hamish keeping an eye on the exchange as if he might have to step in.

"So, you *do* remember me. Of course, I made an impression on you. You certainly made an impression on me."

"I wasn't aware of that." Adam paused in what stretched into an awkward silence. "Would you like a Negroni?" Adam wanted this exchange to be over, or at least different.

The Butterfly nodded with an expression that was at once coy and coquettish, reaching his hands toward Adam but not landing anywhere.

Adam's face became solid. He had gotten used to gay men coming on to him at the Balustrade. Most of them knew he was straight, and it was just flirting like Rosie back in Ur did with her customers. Sometimes, he even flirted in response. It was a harmless game that earned him tips. But the Butterfly was just odd, different, like the stakes had changed. Here at the Creekstone, it felt as unwelcome as it was out of place.

He set about making the cocktail, never looking at his customer. Stirring the cocktail in ice to chill it, he focused his attention on the task, but he could feel the Butterfly watching him, not watching what he was doing, but watching him do it as if he were looking for a place to land.

Adam strained the drink into a glass, garnished it with a slice of orange, and slid it across the bar to him, looking at him only in the last second. "Hamish is buying. Thank you for visiting the Creekstone," Adam said dismissively, allowing a meager smile. Adam didn't let the moment linger. He turned away and began washing glasses.

As the last of the bachelor party patrons filtered out, Hamish returned to settle his bill.

"This is only the top-shelf bar tab; well drinks were included in your contract," Adam said, sliding the register receipt toward Hamish.

Hamish nodded. "I remember. You've done a great job, pal. Everyone had a good time."

Adam showed him the total. Hamish laughed. "I expected it to be double that. So, double it and take the extra as a tip."

Adam raised his brow.

Hamish nodded encouragingly. "Go on. I mean it. And I apologize for the jobbie jabber. If he weren't the bride's brother…"

"Jobbie jabber?"

"That gay guy with the cocktail near the end. He gives us all the creeps."

Adam handed him the bill. "You can specify any tip you'd like."

Hamish more than doubled the bill, rounding it up to an even grand, signed the receipt, and offered Adam a fist bump. "Nice one, pal. Cheers."

"It's been my pleasure. Thanks for booking the Creekstone lounge." Adam had never received a tip that big in his life. He couldn't wait to hear what Jenna would say about it.

Throughout his bike ride home, he couldn't shake the feeling of threat left behind by that Butterfly from the Balustrade.

Eight

When he got home, his new stovetop espresso maker was already by his front door, the package illuminated by the porch light. He made his way into the kitchen and opened the package. He hadn't yet bought any coffee, but he wanted to see it. It was just like the one his grandmother used.

He took it apart, looked at the pieces, and could still see his Nonna filling the bottom with water, tamping in the coffee, and setting it on the stove. He washed it out by hand, rinsed it, and set it on a kitchen towel to dry. It made him feel warm inside and helped calm the creepy feeling planted by the Butterfly.

He climbed the stairs, undressed, and showered. He imagined the long, tedious day peeling away from his skin as he luxuriated in the hot water, rinsing away the soap from his body. He could feel himself settling.

It was after one in the morning. He should have gone straight to bed, but he couldn't resist spending a little more time seated in front of his puzzle.

While he worked on the puzzle, the back burners of his mind simmered with unanswered questions. Why or how did Harjo connect

New Orleans with Broken Arrow? Had it been a result of something Alice had unwittingly said? Was it a mere coincidence that the Butterfly showed up on the very day that Harjo asked about New Orleans? He had never even spoken to Adam before. He had been just a string of Negroni cocktails and furtive glances. Could there really be a connection between the Balustrade and the Creekstone?

A yawn reminded him that it was time for bed. Adam sat back in his chair. He had placed several more pieces in the puzzle and had pieced together a group of four that connected to the border. That was an achievement this early in the process. He stretched his arms toward the ceiling and torqued in his chair, cracking his back and stretching his obliques. He got up, removed his clothing, and crawled into his bed.

In his dream, he was walking down a long, straight road down a ramshackle, dilapidated main street. The shadow feeling was stronger than usual. He could sense someone following him, and every time he turned to look, he saw a woman dressed in widow's weeds—a long black dress and a veil. She kept her distance.

Finding his destination, he turned into a funeral parlor and entered a salon. He recognized two guests in the room: his nephew Jake and Jake's friend Julian. Adam wondered if this funeral home was one of the stops on their vlogging adventure.

As he approached the casket, he saw that it was empty. He turned around. The woman in mourning stood between him and Jake. She lifted her veil, and Adam saw the face of the Butterfly.

He woke up in a cold sweat.

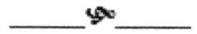

The Moonstone was packed with Sunday morning churchgoers when Stevie arrived. Even the few seats at the counter were occupied, so she had to wait. A booth that could comfortably seat six finally became available, and she felt the need to assure the server that she wouldn't be eating alone.

The server, a girl named Leticia, just smiled and shrugged at her explanation. Her mousy brown hair was pulled back in a ponytail. There was boredom behind her smile. Her job was just a job. At twenty-something, she was less than half Brooke's age, had less than half her energy and none of her personality. She was in constant low-gear movement. She reminded Stevie of a duck in a carnival shooting gallery just drifting from place to place.

Stevie poured a little allulose sweetener into her coffee from an orange prescription bottle she had saved. She had read somewhere that allulose had some weight loss benefits beyond mere lack of calories. Why not give it a chance? To control her diabetes and lose a bit of weight, she had tried every miracle product on the market, everything from cinnamon supplements and chia seeds to exotic teas from isolated tropical islands. What was one more?

Through the window, she saw Adam arrive on his bike. He parked it behind a shrubbery and leaned it against the wall of the diner. She watched him use a chain to secure the wheels. As he stood up, she knocked on the window to get his attention. *Oh, Stevie,* she thought to herself, *You're acting just like a silly schoolgirl.* She felt like one, too.

Adam looked up and saw Stevie smiling and excitedly waving. *I hope I have as much enthusiasm as she does when I'm her age,* Adam thought. He waved happily. He felt glad to see her as well. Though he barely knew her or anything about her, he felt a strong tie to her. He wouldn't call it affection, not yet. Their conversations felt more like catching up after years of separation than getting to know a new friend.

Inside, he slipped into the seat opposite her. He noticed Brooke wasn't serving and guessed that Elf would be in church. "Have you ordered yet?"

"Heavens no. Just the coffee so far."

Leticia approached the table to take Adam's drink order. Stevie smiled to herself. Leticia seemed just a bit lighter and had a little more verve. Adam was easily the most attractive man in the diner, and it was obvious that Stevie and he were not a couple. Leticia probably assumed she was his mother.

"I have a small housewarming gift for you," Stevie said, opening her bag and pulling out a small package of Lavazza Espresso Roast coffee.

"You didn't need to do that." Adam blushed a little.

"Oh, I didn't do anything special. When I opened my cupboard this morning, I saw it and thought of you."

Adam brightened as he realized that Lavazza was coffee. "You must be psychic. I was going to buy coffee on the way home. I just got an espresso maker. It's just like my grandmother's."

Stevie beamed with pleasure.

Leticia returned with Adam's coffee and water and took their orders. The bell on the service windowsill dinged twice. Adam looked up and saw that plates were piling up. Clearly, the cook was faster than the server.

The double bell had less of an effect on Leticia than Adam's smile had. "Brook is so much more pleasant," Stevie said.

"So, you know the place," Adam said.

"I live a few blocks away, less than a quarter mile. I don't eat out often. I prefer to cook at home, but sometimes I feel lazy. You know, I don't know what feels worse, cooking for one or eating alone in a restaurant."

The volume in the restaurant seemed to rise. Some customers who had finished their meals were waiting at the register to pay, and others were waiting to be seated. Just then, a familiar-looking man came out of the back to man the register. It was the same guy who was wrapping silverware when Adam had last eaten there.

"I rarely cook for myself," Adam mused. "I can make a few things. I just never learned how to really cook. So, I eat out alone a lot."

"My grandmother used to say 'Alone, a man can fill his stomach, but a good wife fills his belly and his soul,'" Stevie reminisced. "It's a little sexist, I suppose, but it was true back then."

Adam looked down and smiled.

"What just happened?" Stevie asked observantly.

"My grandmother said almost the same thing, but in Italian," he chuckled. "And then my grandfather would say something back and they'd have a little playful spat."

"Well, I was translating. It seems we have something in common then. When did your grandparents come to this country?"

Adam raised a brow. "It's a long story."

"So, who's in a hurry?" She waved a ringed hand in the air. The bangle bracelets on her wrist jingled loudly enough for the man in the booth behind her to turn around.

Adam challenged himself to organize the story in a concise way. "I don't know when my great-grandparents came here, but right after my grandfather was born, the family moved back to Italy. He says they said it was because of the Depression, but my Nonno told me his father liked Mussolini."

Stevie looked surprised.

"Wait, it gets better," Adam said. "When my grandfather was twelve, he carried messages for the resistance in the frame of his bicycle. My great-grandfather never knew."

"That's amazing."

"It is. My Nonno is very special to me."

"How did your family get back to the States?"

"My Nonno was a citizen. He came on his own after the war. I think he was like fourteen or fifteen."

"On his own?"

"On his own. He met another kid on the boat, made friends, and ended up in Pittsburgh. He worked in a factory and stayed in a boarding house. That's where he met my Nonna. She was the daughter of the couple who ran the boarding house."

Stevie sipped her coffee and winced. "Cold," she said. "That is a beautiful story. Are your grandparents still around? They must be quite elderly now."

"My grandfather is, but my grandmother died a few years ago. He lives alone, but my sister takes care of him. He turns ninety-five this year, I think."

Leticia brought their food. She kept her eyes on Adam and nearly knocked over Stevie's water with her plate.

"Could you heat this up for me, please?" Stevie held up her cup. The server just nodded and walked away.

"I think you are distracting her," Stevie said, rearranging the plate. "She can't take her eyes off you."

Adam bit his bottom lip and had trouble knowing where to look. The shadow feeling was creeping up on him.

"Did I say something wrong?" she asked.

He blushed. "Not really. I'm just uncomfortable being stared at. It makes me feel self-conscious, and I don't like that feeling." Adam didn't want to explain about his shadow.

She smiled broadly. "Well then, it's unfortunate that you are such a good-looking young man." She meant it as a compliment with a twist of teasing.

His face reddened. "How do I respond without sounding egotistical?"

She realized he was more sensitive than she understood and artfully chose more humor to deflect it. "By the same measure, how did I say such a thing without sounding like a dirty old broad?"

Their eyes met in a moment of awkward silence in which they came to understand one another, and they both burst into laughter.

It worked.

At that moment, Elf backed through the swinging kitchen door with a bus tray. Leticia was falling further behind, and there were people waiting for tables that had emptied. As he cleared a table, the old man seated them and got them drinks.

"Looks like Leticia is not long for the Moonstone," Adam commented. "She's not even speeding up."

Elf bussed the table behind Stevie. "Didn't know you were coming in. Glad to see you. Tom and I are planning on moving in this evening if that's alright with you."

He was in such a hurry, there was no time for Adam to introduce him to Stevie.

"It's okay with me, Elf. I'll be at work until midnight, or I'd stick around to help."

He was now wiping down the table. "Tom asked me to ask you if he could teach judo in the living room. He has mats."

Adam's face lit up. "Sounds like a plan. At least it will get used for something. I have no use for it."

Stevie raised her eyebrows.

"You're awesome. I'll text him before he leaves Ur," Elf said, moving to another table.

Stevie looked quizzically at Adam. "Judo lessons in your living room?"

"Sorry I couldn't introduce you. That was Elf. He and another guy he goes to Bible school with are moving in with me."

She nodded. "I've seen him here before. Bible school? And the other guy teaches judo?"

Adam nodded, finishing his last fry. "Yep, he was state champion a couple years back. I met them in Ur."

"My what?"

"No, the town of Ur. Ur, like in the Bible. It's a small town… very small," he added.

"Never heard of the place." She sipped her coffee. Winced again. It was still cold.

Terry Gamble had volunteered for overtime but didn't get the assignment he hoped for. His partner and mentor, Riley, had a week's vacation scheduled, so Gamble pulled front desk duty for the next week. He was clearly in a salty mood.

"Terry, Harjo is ordering burgers. He wants to know if you'd like anything," Lake said, passing by the front desk.

Gamble looked up at him as if the offer had been a patronizing one. "No thanks. I'm off in an hour or so."

Lake understood why Gamble was in a bad mood. He couldn't hide his disappointment over being sidelined on the investigation. After all, he and Riley were the first officers on the scene when the body was discovered, and he'd even sat in on Harjo's first interview with Adam Alba.

He felt bad for the rookie. He remembered his own enthusiasm when first joining the force. Terry just wasn't ready for this level of work. Investigations are sensitive. A lot hangs on procedure and not making rookie mistakes that can get the perp off on a technicality. Gamble was too new, too green. He'd get there eventually, but he still needed the kind of seasoning that Lake had finally earned—had worked hard at earning.

He wanted to say something to Gamble to encourage him, but couldn't think what. It wasn't all excitement and adventure. He had just spent a day, a whole day, on a beautiful Sunday, watching Harjo conduct remote interviews on Zoom with possible witnesses. These were people who had occupied rooms with an alley view at the Creekstone.

More than just running through a checklist like a rookie might, he was amazed at how Harjo could build rapport with each witness in just a few moments. The order of his questions and the way he phrased them shifted subtly from person to person. It struck Lake that Harjo wasn't just interviewing; he was reading people. Lake couldn't help but marvel at the detective's ease and instinct. He made a mental note to ask him about it when he got the chance. Lake wondered if he could ever learn to do that.

Lake hadn't said much or done much, just took notes and tried to pick up on Harjo's strategy. After each call, they'd go over the notes and exchange ideas and impressions.

"All those rooms and no one saw anything out of the window." Lake was exasperated.

Harjo wasn't surprised. "It's not like those rooms have amazing views. I'll bet most people don't bother looking out. It's a business hotel. Most of the time they were working, watching movies, or asleep. The rooms were mostly empty during the day."

Lake was exhausted and bleary-eyed when Gamble knocked on the door with the food delivery.

"Thanks, Gamble," Harjo said.

"Anything else before I go, Detective?"

"No. Who is on next?" Harjo asked.

"Fleetwood, I think." He looked at his large, military dive watch that looked too big for his wrist. "In half an hour."

"Do me a favor; have him check in with me when he gets here."

"Will do, sir," Gamble said. He closed the door as he left.

"Did I just hear his voice crack a little?" Harjo looked at Lake, who was already sorting through the food order.

"I heard it too. He is a little old for puberty," Lake said. "You know what's bothering him, don't you?"

"I do. It can't be helped. Let's go over what we have while we eat. Sorry to keep you so late, but it's been three days since Alba found the body, and we aren't getting very far. I just spoke to the ME. I want to talk it through." He stood up and paced while he talked.

"Estimated time of death is between two and five a.m. That's the best guess, but it was a hot night. He said if the body were stored in a cool environment, it might be an hour or two earlier."

"Stored?" Lake said through a bite of burger.

"Stored. The lividity pattern indicates that she lay flat for several hours after death. Either the perp came back and propped her up, or he killed her somewhere else and moved the body. What do we have from the surveillance footage?"

"Nothing. The camera was shot out. Hotel security said it happened sometime on the previous Monday night," Lake said.

Harjo continued looking down at his notes. "Cause of death, asphyxia. Method: soft ligature strangulation with something like a scarf. There was also blunt force trauma to the right side of her head just before death. The ME says the impact was probably strong enough to disorient her. There was evidence of a concussion. The side of a fist or a rubber mallet.

"Now for the kicker," Harjo continued. "Candy was biologically male."

Nine

The Creekstone lounge was nearly empty when Adam arrived half an hour before his shift started. He knew he had to restock the bar for the busy Sunday evening shift, and it would be a big job. The light was low and amber, reflecting softly off polished wood surfaces. The piped-in music played respectfully in the background, hardly noticeable unless you looked for it. The room smelled faintly of citrus cleaner. The cleaning crew had done a good job restoring the lounge after the bachelor party the previous evening.

There were only four patrons in the lounge. One man sat at a table pecking away at his laptop. Two men huddled near the bar were engaged in what looked like a strategic conversation. And in the shadowed corner booth sat the androgenous customer from previous Thursday. A sweating glass of Diet Coke sat on the table.

Apprehension stirred inside Adam. He had sized up this patron as a local, rather than a hotel guest. Repeat local customers were unusual in this business hotel lounge. It felt like he was being observed and if it weren't for the soft physique, he might have guessed the patron was undercover.

Adam tried to push off the feeling and the thoughts that came with it. There were tanks to check, bottled beer and the well to restock.

Even some of the top-shelf bottles had only a couple of shots in them. They'd be kept under the bar, and the display replaced with full bottles. He ducked behind the bar to take an inventory.

Katja, the platinum blonde college student who normally worked the front desk, stood nearby, posture rigid, hands folded like she was trying to mimic Jenna's poise. He greeted her casually. "How's it going?"

She looked at her watch and seemed pleased he was early. "Very slowly. Can I leave now?"

"I'd appreciate it if you could stay a little longer while I restock the bar. It should be ten minutes, tops."

She shrugged her shoulders in resignation. While he was connecting a new draft keg in the back, Katja approached him in confidence. Her eyes flicked toward the patron in the booth. "That one gives me the willies. I almost called security."

Adam stopped. "For what? Meditating over a drink?"

"She, he, it is just weird. They haven't even touched the drink. After what happened last week…"

He smiled patiently at her. "Don't worry. I recognize that customer and I don't think security is needed. Just let me restock and leave it to me."

She shrugged her shoulders and left him to his job.

The bottled drinks were out of stock behind the bar. Adam could imagine someone like Katja telling customers that they were out of a requested drink despite a full stockroom in the back. He used a dolly to save time bringing out cases of bottled beer.

He moved quickly and efficiently. He could almost hear Harjo's voice advising him to vary his routine, but his system worked well, and it felt comfortable. As he took out the trash, a nervous feeling of entering the dumpster enclosure overtook him once again.

He wondered how long it would take for him to get beyond the guttural reaction of finding Candy's body. He fought his nerves while pulling open the enclosure doors. His eyes involuntarily looked to the ground for the shoe that was not there.

There were two brand new dumpsters in the enclosure. He lifted the lid of one and tossed the trash bag in. He closed the metal doors behind him. He looked up. Two new cameras had been mounted on the back wall of the hotel.

Before he reached the door, he stopped short and stood straight up. His thoughts glazed over his eyes. He could feel the blood draining and that sinking feeling when someone realizes how stupid they have been. Pieces were falling into place, or were they? It could be his imagination. Harjo's speculation that he might be a victim. The odd patron sitting in the back booth. The twenty-dollar bill folded like a fan, the way Candy used to do it.

Maybe it really was just a coincidence that the Butterfly from the Balustrade showed up on the day Harjo questioned him about New Orleans. The more obvious fit could be the odd patron lurking in the back booth while he discovered Candy's body, like an arsonist who waits around to watch the flames. Then there was that tip folded into a fan the way Candy did. Was it a message, a hint, or a warning? That androgenous appearance could just be a kind of disguise to ward off an accurate description.

Adam considered texting Harjo, but how would Harjo respond? If he came himself or sent someone else, what would they do? How would things go down? What if there was really nothing to this? What if the back booth client were just a little odd, depressed, or mentally ill? It could be nothing at all.

That back-booth patron might sit there until last call like they did Thursday evening. Even Katja recognized how odd and weirdly sinister this customer might prove to be. This couldn't wait for Harjo.

By the time he got back to the lounge, Katja was even more anxious to leave. That was all for the better. Let her go. Even with the gentlest approach, the patron might react badly. Katja didn't need to be around for that. He nodded to her. She nodded back with a sardonic smile. Had she shrugged her shoulders? Their eyes were locked. She nodded at him again and walked out of the lounge without saying another word.

Adam could feel his heartbeat increase in rhythm and strength. Was it anger or fear or a combination of the two? It was like going into a new wrestling match with an unknown opponent. It was all to play for. He kept moving, eyeing the booth in his peripheral vision. The patron didn't budge.

Adam's sense of shadow was the strongest it had been in days, weeks, and even months. It felt like he was watching the whole scene from a distance, like a movie, with music in the background building tension. He hadn't felt this kind of anticipation since that night back in New Orleans when the only way to know for sure was to find out for himself.

Adam decided to make the rounds to the existing customers. He filled several small bowls with a salty snack mix as a complimentary offering. He visited each table with a smile, setting the snack down on the table and introducing himself. He approached the back booth last.

"Hi. I'm Adam, your bartender. Just wanted to welcome you to the Creekstone lounge and offer you a complimentary bar snack. Is there anything I can get you?" he asked, keeping his voice even and casual.

The patron looked up as if they had been expecting him. "Got a minute?"

Adam nodded, his heart beating in his chest. "Sure. What's up?"

"I'm looking for Candy. She never came home Wednesday night."

The words landed like a sucker punch to his chest. He tried to keep his expression and his nerves steady. He pretended to think. Hesitantly, he said, "The last time she was in the lounge was Wednesday night." It wasn't a lie; Adam wasn't sure how far he should go.

"I come to pick her up every night. I tried calling her, but it went to voicemail. I waited until two, but she never came out. We're worried about her." The patron's eyes lingered on his own with palpable wariness.

Adam stood tall. "We?" Adam echoed. "Who's we?" He had already begun to soften toward this person, but he wanted to be cautious.

"Her brother and me. Caleb's thirteen. He woke me up Thursday morning when she wasn't there. She didn't come home Wednesday night. It's not like her."

Adam dropped some of his guard. He understood that Candy's positive identification was at hand, and he had the sinking feeling he'd have to be the bearer of bad news, not only for this person but for a thirteen-year-old boy. "Have you filed a missing person's report?"

"No. We were hoping to find her. If she's relapsed, we don't want Caleb taken from her. I've been staying with him since Thursday."

"Relapsed?"

"Your name tag says Adam. Are you Adam?"

He flushed and nodded.

"She told me you knew she was sober. I'm also her sponsor."

Adam glanced around the lounge. Nothing and no one needed his immediate attention. He sank into the booth. "She never drank here," Adam said. "Not when I was on duty, anyway."

"She said you were decent. That you didn't judge her."

"I didn't... don't," Adam said. "I've been sober seven years."

That earned him a nod. A small moment of trust passed between them.

"I'm Alex, he/him, if you're curious. Candy used she/her. That's another reason we haven't filed a missing person's report."

"I don't understand."

"My preferred pronouns," Alex said impatiently.

"Sorry. That part I get, but why would that stop you from making a report?"

Alex pressed his lips together in a grimace. "They wouldn't look for her. She's an adult. And if they found her, being trans might be another reason for them to try and take Caleb. Trans people aren't exactly *people* to a lot of folks."

Adam couldn't imagine living with that kind of fear, but he could easily understand how some people felt about the police. Adam pulled a card from his wallet and set it on the table. "I really think you should talk to the cops. This guy's different. His name's Harjo. A detective. Solid."

Alex picked it up, eyes narrowing. "A detective," he repeated. "You really think he'd care enough to do anything?"

"I do."

Alex set the card down slowly, as if it might detonate. "I'm not ready to call him. We'd rather stay below the radar and keep Caleb." Alex's shoulders sagged and his eyes went dull as if he were accepting the disappointment of the inevitable. "If you see her, will you let me know?"

Adam hesitated. He couldn't let Alex leave. He shouldn't be the one to deliver the news about Candy, but then perhaps he was the best one to do it. Alex and Caleb deserved to know the truth. He deflated. Decision made. The words tangled in his throat.

"I don't know if I'm the *best* person to tell you this…" He recounted the story slowly and as compassionately as he could.

Word by word, Alex's face changed from shock to horror to denial, then to fear to anger to resignation and grief. As tears streamed down Alex's face, he didn't move. He didn't try to hide them. He didn't wipe the tears away. Adam couldn't tell if they came from sadness or anger—probably both.

Adam felt anger at Candy's death. That anger lingered and festered like an infection. Now with the added knowledge that she lived in fear and anxiety, not because of her alcoholism but because of who she was, his anger grew into rage. Unlike Alex, it would never make him cry. It made him want to break something and do something about it.

Time stood still while they sat there in silence until Alex, who had never closed his eyes, probably visualizing the scene that Adam described, pointed a finger at the bar. Adam turned and saw several people now waiting to be served.

"I'll be back," he said, standing up. He chose to comfort Alex as he would any other man with a stoic face and a pat on the shoulder. "With your permission, I think you need to talk to Harjo. Honestly, he's a stand-up guy. May I call him?"

"You're sure I can trust him?" Alex asked without looking up at Adam.

"As sure as I can be." He hoped that Harjo wouldn't disappoint him.

The activity of customers turned into a steady stream, but when there was a gap, he returned to Alex. He brought him a cup of coffee, gently but reassuringly grasping Alex's shoulder again. Adam's dinner arrived from the restaurant shortly before six o'clock. He brought the tray to Alex and said, "You need to eat something. I got this for you." It was a simple burger and fries.

"I'm not sure what I need to do. I have to tell Caleb," Alex said hazily.

"There will be time for that. The detective I told you about is on his way. He'll know more than I do about what comes next."

"Thank you," Alex said. He accepted the plate without touching the food. He was still in shock, still processing his grief.

When Harjo arrived, he had Lake with him. Lake, looking exhausted, greeted Adam with a nod. Harjo was focused, determined. Adam held up a finger, indicating for them to wait. He finished the drink order he was serving and then greeted them. "His name is Alex. He's a friend of Candy's, also her AA sponsor. He and Candy are... were... both transgendered. Alex goes by he/him."

Adam led them to Alex's table and introduced them. Backing away, he went back to work, always keeping an eye on that booth, looking for Alex's reactions.

About half an hour later, the three of them stood up and were leaving together. Adam quickly jotted down his telephone number on the back of a coaster and handed it to Alex. "If you want to talk, just call. Anytime," he assured him.

"Thank you, Adam. For everything." Alex, still in a haze, walked out of the lounge with Harjo and Lake.

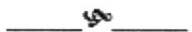

Caleb stood at the window of their apartment, looking at the park across the street. He had eaten almost half the pizza Alex ordered for him; a partially eaten slice lay on top of the box. His eyes scanned the park across the street. It was evening, and the dog walkers were out. Even on hot days, people had to walk their dogs.

Most days, dog walkers were the only people who used the park. Caleb loved dogs. He wished he could have one of his own, but the apartment building didn't allow pets. There were tenants who broke the rules, of course. Candy wouldn't allow Caleb to break the rules because she didn't want anything to jeopardize their lease. It was the best place they had lived in together, and neither of them wanted to move.

It took a lot for Candy to get Caleb back from the foster family. She had to be sober, and she had to have a real job. And... she had to be Andy again. That was a real sacrifice for her. By day Andy worked at a grocery store, but in the evenings, Candy had a different job as a hostess in a gay-friendly restaurant.

The only thing he missed about living with the foster family was Olive. Olive was a scruffy mut that he got to walk every day after school. He hated picking up Olive's poop with a plastic bag, but Olive was worth it. Nothing about that foster family felt like home except for Olive.

The couple he lived with were nice enough. The Hornfelds were older, almost like grandparents. They had rules, of course. He could live with rules. He had to keep his room clean, shower every day before school, wear clean clothes, do all his homework, and go to church.

Sunday school was kind of fun. He was with kids his own age, and they played games, and eventually, he learned how to find verses in the Bible as fast as any other kid. The worst part of that church was the service. The pastor yelled a lot and said terrible things that Caleb knew weren't true. He was obsessed about gay people and preached about sin and how evil gay people were. Caleb had known lots of gay people before living with the foster family. None of them were ever mean or tried to make him gay like the pastor said they would.

The problem was Candy didn't come home on Wednesday night.

He turned to Alex, their neighbor, because he didn't know what else to do. If he reported Candy missing, should it be as Candy or Andy? Alex said they should wait to hear from Candy.

Waiting was hard to do. Too many thoughts ran through his head. What if she didn't come back? What if she was drinking again? What would happen to him? Would he have to go back to the foster family? He was worried and scared.

He had homework to do for summer school and knew he should be doing it, but it was hard to keep his mind on it. Instead, he preferred to watch the dog walkers in the park. He was waiting to see the two golden retrievers. They looked like twins. They were big dogs, but they still acted like puppies. It made him happy to see them scampering and straining at their leashes.

The retrievers had two dads. One or the other would walk them every evening at about six o'clock. After he saw them, he would try and do his homework and wait to hear from Alex, who was out looking for Candy.

That night, when Alex got back. Caleb's life was turned upside down... again.

Ten

"Her legal name is Andrew Yates." Alex found it hard to turn away. Despite the unidentifiable cacophony of smells, Alex took a deep breath that resulted in a long, slow sigh that communicated real grief, at least to Harjo. "How'd it happen?"

Lake started to answer. "He was..."

Harjo intercepted him. "*She* was an attractive woman. I'm sorry, Mr. Duke, we need to withhold certain details pending the completion of our investigation."

Alex nodded. "Can I cover her face?" He wasn't allowed to touch her, and he wanted a way of saying goodbye.

Harjo plucked two nitrile gloves from a dispenser marked "SMALL." "Sure, the ME requires these."

Alex stretched the blue gloves over his hands and plucked the sheet in two places. He lifted the sheet and covered her face, muttering, "Mine eyes dazzle. She died young."

"Do you know who did it?" Alex asked as they left the room.

111

"I'm afraid we don't yet. I know this is a difficult time, but we'd like to ask you for some information that could help our investigation. We'll go to the station..."

Alex felt like he was sleepwalking through a fog, but he agreed.

Adam tossed all night. He knew that he had done the right thing, but he told himself that he could have done it better. In his waking moments, he relived the scene with Alex, trying to figure out what he could have done differently.

The only way he knew he'd slept at all was the dream. Ken Griffen, his last wrestling opponent, was riding a bike just ahead of him. Adam pedaled hard, following him all the way to the Creekstone, trying to catch up and make amends. But when he chased him through the lobby doors, Ken had vanished, and Candy was behind the front desk, checking in a hotel guest.

After the accident, Ken blamed himself and took his own life. Now, with Harjo suggesting Adam might have been the intended victim, it felt like Candy had paid a high price meant for him. He saw the two as somehow parallel.

It was just before dawn when Adam gave up trying to sleep. He climbed out of bed, slipped on workout clothes and headed toward the patch of lawn behind his building. Perhaps a workout would relax him enough to catch up on his sleep before he had to go to work that afternoon.

Dew- and sweat-soaked and breathing hard, he finished three sets of drills and double his normal calisthenics before he felt the shadow feeling that dogged him begin to dissipate. Dawn had broken, and he sat cross-legged on the ground, trying to focus inward.

He kept his eyes closed, focused his attention on his breath and watched his breathing deepen and slow down. When he felt grounded and calm, he opened his eyes, slowly taking in the now much brighter day.

It was the flick of a tail that drew his attention to the tabby cat sitting on the paved walkway, watching him. It was the second time he had the cat as an audience for his exercises. It seemed to be staring him down, occasionally blinking very slowly.

In an artificially high-pitched tone, Adam spoke to the cat. "Hey, kitty, kitty."

The tabby took on a skeptical look and stood up. Tail raised high and swaying its hind quarters, it slowly walked away, never looking back.

Adam laughed to himself. *Rejected by a stray cat.*

Walking in through the back door, he saw Elf and Tom sitting at the breakfast counter. They looked up from bowls of cereal, big smiles on their faces.

"You guys are up early," Adam said.

"Not really. Classes start at 8," Tom said.

Adam looked at Elf. "Don't you have to work?"

"If I were working breakfast, I'd already be there. Frank does his best to work around my class schedule."

It was then that Adam noticed the pile of boxes and other things in the living room. "Wow, that's a lot of stuff." He assumed that the barstools they were sitting on came with Tom.

Tom was grinning. "My mom and I made a list of stuff we might need, and then she spread the word around the church. They filled up my truck!"

Adam beamed at him. He noticed Tom said *his* truck, not his father's truck. It felt like a positive transition. "That's amazing."

"Tell him about his surprise, Tom," Elf said.

"We had breakfast at the Rest. Rosie sends her love."

"And a chocolate cake," Elf added. It's there on the counter."

It had perfectly survived the two-hour drive from Ur and looked delicious.

"Oh, and Henry sent a container of his grandmother's stew and fry bread. It's in the fridge. He says you can microwave the fry bread or just put it in the oven for a while," Tom said.

Adam felt the warmth knowing he was no more out of their thoughts than they were out of his. The care they gave him during his recovery had been remarkable, and he had no doubt the affection was real. "Thanks. I'll call them later and thank them."

"They'd like that, I'm sure. And," he seemed a little embarrassed. "My mom says thank you, too."

"For what?" Adam hoped it wasn't another expression of gratitude for his attempt to resuscitate Tom's father.

Elf spoke through a laugh, "For taking care of her little boy."

Tom rolled his eyes.

Adam reassured him. "Don't be embarrassed, Tom. Mothers are always mothers, and we all know you don't really need anyone to take care of you."

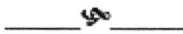

The line at the coffee shop was long. While Stevie waited, she glanced at her usual table. It was taken by two men in suits huddled in a conversation. It was her favorite table. Of course, she could sit somewhere else. Inspiration struck her, and when it was her turn, she asked for a heated cinnamon roll to go.

In her car, her thumbs hovered briefly over her phone screen before she typed. She didn't think it was too early. After all, Adam had shared her cinnamon roll twice before at about the same time. Still, they didn't have a plan. She might be interrupting. She debated for another minute. Then she thought, *what the hell... why not?*

She typed. *Picked up a cinnamon roll this morning—thought we could split it over your grandmother's espresso. What do you think? Is now a good time?* She stared at the message a beat longer, second-guessing her impulse, her teeth pressing lightly into her bottom lip, this time weighing the vulnerability in the offer. She didn't want to be too pushy.

Don't be silly, Stella. A visit from a friend is always welcome. What's the worst that can happen? She could hear her mother's voice in her head. *If he isn't home or doesn't have time, you can go home and make your own damned coffee.*

She hit send. *And if he isn't home, I'll end up eating the whole cinnamon roll myself!*

Stevie was fairly certain she knew the complex Adam lived in, but she didn't remember which unit. Without waiting for a reply, she opened the thread with his contact photo. In it, he sat smiling up at the camera. She tapped on the address embedded beneath it. A few swipes and Google Maps was chirping soft directions through the speakers.

Harjo and Lake sat in the coffee shop with cups of steaming coffee. Harjo had a breakfast sandwich on a croissant; Lake was unwinding his way through a cinnamon roll. Harjo tried not to eye Lake's roll. They were rumored to be the best in town, but as of late, his clothes were fitting a little tighter.

After the events of the previous evening, which included the positive identification of Candy's body as Andrew Yates and an extensive interview with Alex Duke, they decided to confer after sleeping on the information. It had been a very long day.

Terry Gamble had desk duty at the station and was becoming a nuisance. He badgered Lake with questions about the case every chance he got. When Lake said he couldn't discuss it, Gamble took it personally. Lake had tried to tell him that even if he could discuss it, there wasn't much to discuss. Gamble didn't believe him.

Lake was suggesting that they speak with Candy—Andy's little brother—as a next step.

"I want to give him a few days before doing that. He may or may not have information we can use, but it sounded like the kid, Caleb, was kept mostly in the dark. Remember that Duke said the kid didn't know his sister was turning tricks to make ends meet. Duke seems stable enough to help him through this. He must trust Duke to have gone to him for help."

"I caught that," Lake said. "He also said the boy didn't like the foster family he had been placed with. He may not have had anyone else to go to. I'd like to talk to him alone to find out how much he really does trust Duke."

"Yes, social services might have an interest in that conversation. He will need some kind of adult representation in that interview, for his sake and, frankly, for ours," Harjo asserted. "After that, his future will be up to Child Welfare Services. I'd rather wait until after the funeral, if we can. Give the kid time to adjust."

Lake thought Harjo was being too soft. Giving young Caleb time to adjust also gave Alex Duke time to coach him. He didn't like Alex Duke. There was something odd and disconcerting about him. He couldn't put his finger on it. It wasn't just because he was transgender. Being the closest adult to Yates that they knew of, they put Duke on the list as a potential suspect. Harjo hadn't said it, but Lake sensed that Harjo either didn't believe it or perhaps didn't want to believe it.

116

"We also should talk to Andy's coworkers at the grocery store," Lake added. "What did they know about Andy, and how did they feel about him? Did he complain about being harassed, threatened, or frightened? Was he especially close to someone there, someone other than Alex Duke?"

"Talk to some of the neighbors in that apartment complex as well. In fact, start there. Take a uniform with you... not Gamble. Riley said it was all he could do to keep that kid from talking to the reporters when they arrived on the scene at the Creekstone."

"I get the feeling that you think it's going to be a waste of time," Lake said, finishing his cinnamon roll.

"Don't go into it with that attitude, Lake, or you could miss something important. In any case, much of what we do eventually ends up being a waste of time, especially when there is so little to go on in the first place."

"No, but still... " Lake said.

"Something tells me that the crime may not have been *personal*," Harjo asserted.

Lake was hesitant. "A stranger? Statistically, most murders—"

"—are committed by someone who knows the victim." Harjo finished the sentence. He sipped his coffee and took the last bite of his sandwich. "We can't rule out the possibility that someone has it in for prostitutes, gay people, or trans people. It could have been a john who resented the deception of Candy being male."

Lake nodded. "It might be worth checking on reported assaults and potential hate crimes."

Harjo felt a little proud of Lake. He was thinking like a detective who doesn't have any leads. He nodded. "Gamble is on the desk. Give him the task of compiling a list. Just case numbers should be enough."

Lake added, "I could ask Biggs for a list of repeat hotel guests over, say, the last three months."

Harjo raised his eyes but stopped short of rolling them.

"I hope it doesn't come down to that. I just can't get out of my head that Adam Alba found the body and that no one discovered that body earlier in the day when the kitchen and housekeeping staff were in and out of that enclosure. The conveniently damaged surveillance cameras reek of planning and premeditation, damned good planning at that."

"Against Alba." Lake spoke through a long sigh.

Harjo pressed his lips together and nodded. "Daily reports on progress until I get back."

"Back?" Lake was surprised.

"I'm going to New Orleans."

Adam missed two messages in quick succession while steam curled against the bathroom mirror. The first from his sister Cathy was simple: *Call me when you get the chance.* Brief but insistent in tone. There was always a sense of urgency with Cathy. He'd call her back before work.

The second lit the screen with Stevie Tramonto's message. He had meant to try to sleep for a couple of hours before spending some time piecing together his puzzle, but the thought of Stevie stopping by tugged a smile to his lips. Sharing espresso with Stevie suddenly seemed like the better way to spend an hour or two.

If he had expected anything, it would have been from Harjo, but there was nothing.

Adam waited for Stevie's arrival at the end of his walkway, near the curb. He wanted to show her where to park as visitor spaces were few and a little far from his unit. She lit up when she saw him—a hand jingling with bangles and glittering with rings, waving out of the driver's side window. She pulled into the space he pointed to as he walked toward her car.

He opened the door for her as she gathered up her purse and the bag with the cinnamon roll. She climbed out of the car and greeted him with a quick embrace and an air-kiss on both cheeks. She hadn't done that with Adam before, but seeing him was like seeing a relative, and it just happened.

The greeting took Adam by surprise, but he responded naturally. Stevie felt at home.

"I'm so excited to see your new place."

Chagrinned, Adam said, "There's not much to see, but I'll give you the not-so-grand tour."

She sent him a motherly smile, handed him the bag with the cinnamon roll, and slipped her hand into his elbow. Instinctively, he bent his arm. She wasn't feeling his muscles. She wasn't wearing heels. He could feel the companionship in her touch.

After depositing her purse and the cinnamon roll on the breakfast counter, Adam showed her the bedrooms. Tom and Elf's room was still chaotic. His was pristine. She noticed his puzzle and remarked on his cleverness at being able to do a puzzle face down. "I don't think I could do that. I'll bet it's quite engrossing," she said without asking any further questions. It was a part of him she just accepted without qualification. She asked about his roommates.

Adam realized how complicated it would be to explain Tom. He could either say he was merely Elf's friend, or he could reveal a little of his past. He chose to confide in her. "The simple answer is that he is a friend of Elf's, but there's much more to it," he began.

While telling his story, Adam had moved one of the stools to the other side of the counter so they could face one another. "Tom is ten years younger than Elf and fifteen years younger than I am. He's a kid who goes to the same Bible school as Elf. I tried to save his father and failed." He spoke the last bit in a lower, more thoughtful register. He stood up to make the coffee.

"Wait a minute," she said. "You can't leave it there."

He felt comfortable about sharing the story and did. It took some time. They had eaten the cinnamon roll, sampled Rosie's chocolate cake, and had finished their coffee by the time he was done.

For most of it, she just listened without questions. The look of avid attention on her face encouraged him to be as detailed as he felt comfortable. She was sympathetic and also very interested in it.

She asked, "And exactly when did all this happen?"

Adam shrugged. "It started Memorial Day weekend. I was in Ur until a few weeks ago."

Her jaw dropped. She was silent, appearing to take it all in. "That recent!" She was incredulous. She breathed deeply as if letting it all settle in. She stared at his hands, cupping the mug. "Can I ask you about the BAPD mug? It's not just the mug but the way you handle it. It's a police mug, isn't it? I think I've seen ones like it before."

She watched some of the color drain from his face. For a moment, he was silent, considering.

"You don't have to tell me if you don't want to," she added.

"I don't mind. I think it might do me some good," Adam said, and then added, "but it's gloomy."

"Honey, I'm all ears and no lips. I can keep a confidence," Stevie assured him.

Adam began to tell her the story of discovering Candy's body in the dumpster enclosure. It flowed out of his mouth so smoothly and in such detail, it was like a floodgate had opened. When he got to Alex and Caleb, he realized how much he had that poor 13-year-old boy in the back of his mind.

At one point, she raised her hand to her open mouth. "And they think *you* were the intended victim?"

"It's a possibility," he said in resignation.

Eleven

Elf walked out of his hermeneutics class feeling confused and angry. He had just sat through a class that was more sermon than instruction. No discussion of original language, texts, or culture. No historical context. Just an hour of why homosexuals were the tools of Satan to destroy the earth and wage war on the kingdom of God, the devil's revenge.

Herzog had been a terrific professor in Pseudo-Christian Cults. He could easily compare doctrines of religions that claimed to be Christian and demonstrate the ways those organizations changed the translations of the Bible to suit their beliefs. It was fascinating.

Elf had expected hermeneutics, the interpretation of scripture, to be as interesting and enlightening. It was nothing like what he expected. Herzog, energized by political events and trends, focused on making sure everyone was on the same page and following the movement of the kingdom of God. He claimed they were in real spiritual warfare, and they had to fight both practically and spiritually.

Each scripture Professor Herzog referenced sent him off on a tirade of preaching about the gay agenda, the recruiting of children into sexual perversion and the strategic dismantling of American family values.

He did the same thing with the "woke" agenda. He touted conservative leaders as being chosen by God to fulfill the mission of the church. It was difficult for Elf to follow this line of thinking. It seemed to be extreme and virtually ignored the characters of the politicians supposedly chosen by God, especially when it came to establishing policies that were clearly contrary to things Jesus himself said.

It was easy for Elf to understand that what he experienced in prison was sin and was the result of sin. After all, it was rape perpetrated by men who were supposed to be straight. They were never really gay. His protectors and mentors in prison explained to him that their perversion was an expression of dominance and control in a place where they didn't otherwise have any. They said it was the sin of pride or vainglory.

He also could see how much his old girlfriend Grace loved her brother and how tormented she was that he would burn in hell for being gay. He had met the kid and thought he was nice, even if he wasn't a committed Christian, like Grace and Tom. Couldn't love override their differences?

For Herzog, and apparently most of the students in the class, everything was absolutely black and white, Satanic or Christian—no gray area at all. To them, it all seemed clear, so easy. For Elf, it seemed *too* clear, *too* easy.

Elf was no academic. One of the books he got out of the donated section of the prison library was a book called something like *Semantics of Biblical Language*. The author said just translating the texts wasn't enough. We should consider the cultural and historical environment in which those texts were written. We have to understand not only what the authors wrote but what they meant when they wrote it. What did their readers understand when reading those words?

In hindsight, asking a question about the historical or cultural interpretations of those scriptures in hermeneutics was stupid. "The Bible is the word of God. God wrote the Bible" was the professor's dismissive response. The amens and hallelujahs that followed his pronouncement told him he was alone and, in their eyes, wrong.

"I wasn't trying to contradict him," Elf muttered to himself. "I was asking a question about context; that's all." His head swam with thoughts about the consequences of being on Herzog's bad side. The school had rules—many unstated—but everyone knew what they were. It only took an email from someone like Herzog, and a student could be out, expelled, with no appeal, no reprieve, and certainly no refund. It was the one-bad-apple rule.

Most of his professors knew about his background. They knew he had been to prison and what he had done to get there. He wasn't ashamed of who he had been. After all, he was a new creature in Christ, and he celebrated the miracle that his life had become.

Elf also came to realize that he should have been a little less free about sharing his testimony at first. Christians enjoyed the gory details of his life before he was saved. Once they knew the story, however, it changed the way they related to him, always with a little more suspicion. They held him a little more than at arm's length.

If he could only find a copy of that book, he could show it to Herzog and explain where his question came from. He ransacked his memory for the exact title and author. He tried to search for it on his phone, but it just wouldn't come up. Cynically, he knew that even if he found the author and title, he wouldn't find the book in the school library.

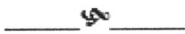

Detective Joe Harjo sat in a crowded Maspero's restaurant, working his way through a Gulf shrimp platter. Detective Batist DuPuis would have preferred to take him to a less touristy place but as Harjo's time was limited, he had to choose somewhere local to treat his guest.

They had been discussing various elements of the case in which Adam Alba had been involved. So far, Harjo wasn't learning much more than he had read in the report. DuPuis seemed like an honest, upfront guy. When he copped to the attitude that caused Adam to call him a dick, Harjo admired his transparency. But, if his hunch were correct, there had to be something missing, some morsel, some twist that somehow communicated that it, whatever it was, wasn't quite over and it had spilled over into Broken Arrow.

"Truth was," DuPuis confessed, "we had no real leads. Lots of forensic evidence, but nothing and no one to compare it to. If Alba hadn't done what he did, we would have never gotten a line on the perp. Alba was arrested because..." he sighed "... under the circumstances, it was easier to suspect him than it was to believe him."

"What got him off the hook?" Harjo asked.

DuPuis explained. "Things weren't fitting together. By the time we arrested Alba, the gay community was mobilized. I had gay men walking through the cemeteries looking inside, beside, and behind tombs. They found one the day after we arrested him. It should have gotten him off, but the time of death wasn't clear. The crime could have happened before we arrested him. But in the next week, there were two fresh ones and, well, he had the best alibi one can get; he was in custody. It was really my fault that there were two more victims."

"Two questions," Harjo said. "What do you mean they were looking *inside* tombs?"

"That's easy. You'll see when I give you the tour. We have family tombs that people can go into. I'll show you. Now the second question?"

"What were you unwilling to hear or listen to?" Harjo ventured.

"Okay, I'll fess up." DuPuis looked around to see who might be listening. The restaurant was crowded and noisy enough to cover his speech. Still, he leaned into the center of the table in a confidential way and lowered his voice.

"The victims were gay, strike one. They were known chemsex guys using GHB. It was no surprise when it was found in their systems, strike two. Also, most had leud conduct records. Exposing themselves, masturbating, or engaging in sexual activities in public, strike three, out. We're not talking about Mardi Gras here, but contrary to popular perception, people can be arrested for such things even during Mardi Gras. Thing is, the GHB alone is enough to explain a death. I'll admit, at the time, I thought if you play with fire, you deserve to get burned.

"The first couple of deaths looked like unfortunate accidents. Some guys seeking a little privacy climb into a cemetery at night, have a little chemsex on someone's grave, and one of them ends up with an overdose. I'm ashamed to admit it, but there it is."

Harjo was more than aware that many cops had similar attitudes toward prostitutes, and Candy was a prostitute. Alex Duke had confirmed it. He wasn't going to allow Candy or anybody else to become "just another dead hooker"—not if he could help it.

DuPuis took Harjo on a unique crime scene tour. He showed him where each victim had been found. Each was in a cemetery, next to, behind, or inside a tomb. Each tested positive for GHB.

"And they were all strangled?" Harjo asked.

"There were signs of asphyxia but no defensive wounds. There were signs of manual strangulation, but like the drug, it's easy to go too far with that. Whether it was the overdose of GHB or the asphyxia or both wasn't always clear."

"Do you think they were unconscious?"

"Any man's guess." DuPuis hesitated. "One of my original assumptions was that they were also into sexual asphyxia... marks around the throat, some petechiae," he admitted. "At first, it was easier and more convenient to assume they went into the cemetery for kicks with a like-minded partner, and things got out of hand."

"It would still be manslaughter. You only found one victim in each case. What about the partner?" Harjo said seriously.

"I have no excuses for you or anyone else," DuPuis said. "We did autopsies and gathered crime scene evidence, all of which came in handy for the trial, but until the killing continued when Alba was in custody, it was easier to think we had found our perp.

"Let me tell you this, Joe. If you're stuck, get Alba to speculate, not what he knows but what he thinks. Listen to him. His perception is uncanny." DuPuis shook his head. "I wish I had paid more attention to him."

Harjo considered. "What can you tell me about the bar where Alba worked?"

"A place called the Balustrade. It's a piano bar that caters mostly to old queens and toyboys looking for sugar daddies. What kind of connection are you trying to make? I don't quite get it, but if you were to explain a bit more..."

Frustrated, Harjo sighed. "I think I might be grasping at straws. I had an idea that whatever happened here spilled over or followed Alba to Broken Arrow."

DuPuis raised his eyes and unconsciously scanned his mind. "Landry, the perp, is convicted and locked up in Angola. Death Row. I don't see how."

"Does he have any family, loyal friends, anyone that might want vengeance?"

DuPuis thought. "Just his grandmother. It's a long shot. If you want to see her, I'll assign someone to go with you, someone who knows their way around. She might open up a bit more with a local."

"And what about Landry himself. Any chance of interviewing him?"

"The Penitentiary is about two, two and a half hours away."

Harjo shrugged. "While I'm here, I should do what I can."

DuPuis looked at him seriously. "Normal visitor hours are on the weekends, but since it's official, the warden might agree. I can probably get clearances. Let me see what I can do."

"I'd appreciate that." Harjo thanked him.

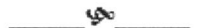

Stevie Tramanto sat at her kitchen table, blankly looking out the bay window at her garden. She tapped a cadence on the glass tabletop with her fingernail. Her cup of green tea had gone cold, and when she pricked her finger to test her blood glucose, it was higher than she expected.

She had hardly noticed. Her doctor was threatening to add an additional medication forestalling the use of injected insulin, the thought of which turned her stomach. But this time, her mind wasn't on controlling her blood sugar. Somehow, her health had diminished in importance after her visit with Adam.

Her latest mystery novel lay open at her place, face down on the table. It was impossible for her to disappear into a novel just now. She just couldn't focus on it. Her mind danced between thoughts about what Adam had said, his astonishing willingness to talk, and how much she felt like she needed to help him.

He hadn't asked for her help. In fact, at the time, she thought he just needed to talk about it, to get it out. She felt honored that he trusted her with the story. It confirmed to her the very connection she felt for this young man.

He had been involved in not one but two real-life mysteries and apparently was in the middle of his third. It was confirmation that their meeting had been ordained. She felt sure there was some sort of past-life connection, but her novice psychic abilities weren't up to the task of defining it. She simply believed it to be true, and that meant their meeting had a purpose.

What he told her had horrified her. It had also drawn her in. It was better than any pulp fiction murder mystery she had read. Breaking the spell of blank contemplation, she reached for the tablet and pen she kept on the table.

She had questions, but she didn't think Adam would be able to answer them. They might give him something to think about, perhaps while he was doing that puzzle. That was an amazing thing to be able to do. It must require a rare ability and a unique mindset to put a jigsaw puzzle together without looking at the picture.

When she finished, she picked up her phone and texted Adam. She hoped he would agree. She could pick him up in the morning, they could share their coffee and roll at the coffee shop, perhaps lunch at the Moonstone grill, and she could drop him off at home with plenty of time to get ready for work.

After his talk with Stevie, Adam felt like he had just come out of a reconciliation meeting with a priest.

They used to call it confession, *Bless me father for I have sinned…* but the priest at Mother of Sorrows wasn't much for formality. He had a remarkable memory and connection with each parishioner. Or, at least, he remembered Adam, and each time they met, it felt like a continuation of the last session.

The priest did offer formal confessions as well. The church, a modern boat like structure, dominated a hill overlooking the Ohio River. It still had confession booths, and Father Dominic used them, mostly with older parishioners. If you called the office and scheduled a reconciliation session, it was face-to-face. You had more time, and Father Dominic gave great advice.

Penance was never just a couple of prayers; it was practical. He suggested things you could do to make amends, to repair relationships, or to make up for lapses caused by human frailty.

Though Adam had to admit that Stevie didn't offer any suggestions along those lines. He could see in her reactions that she listened, really listened. It felt good to get the story out, without fear of judgment or betrayal.

He pedaled early to the Creekstone. Before work, he could take time, sit in the lobby, and use the hotel internet to view Jake and Julian's YouTube channel. When he called to set up his own internet service, he discovered that a technician visit wasn't necessary. It was just a matter of flipping a switch. They would rent him a router for an additional fee, or he could purchase his own. He opted to buy one.

An hour or so in the lobby of the Creekstone was the best option for him now. In fact, it would have been his permanent choice if Tom and Elf didn't need the internet for schoolwork.

A text from Stevie suggesting coffee and lunch came in the middle of watching Jake and Julian eating barbecue in Nashville.

Alex held young Caleb, a brotherly arm draped around his shoulders, while Caleb quietly cried, tears heavily dropping from his eyes, soaking his lap. He had bouts when he would just stop, lower his head and cry. Alex couldn't imagine the pain he felt, the loneliness.

Alex felt the urge to hold him tighter, to show him that he wasn't alone. He should cry out loud, to scream if he wanted to. He knew Caleb wouldn't, couldn't. He was at that age when a boy wants to be a man, and what did being a man actually mean?

It was a question that had plagued Alex all his life, for as long as he could remember. Even as a little girl, he always imagined he'd grow up to be a man. How different it was from young Caleb's experience. Yet, was it really?

Alex knew that Caleb was both aggrieved and afraid. At thirteen, what would happen to him? It had to be in his thoughts. Hell, those thoughts were in Alex's mind as well. Caleb had lost a sister who had once been a brother. Would he accept a brother who had once been a little girl?

Alex would gladly welcome Caleb into his home and become his family. He'd fight for custody if that was what Caleb wanted. Would the authorities ever allow that to happen?

Elf waited outside Professor Herzog's office, glancing at his watch. Herzog said one o'clock and he'd knock on the door exactly on time. His heartbeat in his chest, palms sweating, mind in a revving idle. He was once again thirteen, standing outside the principal's office but without enough rebellion to be angry and defiant.

Now his chest pounded with regret and fear. *How could I be so stupid as to interrupt a Herzog rant?* The hall felt ominously quiet. He could hear the click clop of heeled shoes walking across the tiled floor, the sound of a toilet flushing as someone opened the door to a restroom. It sounded unnaturally loud.

His phone chirped an alarm, and as if he were spring-loaded, he knocked on the door. He waited. There was no response. For a second, he wasn't sure what to do. Part of him hoped Herzog would forget all about the meeting. He knocked again.

"Wait!" Herzog's voice boomed from inside the office, vibrating through the door.

Elf waited.

Eventually, he could hear the undoing of a deadbolt, and the door opened. "Come in, Mr. Flemming." Herzog held the door open, let Elf pass, and closed and locked it behind him. "Sit down." His voice was clipped, curt. He pointed at a chair in front of his desk.

Elf sat down. Facing him was a mall-studio family portrait. Herzog stood behind a stern, robust wife seated stiffly in a chair, bookended by two spit-polished kids, a boy and a girl, in matching Sunday clothes.

"I want to apologize for interrupting your lecture," Elf said, drying his palms on his jeans.

"That's not why you're here. Let me get right to the point, Mr. Flemming. I think my lecture struck a nerve with you. I think I know why, but I want to hear it from you."

Elf wasn't sure of how to interpret what he heard. "I'm not sure what you mean, Professor."

Herzog sat down behind his desk, moved his mouse and clicked, closing a screen. He asked, "Is there anything you'd like to tell me?" He sounded like a suspicious, angry parent giving a kid the chance to come clean.

"I'd like to explain, sir. When I was in prison…"

Herzog leaned forward.

Elf continued. "… I read a theology book that talked about reading the scriptures in the context of the time they were written. I was wondering if—"

Herzog interrupted. "The devil uses a lot of tools, even the words of so-called theologians, to obscure his hidden agenda. That argument has been made many times and most often in the justification of sin, like homosexuality." He sat back, tenting his fingers in contemplation. "I wonder if that was your expectation."

"My expectation, sir? Again, I'm not sure what you mean," Elf said slowly. He could feel the hairs on the back of his neck bristle.

Herzog was almost too self-confident. "I am just wondering if perhaps you yourself struggle with same-sex attraction and were hoping to—"

Elf interrupted him. "I was hoping for a better understanding of the social or cultural environment in which the scriptures were written. That was all."

Herzog looked at him over the top of his glasses. "Are you sure that's all?"

"Yes, sir. That's all." He didn't think Herzog believed him.

"God wrote the Bible, full stop. God is the same yesterday, today, and tomorrow. That's all you need to know."

Elf looked down at the floor while Herzog pecked at his keyboard. "*Hermeneutics, my ass,* Elf thought, *there's no interpretation of scripture if it's all meant to be taken literally.*

Herzog clicked the mouse a couple of times. "I see you are graduating in June. I think for the sake of the rest of your time here, Mr. Flemming, we should spend time in private counsel."

Elf's heart sank. The last thing he wanted was more time with Herzog. He decided to tiptoe. "I'm grateful for the offer, sir. May I ask what you have in mind?"

Twelve

"Cathy, take whatever you need from the trust account. You know I'm not using it," Adam said into his phone, hoping to make his sister feel better. Her husband's job was on-again, off-again under the mercurial threats of presidential tariffs.

"Adam, that's your retirement money. You may need it someday."

Adam sat back down on his chair in the Creekstone lobby. This was going to be a longer conversation than he had time for. A hotel guest, an older man with grey hair and a tired face, sat nearby pretending not to listen.

"What did Ma always say about *someday*?" Adam muttered.

"It never comes. But two months ago, when you were in the hospital and I couldn't get to you, we thought that someday had arrived. Thank God you came out of it, but what if...?"

"What if? What if? What if? Cathy, there's more money in that account than I could ever use. I could retire right now if I wanted to. That trust fund that the Griffens set up for me... I just don't use it. I've *never* used it."

"You don't still feel guilty over that, do you? It made *them* feel better."

"Jake and Julian are doing well. You must be proud." Adam abruptly changed the subject.

Another sigh. "I'd feel better if he were home."

"No, you wouldn't. He'd be miserable and you'd feel guilty."

"Adam, they sleep in that van."

"They *camp* in that van. There's a difference. It's like an RV. Have you seen it? It's amazing."

She lowered her voice. "Sometimes they just park on a street somewhere for the night. They could be arrested or worse. Anything can happen."

"Cathy, I watch their channel. From what I can see, they're having the time of their lives. Would you deny them that?"

His sister was silent. He went back to their original topic in a way that wouldn't brook argument. "Listen, I have to start work soon. If you need money…"

He listened to his sister sigh. "I don't think it will come to that. If it does…"

"If it does… use it, for Christ's sake. If we learned anything from two months ago," he used her own reasoning against her, "it was that I might never need that money, ever. That's why you are on the account, too. If we both go, Jake gets it."

"Don't say things like that, Adam," Cathy snapped.

He had gone too far. He tried distracting her again, and it worked. He tossed out, "How's Nonno? I called and he didn't answer."

"He spends most of the day in the garden or in his workshop. The garden is beautiful. I don't know how he keeps it up at his age. He started taking Nonna's jars out of the basement. He wants me to can tomatoes."

Adam smiled to himself. "You know how, don't you? You used to help Nonna all the time."

"Of course I do," she said.

"Well then? Anyway, so, he's doing pretty good."

"Better than can be expected. He always asks for you." He could sense her deliberation. "Adam, please come home for Christmas. He's not getting any younger and, well, you never know."

What was she hiding from him? He felt a knot swell in his throat. After a moment, he said, "I'll do my best."

"Make your best good enough, Adam."

He sat in the lobby for another five minutes, digesting the conversation with his sister. Adam always had difficulty pinpointing her motivations. She was a worrier. That was to be sure. But she could also manipulate him, or at least she tried.

Was she more worried about her husband's job, her son's travels, or Nonno's health and well-being? Her gallivanting son, Dan's insecure employment and her taking care of Nonno, were all in the mix.

They had covered all the bases and visiting Pittsburgh at Christmas was not a bad idea. He stood up again, slid his phone into his pocket, and headed for the lounge. It was almost four o'clock.

Jenna was behind the bar when he walked through the smoky glass doors. There were a few patrons scattered around the lounge working at laptops. Adam could almost guess what rooms they were in. He had learned that the last few rooms on the third floor had questionable Wi-

Fi connectivity. Guests in those rooms invariably ended up in the lobby or the lounge.

"I saw you sitting out in the lobby," she said as he slid past her. "Everything is all stocked. It has been a slow afternoon, and I had lots of time."

"Katja is not working today?

"She quit. She said things were getting weird around here. Did you know she and Hector were dating?"

Adam shrugged. "Never thought about it but it doesn't surprise me. Speaking of Hector?"

"He's back in Venezuela. Katja told Biggs when she resigned. Apparently, his father could pull a few strings."

"At least he didn't end up in El Salvador like those others," Adam said.

Jenna neared Adam to whisper. "Gang members, my ass. Hector was a premed. Have you ever heard of a gang member who was a serious premed student?"

Adam smirked. "Is that what they thought? I avoid the news. It's always bad news for someone."

She looked away in mock frustration. "You're always so fucking calm, Adam. That's what I like about you."

"And you, Jenna, are passionate about things you care about. *That's* what I like about you. And I'm not always so calm on the inside."

She looked at her watch. "Biggs and I are going over applications. He needs to replace Katja and a few housekeeping staff. I need to replace Hector, and half the kitchen staff is afraid they'll be taken in the next raid. Don't you leave me, or I'll hunt you down."

He turned to look at her. His face betrayed the confusing thoughts that had been cluttering his mind since finding Candy's body. He had thought he understood Jenna. Prim, proper, and reserved when she was on display. Harsh, brassy, and tough on the inside, and when she let her hair down.

"Adam, just kidding, of course. Are you thinking about leaving?"

He saw her now in a different light. Who knew his schedule and even his routine better than Jenna? She knew the hotel schedule and the security system and could control who on her staff did what and when. He shook his head. The motion doubled to answer her question and, at the same time, clear his head. Here was something new to think about, like finding a missing puzzle piece under a piece of furniture.

Her poise restored, Jenna smiled. "I'll be in Biggs' office for a couple of hours if you need anything. Then I'm out of here. You have my number." She reached under the bar to get her purse. As she left, she said, "Hey, everything okay with your direct deposit?"

He had forgotten all about getting his first paycheck. "Wow, I haven't even checked."

"The next one will be a real treat after that tip from the bachelor party. I meant to thank you for covering and for doing a great job."

Adam smiled and shrugged off the compliment.

At six, Adam ducked into the back to take a few bites of his dinner. When he came out, Terry Gamble, out of uniform, in street clothes, was standing at the bar. Adam recognized him at once despite the glasses and emerging caterpillar beneath his nose. He wore a Dodgers baseball cap backwards and a merch T-shirt that read "Festival Muscogee."

Gamble didn't seem to recognize or acknowledge Adam at all. He ordered a draft beer and took it to the back booth where Alex had stationed himself. The booth offered the most complete view of the lounge. Subdued, lacking his normal enthusiasm, Adam assumed Gamble was undercover as part of the investigation into Candy's murder. Not even a wink of acknowledgement. Adam's expression contorted. Did Gamble actually believe that Adam wouldn't recognize him out of uniform with such a minimal disguise? What could he possibly be looking for?

Harjo's first impression of the Balustrade was that it would be a good place to bring his wife. It was more elegant than he had expected. Soft lighting, a quiet crowd, a man in a worn tuxedo played soft, slow improvised jazz on a baby grand piano. On the headboard sat a glass pitcher filled with cash tips.

Harjo's wife was on his mind. When he told her he'd be going to New Orleans for work, she hadn't complained, but after thirty years together, he knew what she must be thinking. They hadn't had a real vacation, just the two of them, in several years; he felt a twinge of guilt. He promised himself that they would plan a trip when this case was over.

He sat down at a small table, one that gave him a decent view of the comings and goings of the place. Harjo didn't know what he was looking for. but thought he would recognize it when he saw it. The other tables were mostly occupied by older gentlemen wearing fine clothes and the glint of a gold wristwatch reflecting in the light of a tabletop candle. There were a couple of women, but in the lighting, Harjo wondered if they might not be drag queens.

The bartender, a handsome, almost pretty man in his thirties with pecs and biceps challenging his form-fitting white shirt, glowed in a soft spotlight behind the bar. Between filling orders, he wiped down the bar, washed glasses, and dusted off the backlit bottles of expensive liquor. Harjo guessed Alba would have been eye candy for both the older and the smattering of younger men in the room.

Several minutes passed before Harjo realized there wouldn't be table service. He never drank more than a beer now and then, but thought he'd have to order something. He walked over to the bar, passing a small group of younger men. *Young enough to be carded*, he thought. As he passed them, his eyes met the gaze of one of them. The boy's eyes softened and demurred the way a woman's might.

Harjo was abruptly reminded of where he was. He felt himself close off. He wasn't sure what the dynamic was. All DuPuis had said was "old queens and toyboys." What did that mean exactly? He guessed the boy thought he was an old queen.

He wasn't sure how to handle the situation. The opportunity to talk with one of these young men might give him valuable insight. Or, to the contrary, might become an annoying distraction. He wanted a feel for the place.

Harjo returned to his table. His fingertips gently tapped on his glass of perfectly poured beer. He let his eyes travel the room, seeking out overlooked details. He noticed that there were unobtrusive security cameras discreetly embedded in the molded decorative ceiling. An alcove, more brightly lit, next to the bar led to the restrooms and an emergency exit.

He observed a number of interactions between the younger and the much older patrons. Suggestive glances preceded an invitation to a table. The unspoken invitation somehow extended through eye contact. The younger would join the table and then, in a few minutes, the older guy would gallantly get up, approach the bar, and buy a drink for his new friend.

A patron walked past Harjo's table with seeming intention. He walked toward another alcove, this one dark. Harjo had barely noticed it. A small brass plaque to the side of the door read "Private." He watched the man disappear into the alcove. It was like a magic trick.

He was real, and then he was gone. Harjo's curiosity and suspicion were aroused.

He got up and approached the alcove archway, touched the frame, and peered inside. It was absolutely dark. His heart beat in his chest, but caution prevailed. Without backup or jurisdiction, he dared not go further. Pressing his lips together, he turned away. He'd ask DuPuis about it, and if DuPuis didn't know, Alba would.

The large window above the kitchen sink filled the room with light. The old-fashioned Formica countertop glistened in the light and boasted evenly spaced small appliances: a toaster, a Mr. Coffee, and a stand mixer. The cabinets were white enamel and might have been considered antiques.

Officer Lake and Mr. Hornfeld sat at the table while Mrs. Hornfeld fussed about making instant coffee and plating cookies. The Hornfelds were an elderly couple who, in their retirement years, took in foster children, just one, at a time.

"Oh, I'm too old for young ones," Mrs. Hornfeld said as she placed a cup of murky liquid in front of Lake. "They have to be in school for us to accept them, even in the summer." Her husband took a sugar cube out of a bowl and pushed the bowl toward Lake. His wife set down a creamer in the form of a cow in front of him.

"It's our ministry," Mr. Hornfeld offered. "These kids have had a rough go. Stability is what they need. Stability and order."

Setting a plate of cream-filled cookies on the table, Mrs. Hornfeld said, "That's why we have rules. They are simple, the kind any good parent would have for their children. We raised three of our own and have fostered over twenty."

"Do you get involved in their schooling, say, attend parent-teacher conferences?" Lake was curious.

"We do," Mr. Hornfeld said. "Most often, they are about adjustment issues or disciplinary issues."

"That's interesting. With all your experience, I wonder how you handle such issues?"

"Well, they all have adjustment issues at first. Don't they, Hugh? We find that time settles most of it. They just need to get settled, that's all."

"You're right about that, Ida. Just takes a little time. Being the new kid in school has never been easy for anyone."

"We did sign up Mark for the scouts, remember Hugh? That helped him a lot. He just sent us an invitation to his Eagle Scout ceremony. Imagine that. We can't go, of course. It might as well be on the other side of the world. I'll send a card though," Ida said.

"As for discipline," Hugh went on. "If they know what to expect and what is expected of them, outright discipline, I mean things like punishment, just aren't needed." He sipped his coffee, made a bitter face, and motioned for Lake to pass him the sugar bowl.

"I'm wondering if Caleb Yates experienced any of those issues," Lake asked.

"Oh my, Caleb. How long has it been, Hugh?"

"He left us a little less than a year now. He was with us for almost a whole year," Hugh said. "Good kid. Very polite."

Ida sat down at the table. She was dipping a teabag in her cup. "Young Caleb was a good boy. Two feet in one shoe most of the time. I think he adjusted fine. Never any need to speak to him about his behavior."

"He got squirmy in church, you remember, Ida?" Hugh said.

"Yes, he did get squirmy, but kids at that age often fidget."

"Didn't memorize many verses, but he sure could look them up by the time he left us." Hugh seemed proud.

Ida pursed her lips. "He's not in trouble with the police, is he? We've never had a police officer ask us about one of our children before."

"No ma'am, he's not in trouble."

"Oh, I'm glad to hear that. He is such a good boy. Hugh, you know I've said it before, I think Olive misses him."

"Olive?" Lake asked.

"Our dog. Caleb was very good about walking her."

"Who were his friends from school or church?" Lake asked.

The Hornfelds looked at each other. "I'm sure he met kids at Sunday school, and I'm sure he knew lots of kids at school, but he never brought any of them here," Ida said thoughtfully. "Now that you ask, he never went anywhere either. No birthday parties, no pizzas with friends, no after-school activities, no sports, nothing. Don't you think that's odd, Hugh?"

"Never thought about it," Hugh said.

Thirteen

arjo's partner for the day was Officer Clarie Fontenot. She was waiting for him in the lobby of his hotel when he stepped out of the elevator. DuPuis had told Harjo to dress casually and hinted at an adventure, and Landry's grandmother was reportedly a suspicious old woman who distrusted authority.

Officer Fontenot politely asked him to change. "The warden is going to let you visit with Landry today, but there's a dress code: no camo, no denim, and no white clothing. If you don't mind changing, sir," she said respectfully. "Also, please bring your police-issued ID. You'll need it to get into the penitentiary."

Fontenot was an attractive woman, sturdily built, in her thirties with long, curly brown hair pulled back in a bun. She was dressed in chinos and a blue shirt. She was armed, but with a weapon that was not a typical police issue.

"I thought we were going to talk to Landry's grandmother first," Harjo said.

"We are, sir. Trousers and a casual shirt would be fine for both visits."

Fontenot drove a Jeep Wrangler that had the jarring ability of finding every bump and crack of a degraded road. The further they traveled, the more rustic the road became. At one point, it seemed to Harjo that they were driving along the top of a levee on an unpaved road so narrow that if they had faced an oncoming vehicle, one of them would end up in a swamp.

DuPuis was right; even if Harjo had the best possible directions, he could have never found this place. He had no idea how complicated the trip was yet to become. Fontenot, however, seemed unfazed by the route. Eventually, they parked in a small field of long grass that led down to a crumbling cement boat launch.

They walked toward a shack that clung to the water's edge. An overpainted metal Coca-Cola sign that now read "Live Bait" swung from two rusty chains hanging off the eaves. They descended four steps down to a warped wooden deck that wrapped around the shack and terminated in a dock where a small boat with an outboard motor was moored.

The interior was a simple square room. An elderly man sat in a rocking chair listening to talk radio.

"Hey, Bertrand, comment ça va?"

He shook himself awake. His face brightened. "The day just got better, cher," he said, blatantly eyeing her figure.

A propane refrigerator that had once been white rumbled in a corner. Written in thick black permanent marker on the door was "COKE $1."

"I need to rent your boat. It's not booked, is it?" She knew it wasn't. It was tied to the dock.

"How long for?" he asked, looking skeptically at Harjo.

"An hour or so. Not long. Just giving my friend here a bayou tour."

He nodded.

Coffee on the table, the cinnamon roll cut in half, Stevie pried her notebook out of her purse and opened it to the red ribbon she used as a marker.

Curious, Adam tried to read it upside down, but the only way he could tell it was a list of questions was the elaborate question mark at the end of each item.

She started talking in mid-thought. "So I wrote down these questions. None of them have simple, straightforward answers. If you don't mind, I'd like to play detective."

Adam grinned his permission. She had been the only one in whom he had confided, not only the events but how he felt about them. He instinctively trusted her and knew she wasn't really *playing* detective. He thought it might help him to clear his own head. Working this puzzle left him with more questions than resolutions.

"In Ur, they told me not to investigate on my own," he playfully cautioned her.

"That's bullshit, if you ask me, and, well, you're not on your own, are you? I'm here." She waved her hands, taking in their table and its surroundings.

"Okay, what do I do?"

She turned the page, and in the middle of it, she drew a circle and wrote "Candy." "We're going to start with Candy. After all, she was the victim, even if that detective thinks you might have been the target."

She asked Adam to list everything he knew about Candy. She insisted on distinguishing between what he knew, what someone else had told him, and what he surmised. Each statement got a bubble that she connected either to the center circle or another bubble.

"It's only your surmise that she was a prostitute. She could have been selling drugs," Stevie suggested.

"I don't think that was the case," Adam objected.

"Honey, I didn't say that she was, but nothing we have here rules out the possibility."

She then began to brainstorm with Adam about the reasons someone might want to end her life. These bubbles were relegated to the lower right-hand corner of the page.

"I think we're missing one. Caleb," Stevie said.

"Caleb? Are you suggesting that a thirteen-year-old boy—"

Stevie interrupted him. "No, not likely, though not impossible. It's more likely that someone would want to get the boy away from that living situation. You said she scanned the page. Alex said they were afraid of losing him."

Adam conceded.

Together, they did the same for Adam as the target, not the victim. And even a third one for the crime itself. As they finished, she reviewed their work, and on each page, in the farthest corner of the page, she drew an X and circled it. She connected the X to the center circle.

"What's that for?"

"Algebra. X is the unknown factor. Something or someone who is not yet recognized but whose presence may or may not be deduced from what we have on the page." She was suddenly inspired. "It's like one of your jigsaw puzzles. Which piece fits where? But imagine buying a puzzle from a thrift store and, by chance, some pieces from another puzzle were included in the box. In the world of mysteries, those are red herrings. The problem is we don't know which pieces are which or if there are missing pieces."

"By that logic, we might never get an answer," Adam protested.

"That is precisely what 'reasonable doubt' is for," she said with another wave of her hand.

As they sipped their coffee refills, Stevie toyed with the tiny hair at the nape of her neck. "Adam, sweetheart, I know I promised you lunch, but if you don't mind, I'd like to skip it today. I offer you a raincheck."

"Is something the matter? Are you okay?" Adam asked.

"Oh, I'm fine. I'm just thinking," she took a deep breath. "You have a lot to think about, and I'll just bet you can't wait to get to that puzzle of yours."

Adam felt as if she had read his mind and told her so.

"Well, in that case, we'd better be off, but I want to add one more thing for you to consider."

"That is?" Adam asked.

"You said that the detective told you to vary your routine, right?"

"Yes, but it's hard to do," Adam replied.

"Precisely. Listen, honey, it occurs to me that if Candy arrived at the Creekstone lounge about the same time and left at last call every day—"

"Only Sunday through Thursday, as far as I know."

She pressed her lips together. "Well, it occurs to me that her routine was as predictable as yours. Easier, in fact. All that killer had to know

149

was when was last call. Anyone who planned to do what they did could easily see their window of opportunity. They wouldn't even have to enter the lounge."

Adam thought about it. "But we have no idea who that might be."

"We can name *one* of them," Stevie asserted.

"Who?"

"Alex. You said he said that he picked up Candy from the hotel every night. Out of the three pillars of mystery solving—motive, means, and opportunity—he has two of the three, and you should know that in the legal system, motive is the least persuasive."

"How so?"

She looked at him knowingly. "Remind me of how long *you* were held in New Orleans without bail?"

Fontenot kept the motor low and slow as they navigated the narrow waterways.

"Lucky you," she said to the back of Harjo's head. "This Bayou tour goes for at least fifty bucks, and you get it for free." He could hear the smile in her voice.

As they wove their way down inlets, cutting through water-top blankets of green algae and around clumps of cypress trees, the calm, murky waters had a magnetic effect on Harjo's eyes. He could imagine all sorts of creatures swimming beneath the surface. So distracted was he searching for surfacing alligator eyes, he could not have replicated the twists and turns Fontenot had taken. He was utterly clueless as to where they were.

They sputtered into a small clearing where a woman was hanging laundry on a rope strung between two pecan trees.

"Bonjour," Fontenot greeted the woman.

"Bonjour, cher." The woman turned around. Her voice was clear and strong.

Fontenot tied the boat to a metal post protruding at an angle out of the water and then pulled the boat close to a set of half-rotted wooden stairs that climbed the bank. She held the boat steady while asking Harjo to climb out. He felt the stairs sink disconcertingly into the bank under his weight.

As he climbed out, he gallantly turned to offer Fontenot an extended hand to help her get out of the boat, a gesture the old woman seemed to approve of. Fontenot gave a short, graceful leap to the second step up and smiled at the woman.

The old woman stood staring at them, hands at her side. As they gained their footing, she said something in Cajun French and turned toward her house.

"She's inviting us to her porch. If she offers tea or lemonade or something, take it, drink it, and tell her it's delicious. It will be very sweet. I hope you aren't diabetic," Fontenot said under her breath as they followed the woman to the house. They sat down on porch chairs and waited for the woman to return.

"She doesn't speak English?"

"Of course she speaks English, but this way is better. I've known her for a year or so; I've known *of* her for years. Detective DuPuis thought I could get further with her than someone she had never met before. We're going to speak French. We've gone over what you need to know. If you want a transcript, use this." She handed him a small voice recorder.

In a few minutes, the old woman came out with a small tray with glasses of iced tea. Sprigs of mint lodged between ice cubes sprouted out of the tops of the glasses. Fontenot was right. It was very sweet.

At first, the conversation was almost perfunctory, little more than a discussion of the weather. In some ways, she reminded Harjo of an old Creek woman he had known. After a few moments, the woman became serious. Fontenot later translated the conversation for Harjo.

"You come with news about my grandson? They... they told you something? What news do you bring me, chère?"

"No, ma'am. No news like that. Have you been to visit him?"

The woman went quiet. "Only once. It's too long a trip. The bus, the waiting, and no place I can stay there. That terrible place. It changed him. He isn't the same anymore. He was like a balloon without any air. They wouldn't even let me touch him. How can they do that to a grandmother, huh?"

"They were trying to protect you."

"Protect me?" She snorted softly. "From my grandson? I smacked his ass at least as many times as I cleaned it." At this, she chuckled, apparently lost in a memory of Landry's youth.

"Do you think somebody out there wants to get back at the folks that put him away?"

Her head snapped toward Fontenot. She sat up straighter. "No brothers. No cousins. No friends. Not even me. I know what he did. I can't understand it. I don't know what I did wrong to make him turn out like that. He was a sweet child. I know what he did, but he is still my grandson. I love him, yeah. I always will." She looked away, and Harjo saw tears pooling in her eyes, but didn't know why.

"Maybe he's got friends in prison. Maybe they got friends outside. Maybe they want to get revenge. For him, or for you."

She looked surprised.

"Friends? No, he doesn't have friends in there. He told me so. Said he keeps to himself. Why would they do that for him when it won't do no good anyhow."

Harjo touched Fontenot's elbow. She turned to him. He mouthed, *Aryan Brotherhood?*

She understood.

"Did he ever say anything about the Aryan Brotherhood? That club for white folks?"

"No. He got nobody. No friends." She looked down, then up at Fontenot again. "When I saw you coming. I remembered you. You brought me to court that day. I thought—*mon Dieu*—they done killed my boy in that place, and now you come bringing the bad news. Tell me he is still alive, cher."

Fontenot nodded. "We're going to see him today. What do you want me to tell him from you?"

"Tell him his grand-mère still loves him. And if I go first… I'll wait for him to come."

By eleven, they were on their way to the state penitentiary, commonly known as Angola. They stopped for lunch at a Popeyes along the way and while they ate in the air-conditioned interior, they listened to the recording. Each with one earbud in their ear. Fontenot translated sentence by sentence.

"Do you believe her?" Harjo asked.

"I do." She nodded. "When he was arrested, Landry had only one so-called friend. A guy who lived across the street from him, who said Landry seemed like a nice but private guy. He said he had tried to reach out to him, invited him once or twice to socialize with friends because he knew Landry was gay by the people who came and went from his place. He said Landry was pleasant but never showed up."

"Did you find any of those people that visited him?"

"A few; hookups mostly. Nothing much from them except that Landry was into asphyxiation—receiving as well as giving. The few we found and questioned were the ones who wouldn't do it and left. What made you think of the Aryan Brotherhood?"

"It just occurred to me. Landry is white. He may not have had a choice. Prison gangs."

"I thought they hate gay people," Fontenot said.

Harjo closed the box on his remaining lunch. "In prison, especially one with as many lifers as Angola has, anyone can be situationally gay, even the Aryan Brotherhood."

"You think the Aryan Brotherhood is behind your murder, and they offed that prostitute to frame that guy, Alba?"

Harjo shrugged his shoulders.

Brooke slid a plate back onto the service windowsill. "Something bothering you, honey? You don't seem to be yourself. This one was no mayo."

Elf pulled the plate off the sill, lifted the top burger bun and saw the mayo. He set the plate aside. He'd eat it for his dinner.

Service was slow enough that he had time to prep for dinner, yet steady enough to keep him moving. From the moment he left Herzog's office, he didn't feel right. It wasn't butterflies but lead in his stomach, and he couldn't shake the feeling of being trapped. He hadn't felt that way since prison.

Herzog refused to say what he had in mind for their weekly counseling sessions. All he said was that he'd let the Holy Spirit lead him.

Elf distracted himself by imagining telling Herzog that the Holy Spirit was leading him away from weekly counseling with the professor. It felt good to think it, but he knew it would never fly.

The lead in his belly got heavier when he calculated that it would be eleven months until he graduated, and he still had half that time left of his probation. That meant forty-four weekly meetings with Herzog and twelve more meetings with his probation officer.

He remade the burger and almost put mayo on it a second time. Putting the plate up on the sill, he hit the bell and watched Brooke check the order before taking it to the customer. She winked at him.

He felt trapped and needed friends around to help him through it. He'd talk to Tom after work. Maybe Adam, too, if he were still up when Adam got home. He prayed, "Lord, if possible, let this cup pass from me, but not my will but thine be done." He still felt trapped.

Landry sat on the other side of the plexiglass partition from Harjo. He looked hollow, sunken, just a shell of a human being. His eyes were vacant. He was unshaven, tired, wilted. He slouched on a folding chair. A guard stood behind him.

"Thank you for seeing me, Mr. Landry." Harjo was polite.

"I didn't have a choice, but anything is better than being in the fields." His voice was without inflection.

"Still, I thank you."

Landry stared blankly at Harjo and then, with a sarcastic Cajun flourish, he said, "Laissez les bon temps rouler!"

Harjo knew what that meant, but figured it was Landry's way of saying 'get on with it.'

"I have a few questions for you."

155

Landry looked confused. "Who the hell are you and what the fuck do you want?"

The guard cleared his throat in what Harjo took for a warning.

Harjo made light of it. "Mr. Landry, most people go through their entire lives not being able to answer either of those two questions."

Landry arched a single eyebrow. He seemed to be a little more alive, a shade more present.

Harjo continued. "But I have a purpose for being here. I'm a detective from Oklahoma, and I'm investigating a murder. I think you might be able to help me."

"I ain't never been to Oklahoma.

"No, you aren't a suspect, Mr. Landry."

"Then what do you want?"

"Tell me who believes in you enough to avenge your incarceration?"

"What?" His face was incredulous. "*Believes* in me?" He looked around the tiny room theatrically as if he thought he was being pranked.

"Who would want to take revenge on the people responsible for your being here in Angola?"

Landry jerked his head back as if he had gotten a whiff of something putrid. "You are fucking nuts, Detective. I am the only one responsible for my being here. I own that and anyone who thinks differently is just... crazy."

He leaned forward and spoke as if in confidence. "Listen, Detective, there is something fucking wrong with me. I know it now, and I admit it. I even knew it when I was doing that shit. I knew it was not right, but I liked it. The first time it happened, it was an accident, but every time after that, I wanted the high. If I got out, I'd do it again. I'm not normal."

Harjo had never heard of a serial killer talking this way. Did he believe what he was saying, or was he saying it to manipulate Harjo in some way?

Landry looked around as if there were other people in the room. "Nobody in here is normal; guards and inmates alike." He glanced up at the guard behind him. "No offense."

The guard responded with a smirk.

Harjo wiped his mouth with his hands in thought, planning his next question. Before he could formulate it, Landry continued. "Are you Catholic?"

Harjo shook his head.

"Well, we Catholics have a place called purgatory. Guys in here will tell you this is hell, but hell has to be even worse. To me, this is purgatory, yes. It's a place where we sinners go to be cleansed before we're ready for the pearly gates. I figure that's where I am, purgatory. I belong here. This is my penance for being so fucked up."

Harjo was quiet for a few moments, reorganizing thoughts in his head. He was aware of, could feel, Landry observing him, calculating. He didn't think Landry was hiding anything. That itself was confusing. He had expected Landry to be cocky, to play the hand like he still had cards even if it were a bluff. Instead, Landry went all in and then folded his hand.

Finally, Harjo spoke softly. "I met your grandmother this morning."

Landry froze.

"She sent a message for you."

Landry looked away.

"She says she loves you no matter what. She always will, and if she goes first, she'll be waiting for you on the other side." Harjo stood up. "Mr. Landry, it may be an odd thing to say under the circumstances, but I'm glad I met you."

Fourteen

There was a call from Harjo. Austin Lake flicked the screen of his cell phone and held it to his ear. "Lake here." At the same time, he stood up to close the office door. Terry Gamble was still on desk duty, and if he overheard the call, he'd pester Lake with questions.

"What's up, Joe?"

"Lake, I'm at the airport. I just changed my flight. I'm heading to Oklahoma City to meet Jesus." Harjo sounded tired, his tone sardonic.

"Huh? Jesus?" He couldn't have heard right.

Harjo snorted a half-hearted laugh. "My attempt at humor. Jesus Ramirez." This time, he pronounced Ramirez' first name as Hey-soos. "He's the DEA agent who worked on the drug trafficking case in Ur. Baxter, the local sergeant, will be there too."

"So how did it go in New Orleans> Did you *Laissez the bon temps rouler?*"

Harjo's disappointment sank almost to the point of despair. "I think I just wasted the taxpayers' money." Even as he said it, he didn't believe what he said. The thought that Alba was the link between something in New Orleans and the murder of Candy Yates wouldn't fade despite the lack of any indication, much less real evidence.

Just maybe the link led back to the case in Ur. He didn't really think so. If someone from the drug world wanted revenge on Adam Alba, they could have just as easily shot him as he walked or biked back from his job after midnight. If they wanted to see him suffer more than he had, they could have done that almost as easily.

"How about your interviews with the grocery store employees?"

"I have statements and transcripts, but honestly, there wasn't much. It seems Andy Yates showed up, did his job, and left. The manager said that he suspected Yates had another job because he insisted on working only the day shift, despite the pay differential for the restocking night shift. He just didn't know what it was."

"Anybody know about Yates's alter ego?" Harjo didn't like what he had just said. It sounded disrespectful. "I mean, did anyone know Andy was Candy?"

"Just one. A kid who worked in fresh produce. He said he didn't know for sure, but he thought Andy might be a drag queen. He almost spat when he said it."

"You have my attention." Harjo encouraged him to continue.

"I'll quote him." Lake opened a file and found a page of the transcript. "Quote, 'You mean that drag queen?' He said it with contempt in his voice. When I asked him why he thought Yates was a drag queen, he said, 'He plucked his eyebrows. What kind of real man does that?'"

Harjo sighed. "You think he hated him enough to kill him?"

Lake puffed out a breath. "Hurt him, maybe. The kind of guy who, under the right conditions—out with friends, a little too much to drink—might enjoy beating the hell out of someone, but to pull off a murder, not seriously."

"How about the neighbors in the apartment complex?"

"We knocked on doors but didn't get very far. The management company gave us a list of tenants. I've got a few appointments this afternoon."

Lake didn't talk about his meeting with the Hornfelds. He had done it on his own, and all he had gotten out of it was that Caleb Yates had a lonely and grim experience.

"Good work, Lake. I'll be driving back from Oklahoma City late tonight. Is Gamble still on the desk?"

"Yep. Friday is his last day."

"Let's meet at that coffee shop again tomorrow at, say, 8:30."

"Done. See you then. Good luck with Jesus," Lake quipped.

Stevie dropped Adam off at home just after noon. Inside, he stopped in the doorway to the living room. Tom was decked out in judo garb; he was coaching two twelve- or thirteen-year-old boys. They too were dressed like their teacher. Tom noticed Adam watching and winked at him.

As Tom spoke directions, the two boys would approach one another. It looked as if they were dancing in step. Then one would grab and throw the other, who landed on the pads with a thump. Adam winced, feeling the muscles in his neck tighten. Tom passed back and forth watching them, commenting on posture, balance, and form along the way.

Adam most appreciated how Tom coached both of them, the one who was to be thrown, the uke, as well as the one doing the throwing, the tori. He had learned the terms from Baxter.

He pulled himself away. He was looking forward to some of the stew Henry sent him and then spending a couple of hours with his puzzle. Details from the brainstorming session he shared with Stevie swam in his thoughts like a vigorously stirred pot of soup.

A woman with stiffly coiffed blonde hair and vibrant red fingernails sat hunched over her cell phone, swiping the screen with the pad of her ring finger. Adam couldn't help noticing the size of the diamond on that finger from across the room. It was big enough to be fake.

She didn't notice him until the alarm of the microwave sounded. "Oh. You startled me." Her red taloned hand rested on her chest.

"I'm sorry. I didn't mean to…"

She deftly removed earbuds from her ears and set them on the counter. The tinny sound of some video emanated from them. "Sorry, I didn't hear what you said."

"I didn't mean to startle you," Adam said.

"Oh, I was in another world. Who are you?" the woman asked.

"My name is Adam. I live here. I'm about to make an espresso. Would you like one?"

"Oh no, thank you." She held up a large plastic cup of something orange and frothy. "I hope you don't mind my being in here. There was no place else to sit."

"I don't mind. Those your boys out there?" It was a stupid question with an obvious answer, but conversation made the shared space feel less awkward.

She nodded. "One of them. Mine is the redheaded one, Clint. The other is Clark. Clint and Clark, Clark and Clint. They're inseparable, like twins. Clark's mother and I switch off. A parent has to be present when Mr. Delgado is teaching kids. He insists on it. The boys love judo, though I can't imagine why."

"He was state champion a few years ago." Adam needed something else to say.

She wasn't impressed. "He's great with the kids." She shrugged. "Well, it was nice meeting you, Adam. Don't let me keep you. Enjoy your lunch." She grabbed the earbuds and within seconds, she was back inside her cell phone.

Balancing a fry bread on top of his bowl of stew, his coffee in the other hand, he climbed the stairs to his room. Sitting down at his table, he disappeared into his puzzle almost as quickly as Clint's mother did with her phone scrolling.

Back at her kitchen table, Stevie felt unsettled. Together, she and Adam had painted a complicated image of Adam's current situation. In canceling the lunch, she wondered if she had somehow cut off the flow. She believed that Adam needed time. Perhaps he needed to talk through the details rather than work on that puzzle. Still, at the same time, she could envision him sitting at his puzzle, clearing his head, and making sense of what was happening around him.

She reached for the deck of Tarot cards she kept wrapped in a silk handkerchief. She'd do a reading about Adam and his situation. She didn't think for a minute that she would share the results with Adam. After all, she wasn't that good, and she wasn't quite sure how he would react to the Tarot.

She shuffled and cut the deck several times. Fanning out the deck face down, she pulled out the Eight of Cups, a man using a walking stick, leaving behind apparently good things, under the light of the moon. Some pain had caused Adam to abandon something good and move toward the unknown. *Well, Stevie, you know that much from his story,* she mentally commented to herself.

The second card was the Five of Cups. Three spilt cups, two remain upright, a cloaked figure with his back to the cups mourns loss. He faces the challenge of crossing a rapid river and lots of trials to reach what comes next. *He's lost more than he now has, but instead of clinging to what remains, he has learned that mourning loss is one thing, but settling for what remains is stagnation.*

The final card was the Six of Swords. A man ferries a woman and a child in a boat from turbulent waters to tranquility. She pondered the possibility that Adam could be the man, helping others or the child, being cared for. *A difficult but life-changing decision to move toward the unknown, moving away from turbulence toward tranquility. In some cases, a wise decision; in others, it might be better to weather the storm. In any case, the decision has been made, let the past be the past and let old wounds heal.*

She felt much better. Adam was on a journey, perhaps an epic one. But what was the purpose, she wondered, of her meeting him and the quick friendship they seemed to have established. She shuffled and cut the cards again, thinking about her relationship with Adam. Was she part of this puzzle, or was she a stray piece from a different puzzle?

The first card was Temperance. A divine, angelic figure pours water from one cup to another with one foot in turbulent waters, the other on firm ground. *He does seem calmer after our visits, perhaps I help him find balance and equilibrium.*

The next card was the Ten of Cups. A man sits confidently in front of a table filled with cups. *Wow,* she thought. *How is it that I help him feel safe? We are certainly connected, but that could just be the Italian in both of us. But I suspect it is more than that.*

The third card confirmed what she suspected: the Queen of Pentacles. A queen sits on an elaborate throne, cradling a large pentacle. Nature and wildlife surround her. She is perfectly calm, perfectly confident. Stevie considered. *Yes. Nurturing, motherly support, grounded, reliable. I can certainly be that for him. But am I opening myself up to the grief of watching him struggle?*

She pulled one last card to answer her final question. In the Four of Swords, three swords adorn a wall above a tomb upon which is engraved the fourth sword. A stained-glass window in the background shows the holy mother in front of a supplicating child. *I'll need wisdom and a peace beyond understanding, but I can do it, and that's my job.*

"I'm sorry I didn't open the door for you yesterday. I wasn't expecting company and was frightened," she said as she led Austin Lake to an easy chair. She was an elderly woman with soft, pleasant features. She had dressed for the visit and wore a pair of reading glasses dangling from a gold-colored chain. The scent of an old-fashioned perfume, White Shoulders, hung lightly in the air. Lake recognized it, could even name it. His grandmother wore it for church and special occasions.

Her living room was small, crowded with framed pictures and porcelain figurines. On the coffee table, there was a tea service and a plate of homemade cookies. The tiny apartment had the scent of baking. Lake thought she must have baked those cookies for their visit.

He thought it rude to refuse the offer of tea. And the cookie he accepted was still warm.

"Well, I don't know them very well. They keep to themselves mostly." She was speaking about her neighbors across the hall. "The young boy is very polite, as is the sister. But the older brother is less so. I wouldn't say he is exactly rude, but he does seem to always be in a hurry."

Lake was fascinated. "Older brother?"

"Yes, odd creature. He must work in a bakery or something."

"What makes you say that?"

"Well, he leaves quite early in the morning and wears his hair in a kind of topknot. I haven't seen that since my late husband and I spent two years in Japan. He was in the military," she said, sipping her tea. "I've seen him leave through my peephole in the morning. I wake up quite early—as one gets older, one does get up earlier. I've never spoken to him in the morning as I am still in my housecoat, but I've run into him in the afternoon at the mailboxes."

"And what about the next-door neighbor?" He pretended to look at his notes. "Alex Duke."

"He probably can give you a lot more information. Quite friendly with them, I think. In and out of each other's apartments like they are one big happy family."

"Do they cause any problems or disturbances?"

"There haven't been any loud arguments, if that's what you are asking. Only the opening and closing of doors. Honestly, when they moved in, I was at that peephole fifty times a day until I realized it was just them." Her face took on a saddened expression. "I'm sure you think I am a nosey Nellie, Officer Lake. I'm alone and old. The older I get, the scarier the world becomes." She paused. "They aren't into drugs or anything, are they?"

Lake smiled. "Why do you ask?"

She pursed her lips. "The real question, Officer Lake, is why are you asking about them? Have they done something wrong?"

Lake avoided a direct lie. He didn't want to tell her he was investigating a murder, thinking it would further frighten her unnecessarily. "Social services is interested in the welfare of the young boy, ma'am."

She leveled her eyes on his. "It's my understanding that they're siblings. It is a little odd that the three of them live in a one-bedroom apartment the same size as mine. I assumed that was a financial decision. The boy seems well cared for, but I've never been inside that apartment since they moved in. You can tell *that* to social services."

Adam barely made it to work on time. Absorbed in his puzzle and in his thoughts, the time passed quickly, and before he knew it, he needed to shower and bike to work. When he arrived, a note from Jenna told him that a case of Scottish lager that she had ordered for the bachelor party had finally arrived and that he should push it as a new bottled import they were testing.

He no longer felt guilty about taking full advantage of his one free meal. His standard order was now a New York strip steak, medium rare, with a loaded baked potato and a salad. Any real meal in his mind always ended with salad. "The vinegar helps you digest," his grandmother used to say.

His Nonna made the best salads in the world. In the summer, she used what Nonno's garden provided. She sometimes embellished her salads with a chopped apple, olives, peeled grapes, or some thinly sliced salami or cheese. Never croutons. Croutons belonged in soup, not salads. The dressing was simple: red wine vinegar and high-quality olive oil seasoned with salt and pepper.

When Nonna made salad, she was like an orchestra conductor at a rehearsal. She'd add a little of this or that, toss and taste, and repeat until it was perfect. His mother could never pull it off, but his sister, who had grown up in Nonna's kitchen, could. The thought of his sister's salad was one more reason to consider Pittsburgh for Christmas.

His belly full, he ducked out of the lounge to bring the tray back to the restaurant. As he handed the tray over to a busboy, he noticed Hamish, the burly guy from the bachelor party, and some of his friends sitting at a table.

Hamish noticed his approach and smiled. "Hello, mate!"

"You guys leaving?" Adam's eyes scanned the luggage surrounding their table.

Hamish stood up to shake his hand. Towering over Adam, he said, "It's about time. We stayed a few extra days for a wee holiday. But it's time to go home. We're off to New York, then an overnight flight to Glasgow."

"It was a pleasure meeting you. Hey, stop by the lounge before you go. I'd like to buy you guys a round. My boss ordered a case of Tennent's for the party, but it didn't come in until today."

Hamish beamed. "Aye, we'll take some of that off your hands. Our pleasure!"

It was about half an hour later when the lounge seemed to fill up with Scotsmen. Most of it was down to Hamish's stature. The man was huge. Adam began popping bottled tops and setting the bottles of Tennent's Lager on the bar. They helped themselves each with a healthy "Cheers, pal." Hamish was on his second when Adam asked him about the wedding.

"It was beautiful. She's a bonny lass and Derek is a lucky man, to be fair. We're glad to see him so happy."

"Where did they go for a honeymoon?"

"Ah, now that's a sad story. They were all set to go to Turks and Caicos, but our Derek worried he might not get back into the country." He shook his head. "It's a mad time. They went to Disney World instead._Aye, and what's worse, her brother disappeared from the reception."

"Her brother, the one I met?"

"Aye, the Jobbie Jabber. Not that I was sad to see him go. It was all I could do to settle the lads down after some of the things he said or did. They would'a gie him a laldy if I didn't step in… more than once."

"I'm sorry, what does that mean?"

Hamish spoke in clearer English. "I think it's bad form to beat the living shit out of the bride's brother, no matter how much it's deserved."

"He disappeared?"

Hamish shrugged his shoulders. "He just left in the middle of the party. When they realized he was gone, the family was in a right state."

"Any idea what happened to him?"

Hamish seemed to get more comfortable and more Scottish as the moments passed. Adam wondered if he had started drinking well before their dinner. He'd watched him put more alcohol away at the bachelor party without any effect at all. But now he was showing effects. Adam struggled to understand him.

"Aye, nae idea where he's bouncin', mate. Dinnae gie a toss either. Fair chuffed to be rid o' the daftie! Ah've got nane against gay folk, nae way! Each to their own, but that lad was always spillin' the beans. Disrespectful he was. He was flauntin' his rig in his kilt, swingin' his hips like a lass keen for a lad. Naebody wears a kilt like a lassie wears a frock."

Within half an hour, the whole case of Tennent's was gone, and Adam owed the lounge seventy-five dollars. He had new questions to consider. He didn't like the Butterfly either, but what would cause him to leave his own sister's wedding reception? Did he fear the groomsmen from Scotland or was it something else? Adam pulled out his cell phone and texted Stevie. "Just got another possible piece of the puzzle. Not sure." Then he texted Harjo. "Just thought of something more about New Orleans. When can we talk?"

Fifteen

Elf tried to stay awake, waiting for Adam to come home. Tom had been of little help. When Elf tried to explain how uncomfortable he felt with Professor Herzog, Tom's face was blank. To him, Herzog was an authority in the kingdom of God. Herzog operated on a higher spiritual level than most, and if he felt he had to spend time with Elf, God was in it, and Elf should be thankful for the added attention. The best advice he had for Elf was that he needed to trust in the Lord and all would be well.

Now, as Tom breathed the deep breath of sleep, Elf lay awake, hoping for the sound of the front door. Tom wasn't stupid. He knew the difference between right and wrong, knew his Bible better than most, but he was also naïve. He wasn't likely to question a spiritual authority.

The phrase "blind faith" never sat well with Elf. Faith wasn't blind but saw through things. Blindness came with addiction. Elf had known both, and he recognized the difference. The determination to use drugs despite the harm, despite the lack of satisfaction, despite the emotional costs and the damage to relationships. Addiction is blind. Faith is not.

Blind faith is dangerous. Blind faith demands unconditional obedience, not out of conviction but of unconscious fear of consequences and men who create systems to protect their power.

Elf checked his thoughts, the inner voice that narrated his life. *Dude, you just don't want to spend that much time with Herzog because you don't like him. Dude, it's less than a year, and in the end, you'll be able to live out your ministry. Dude, maybe God has a purpose in putting you through this, like Jesus in the desert, preparing you for what is to come. Dude, just do it and get it over with.*

A deep breath, a yawn, and the rhythmic sounds of Tom's breathing pulled him down into a deep but restless sleep.

In his dream, he was meeting with Ridgway, his parole officer. Ridgway was a man who tightened the screws whenever he could. He was accusing Elf of lying even though he knew the truth. He enjoyed watching Elf squirm inside. Elf was trying to remain calm, but Ridgway towered over him. Threatened, afraid, emotionally violated, and backed into a corner, Elf's only physical sensation was a pounding but fading heartbeat. Beat by beat, his heart seemed further and further away. He was losing touch. He was going back to jail. Then it wasn't Ridgway; it was Herzog. And suddenly, he was being led off campus in handcuffs.

The apartment never felt so empty. It now felt as lifeless as his room at the Hornfelds. It wasn't *his* room; it was the room they lent him. Olive wasn't his dog, except when he was out walking with her. All those quiet roads, the paths through the woods, and even through the cemetery, when he could talk to Olive and tell her things, his thoughts, his feelings, and occasionally, his dreams. She always seemed to listen to him. When he talked, she even looked straight at him like she was really paying attention.

172

Before the Hornfelds, it was the Wilsons, where he shared a room with their real-life son Timothy, who always made sure that Caleb was aware that the room was really his—he was just sharing. Before that, it was the Parkers. The Parkers were the worst. There, they didn't even lend him a room; they lent him a bed, just a bed, the upper bunk in a room with three other foster boys.

With Candy, it was different. The apartment was theirs, not hers, theirs. Everything was theirs except for his phone. His phone was his phone, and her phone was hers. There were a few weeks until the end of the month, and he understood that the apartment would no longer be theirs. He'd have to give it back and either move in with Alex or go to some other borrowed room, bed, or mattress on the floor. When Candy was out working, he was alone in the apartment most of the time, but it was still their apartment because Candy was coming back.

Now she wasn't coming back. He needed a plan. He could stay with Alex if he wanted to. At least that's what Alex said, but Caleb knew that the decision wasn't completely Alex's to make. Sooner or later, that woman would come to check on him, and the decision would be hers more than his, more than Alex's. Until then, Alex stayed with him at night and slept on the couch the way Candy did. But it wasn't the same.

Now he sat on a shaded bench in the park waiting for Jason or Will to come by with Cagney and Lacy, the two golden retrievers. He started leaving the empty apartment after school. He couldn't stand being there. It was like a constant reminder that Candy, the only blood relative he had, wasn't ever coming home.

He had met the dogs and Jason in person the day before. Both dogs nearly climbed all over him. It was all Jason could do to control them. They were all wagging tails, sniffs, and licks. Jason let him pet them. One of them, Jason or Will, always walked Cagney and Lacey in the park around this time. He had watched them from the window. He hoped that if it was Will that he would let him play with the dogs like Jason did.

Harjo read Adam's text as soon as he received the alert. His phone sounded just as he was backing out of his parking space in the lot of a nondescript office building used by the Feds in Oklahoma City. Putting the car in drive, he inched back into the same space and considered the text.

He had just spent two hours of back and forth with Sergeant Baxter and Jesus Ramirez. He learned the ins and outs of the case they recently solved. He also learned that the FBI was involved as well. Baxter suggested he talk with Cayce if he wanted the FBI angle.

Harjo met Justin Cayce once before and still had his number on his phone. But by the end of their discussion, he didn't think it would be worth calling him.

Baxter and Ramirez were probably right that the loss of the small-scale trafficking through Ur was chump change compared to big operations.

"The only reason we were interested in the Ur route was that we thought it might be part of a bigger, more subtle picture, that we were picking up on a dripping faucet that was running full force behind the scenes." Ramirez sighed. "We were wrong."

Baxter added, "It turned out to be an entrepreneurial operation."

Ramirez finished the thought. "It's a wonder bigger guys didn't just finish them off."

Baxter pursed his lips and said, "Maybe they would have sooner or later. I'm glad we got there first."

After Harjo read Adam's text, he looked at his schedule and replied. "I have a meeting at eight-thirty. I could stop by your place at seven if that isn't too early, or I could see you at the station around four-thirty."

At ten minutes to seven in the morning, Harjo walked around to the courtyard behind Adam's building as instructed. There he watched as Adam engaged in a kind of push-up, placed the top of his head on the ground and then gingerly removed the support of his arms for brief spells. He moved slowly, methodically, turning his head and shoulders. Given what Baxter had said about Adam's recent injury, the move surprised him. He waited until Adam assumed a more easily interrupted position.

Adam noticed him standing at the curb and bracing himself on his hands, took the pressure off his neck muscles and in one smooth motion, stood up. He motioned for Harjo to follow him through the back door.

"Was that cat watching you?" Harjo had noticed the cat walking away when Adam stood up.

"Every day. He shows up almost as soon as I start my drills and then leaves when I'm finished. My friend Stevie says she thinks he's a familiar."

"A familiar what?"

"That's what I asked. I didn't understand either. She said a familiar is like a guardian angel in animal form. You want coffee?"

Harjo nodded.

Cups poured, Harjo took cream. Adam also heated up his last fry bread and cut it in half. "Here, Detective. Made by an ancient Choctaw woman in Ur."

"She must like you."

Adam nodded again, this time with a warm smile, thinking of Halona, Henry, and Rosie.

"Baxter speaks highly of you."

"He's become a friend," Adam said.

Harjo saw his segue. "I just spent a couple days in New Orleans. Detective DuPuis also speaks highly of you. He gave me a tour of the crime scenes in the case you got involved with."

Adam involuntarily shuddered. "I don't think what I have to say has much to do with that case."

Adam proceeded to tell him about the bachelor party and his encounter with the Butterfly. He explained the connection with the Balustrade and ended with the Butterfly's disappearance from the wedding reception.

Harjo took out his notebook. "Do you know his name?"

Adam shook his head. "All I know is that he drinks Negroni cocktails. I can still see him sitting in the Balustrade, entertaining a few older guys. He gave me the creeps even then."

"You say he went missing?"

"Disappeared is what Hamish McFadden said."

"Where can I find this Hamish McFadden?"

"Presumably Glasgow. They flew out last night."

"Anything else you can tell me?"

"The wedding was Sunday. The groom had a Scottish accent. His name is Derek. According to McFadden, the Butterfly was the bride's brother. Sorry, I don't know more."

There was silence while Harjo jotted notes and sent a text. Adam leaned forward, elbows on the counter, hands under his chin.

"Detective, what is Officer Gamble doing undercover at the Creekstone? What's he looking for?"

Harjo was either surprised or confused; either way, he was speechless. "I've been out of town for a couple of days. There may have been developments that I don't yet know about," he said, thinking that Lake might have some explaining to do. "You say he was undercover?" Harjo was cautious.

"He was in street clothes, pretended not to know me, was starting a mustache, and sat in the lounge for hours. I figured he didn't want to be recognized, but for the life of me, I couldn't figure out what he was looking for."

"When was this?"

"Just the last couple nights."

Harjo made another note in his notebook and sent another text.

"Now, Mr. Alba, I have a question for you, if you don't mind."

"Shoot."

"What's behind the archway marked 'Private' in the Balustrade? DuPuis didn't know."

Adam's face hardened. "Private entertaining rooms. Members only. There is a bartender, a waiter, and a bouncer. I met the bartender and the waiter on separate occasions. I never met the bouncer. I don't really know what goes on back there. Reservations are required. Guests usually enter through the alleyway. I never worked back there myself."

"Why?"

"They never offered it to me. But I don't think I would have done it anyway."

"Why is that?" Harjo asked.

Adam huffed. "I don't think that the members of such clubs like unfamiliar, unvetted faces."

"That's why they didn't ask you to do it. Why would you have refused?"

Adam considered his answer and chose to answer carefully. "If I learned those secrets, I'd have a target on my back. I suspect that some of Louisiana's most prominent citizens are members."

"Can't you keep a secret?" Harjo wondered how Adam would reply. He wasn't taunting him, but he hoped to get a bit more out of him.

He spoke slowly, looking Harjo in the eye, without blinking. "My grandmother used to say, 'Curiosity can kill. If you don't need to know, don't ask.' Being trusted with secrets, Detective, demands loyalty. I don't pledge my loyalty flippantly. The Balustrade was a job, a good-paying job, but just a job."

Harjo smiled cautiously. "Do you have any idea who some of those prominent citizens might be?" Harjo was again exploring the hypothesis that Adam might have been the target, if not the victim.

Adam smiled to himself. "I'm afraid not, Detective. It would only be speculation, and I'm not willing to speculate on things like that. In fact, I understand that our conversation isn't off the record, and I really don't like where we have gone." He paused and then added, "I think I can guess what you are getting at. I really don't know anything that isn't a surmise or speculation. But there is one thing I do know, and that is, I've seen the Butterfly go through that door."

Harjo stared at Adam. "I've been told your surmises can be quite insightful."

Adam snorted. "DuPuis, no doubt. He should have listened to me. Unfortunately, I don't have any ideas for you. If I did, I'd share them. To be honest, I don't think Candy's death had anything to do with me. Her routine was as predictable as my own. Whoever killed her intended to kill her. I have no idea who or why. I knew the woman only two weeks."

Harjo was convinced it had something to do with the backrooms at the Balustrade, but Alba claimed to have never even seen them. In the few seconds he had time to think, his analytical mind mapped out several ways he might tie Candy's murder to that room. How long had the Butterfly been in town? Without realizing it, he thought, Alba had just introduced him to another potential suspect. Now he had to find the Butterfly.

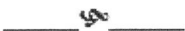

Lake had to stop at the station before meeting Harjo at the coffee shop. Terry Gamble was already at the front desk.

"Hey, Terry. How's it going?" He stopped and squinted at the young rookie. "Growing a stash?" Lake smiled. *Well,* he thought, *that confirms one thing in Harjo's text. Terry Gamble was growing a mustache.*

Gamble looked embarrassed. "Just seeing what it's like. How's the investigation going?"

"It's going." Lake didn't elaborate. He knew Gamble was anxious to know more, to involve himself in some way. "Sorry, not much to report yet." He noticed the hint of a smile on Gamble's face. It was like he enjoyed seeing him struggle.

Lake changed the subject. "Any missing person reports happen between Sunday and now?"

"Just one. Took the report myself." The smile was more obvious, reaching the crow's feet in the corners of his eyes."

"Did you put it in NamUs?"

"Not yet. He's an adult. A guy left his sister's wedding, and they can't find him. Get this, he was wearing a skirt."

Lake furrowed his brow. *What is Harjo on to? Yesterday, it sounded like he had come up empty, and this morning, he's asking about a missing guy in a kilt.* "A skirt or a kilt?"

"A kilt. He was one of the ushers. The groom was from Scotland." The smile faded a little.

"Do me a favor, call the family, see if they've heard anything, and if they haven't, tell them we're on it. Oh, and print out your report. I think Harjo might want to see it. Good work, Terry."

"When do you need it?" Gamble asked.

Looking at his watch, Lake cringed. "Ten minutes ago."

Harjo was halfway through a breakfast croissant sandwich before Lake pushed his way past the line of people waiting to order. A slightly smaller group waited at the opposite end of the counter for their orders to be filled. The tables, however, were sparsely populated.

Lake sat down across from Harjo. "Is this for me?" He glanced down at a coffee and a hot cinnamon roll cascading with frosting and melted butter.

"Good job, Sherlock!"

The sarcasm wasn't wasted on Lake. "Thanks. Glad I don't have to wait in that line." He scooped up some frosting and butter with a spoon and stirred it into his coffee.

"You know they do have cream and sugar," Harjo informed him.

Two tables away sat a woman, her arms adorned in bracelets, and her fingers with rings holding a paperback novel aloft.

Lake smiled broadly. "So, when did you get psychic abilities?"

Momentarily, the comment snagged Stevie's attention.

"Gamble has a mustache," he snickered. "What there is of it. How did you know?"

"I'm not psychic. Adam Alba told me," Harjo said. "He has apparently been hanging out at the Creekstone lounge in plain clothes for the last couple of nights. Alba thinks he's undercover. Anything I should know?"

Hearing Adam's name got Stevie's full attention. She dog-eared her current page in her book and turned the page to make it look like she was still reading.

"Joe, you know he's been itching to get involved. Maybe he just had a hunch of his own and thought he'd give it a shot."

"Let's hope that's all it was. From now on, he gets nothing, absolutely nothing about this case. Take notes and document any comments and questions he asks about it from now on."

Lake furrowed his brow. He was beginning to view Terry Gamble in a different light. "Done, Joe. So how did Alba know about the missing guy in the kilt?"

Stevie turned another page, listening intently.

Harjo explained.

"Tell me about the missing person's report."

"Christian Rhome, twenty-two, five feet seven, 130 pounds, slight build, dark hair, brown eyes, tattoo of a striking wasp on the left side of his chest. He disappeared from his sister's wedding reception on Sunday before the bridal dance. He was one of the groomsmen, and..." Lake paused for dramatic effect. Harjo and he spoke simultaneously. "... He was wearing a kilt."

"You say Gamble took the report?" Harjo's eyes grew serious.

"Yes, sir." Lake picked up on and mirrored Harjo's expression. "I asked him to get an update this morning. As of half an hour ago, the family still hasn't heard anything. He had to add that to his report. That's why I was late. You going to tell me about New Orleans?"

It took the better part of half an hour for Harjo to describe his experiences in several cemeteries, his bayou adventure, and meeting Landry in Angola. When he was finished, his face took on an expression of relief and just a little smugness. "As it turns out, my hunch wasn't completely wrong. I was just looking in the wrong direction. Dollars to donuts it has something to do with where Alba worked and this character Christian Rhome, not the serial case he got himself tangled up in. Any idea how long Rhome was in town before the wedding?"

"Family says a week to the day he went missing."

"So," Harjo pondered out loud. "He was in town."

Sixteen

Terry Gamble was back again. The only thing that had changed was that his feeble mustache was a bit darker. It made Adam want to laugh. It reminded him of the time a sneezing fit in the lunchroom revealed that a guy in the year ahead of him had used mascara to embellish his fledgling mustache.

After telling Harjo about Gamble's behavior, he had hoped for enlightenment or expected it to stop. A new development was how Gamble used his phone. It looked like he was taking photos. Adam noticed him lift his phone and pose once or twice for a selfie. He recognized the move. He'd used the same trick to snap a covert photo of Tom Delgado in the park back in Ur. He seemed to find interest in his phone when new customers came into the lounge, especially when they interacted with Adam beyond a simple drink order.

It became a game for Adam. Several times, he chose to initiate engagement with a client to see if Gamble would pick up his phone. That was fun and interesting for a while.

When Adam arrived for work on Thursday, he placed a reserved sign on the booth favored by Gamble. Adam was getting tired of the game. Night after night, photo after photo, Adam's sense of shadow rose. He hated being observed. His mind would obsessively look for the logic behind the observation. When the logic was obvious, it was better, like the people who watched him do his wrestling drills. The behavior was worth a look. Or even when he noticed a person, woman or man, checking him out. That didn't last long, and on a certain level, it was flattering.

It got weird when the gaze lingered or habitually returned. If someone focused on his pants, he'd have to check his fly. If his zipper was fine, what the hell were they staring at? Even that was a kind of explanation that helped ignore the shadow.

When all was said and done, he understood that it all went back to the brain injury he had suffered in college. Understanding, however, didn't remove the uncomfortable feeling that came with it.

When Gamble once again stood at the bar and ordered a beer, Adam winked and said, "Ignore the sign. I saved the table for you."

Gamble's face reddened, then went solid and expressionless. "Thanks," he said and retreated to his table. Was it fire, hate, or bravado in his eyes? Adam decided to press Harjo for an answer when he got the chance.

"Hi. I'm Elliot. Are you Adam? Jenna said you'd show me around." He was young, in his early twenties, a good-looking kid, a bit overdressed, with short-cropped hair. He had a warm face of smooth, mahogany skin, an infectious smile and a calm, quiet demeanor.

Adam stumbled over his response. "Show you around?" Then he caught on. "Oh, she hired you! Congrats on the new job." He chuckled, thinking Jenna must be frazzled. "Sorry, she must have forgotten to mention it to me. I'll be glad to do that. Welcome to the Creekstone. Will you be staying for the rest of the shift, or is this to be a quick tour?"

"I don't know. She didn't say." Elliot shrugged his shoulders. "I can stay as long as necessary."

Adam's estimation of Elliot quickly changed from timid to quietly confident. He was impressed and imagined Jenna had been too. "I'll text Jenna. She's good at responding, and don't worry, she doesn't often forget things. I don't want you to have the wrong impression of her. In the meantime," Adam continued, "did Jenna give you an employee number?"

Elliot rattled it off.

Adam led him to the POS. Out of the corner of his eye, he noticed Gamble taking another selfie, his phone conveniently aimed in their direction. As he guided Elliot through the process of signing in, he explained, "Every time you ring up a sale, the system will always ask you for your ID number. It doesn't mean that you've been logged out or anything; it's so you get credit for your sales and tips. You have to log out at the end of your shift."

Jenna's reply came through. *Keep him the whole shift, put him through his paces. He'll be on his own tomorrow.*

At five-thirty, Alice arrived with a tray and a burger and fries for Elliot, and Gamble took another selfie.

Adam showed Elliot where to eat his dinner in the back. "When you're on your own, you'll need to keep an eye out on the lounge. You can see the bar from here."

Elliot nodded. "Gotchu."

"My dinner usually comes about six, so I'll cover. Enjoy your dinner."

Training Elliot was a breeze. He was a quick learner. He already knew how to pour a beer properly. He still used a jigger for shots. He knew more about cocktails than Adam expected.

"I'm taking an online mixology course," Elliot confided. The more secure he felt, the more talkative and companionable Elliot became.

Adam enjoyed working with him and nearly forgot about Gamble. Elliot also distracted him from thinking about Candy. It was exactly one week ago that he found her body.

At the end of the shift, Adam showed him how to check the tanks, restock bottles and the well, and check the top-shelf supply. "First thing every shift, fill the ice bin. We don't have a barback."

After closing, they walked out together. Adam handed the lounge key in at the front desk and introduced Elliot to the clerk. "Unless Cody Biggs has told them to expect you, you might want to arrive a few minutes early tomorrow to introduce yourself to get the keys to open up."

Friday morning was unusually cool. It was an overcast day, with dark clouds streaming across the sky.

There had been light rain the previous night as Adam pedaled home, and the forecast predicted intermittent rain all day.

When Adam came in from doing his wrestling drills, he found Elf at the stove and Tom pouring juice into glasses. "Hungry? I'm making pancakes and eggs."

"I'm not much for breakfast," Adam confessed. "Thanks anyway."

"They say it's the most important meal of the day," Tom said.

Adam shrugged pleasantly. "I'm not a growing boy anymore, Tom." It was a playful dig that he softened by saying, "I just don't get hungry in the morning."

Elf meekly asked if Adam would meet him for pizza later.

Being a pizza snob had never done him well. "Sounds good. Tom, too?" Adam didn't want him to feel left out.

"Can't. I'm going home for the weekend."

Adam said, "Give them my regards, and tell your mom I'm taking good care of you."

Tom feigned a scowl and then smiled. His sarcastic tone was good humored. "She'll be glad to hear it. Thank you from her in advance."

"Elf, I'm going to a meeting tonight at 7:30. Can we make it about five?"

Elf slid a plate in front of Tom and went back to the stove.

Tom looked up. "Meeting? You have a date?"

"No, just a meeting," Adam answered, not embellishing and hoping Tom didn't press the question. Elf knew that Adam was living sober, but Tom didn't, and Adam didn't want to explain. He wanted to attend an AA meeting, hoping to run into Alex. He could have asked Harjo or Lake to relay a message, but that might require even more explanation.

Alex had said he was Candy's sponsor, and if Candy attended an evening meeting, it would logically be Friday or Saturday night because she was in the lounge the other nights. There was the possibility, of course, that she would attend a morning meeting, especially if she worked Friday and Saturday evenings, either at the lounge or somewhere else. Anyway, it was about finding Alex.

"Five is fine. Where's your meeting?" Elf said.

Adam thought it would be safe to name the church. "It's on Kenosha. Do you know it?"

Elf nodded. "Yeah, there is a place a couple blocks away called Rizzoli's. Good pizza."

Adam thought to himself, *I'll be the judge of that*, but all he said was, "Wait a minute, I thought you worked Fridays after school."

Elf's voice lowered, like he was confessing to a punishment. "I had to change my schedule. One of my professors wants to meet with me on Fridays at three. Five should be fine."

Tom sliced off a wedge of pancake and slid it through the yolk of his eggs. He said, "Elf, it's not that bad. The Lord has something special for you."

Elf slid two over-easy eggs onto his own pancakes. He didn't look at either of his friends. "Special, yes, I'm sure of it." He didn't sound convinced.

Intuitively, Adam thought it was that meeting that Elf wanted to talk about, and for some reason, he didn't want to do it with Tom. Adam didn't know whether to worry or feel flattered. "Well, I need to shower." He pretended to sniff at his armpit. "If I hang out here any longer, I'll put you off your food."

Tom laughed.

Elf said, "I've smelled worse, believe me."

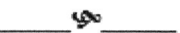

Stevie looked out her bedroom window at the darkening sky. She sensed the weight of the clouds pressing down on her. As darker clouds gathered, she found herself singing an old, melancholic song by the Carpenters. "Hanging around, nothing to do but frown, Rainy days and Mondays always get me down." She stopped herself and said out loud, "Stella Vera Tramonto, you are being silly. You like rainy days, and today is Friday, not Monday, for heaven's sake."

She opened her window and took a deep breath. Rain changed the air. Whether it was some difference in ions or just the dust cleansing from the air, she couldn't say. She just loved it.

She closed the window, picked up her purse, and headed out to her car. She was going to *get grounded*, something she did several times a year.

The labyrinth was almost an hour away in an isolated corner of a family ranch. Years ago, it had been carefully laid out in flat stones and broken bits of ceramic tile. The couple that had created it had died a few years back but had specified in their will that it remain untouched and available to anyone who wanted to use it.

For the whole drive, the rain came straight down, not borne or tossed by wind. Just a constant, steady flow. She left the windows of her car partially open to enjoy the air. Just before she arrived at the place to pull off the road and park, the rain stopped.

Hers was the only car parked in the graveled space. She squeezed past the fence post with a hand-painted sign with an image of the labyrinth.

She followed the path that led the way through wet prairie grass to the clearing. When she arrived, she saw that someone had pulled tufts of grass out of the pathways. The labyrinth itself was almost pristine. She felt connected to the person who had made that effort and sent them her feelings of gratitude.

This, she thought, *is a place of energy, like those vortexes in Sedona.* Stevie stood at the entrance and mentally prepared herself to enter a sacred place. She felt compelled to make the sign of the cross and genuflect despite the lack of a tabernacle. She hadn't done either in years.

This, she thought, *is a tabernacle of the spirit.*

She began to follow the winding path of the labyrinth, each contemplative step assuring her that she was somehow one with everyone and everything. She thought about how the labyrinth symbolized the winding, unpredictable path of life and felt gratitude for her life and where her own path had led her.

Upon reaching the center of the labyrinth, she closed her eyes and raised her arms toward the sky in an open gesture of acceptance.

At first, the rain came as just a few drops. She didn't move. A few more. These a little heavier, closer together. She still didn't move. Then the steady, heavy rain that escorted her all the way to this place drenched her from head to toe. She luxuriated in it and began to laugh out loud, enjoying the sound of her own laughter as her spirit lifted.

As the rain fell, Adam sat down at his puzzle and began to work. At first, his thoughts bounced around. But as the shapes of the puzzle pieces began to fall into place, so did his thinking. His hands worked methodically while his unconscious mind sorted through deeper questions.

Whatever Gamble's purpose in staking out the lounge, he could do nothing about it. He might press Harjo for information. He was also aware that Harjo was not a man to be pushed around, a stand-up guy.

Adam understood that he might have been under surveillance, possibly as a suspect, and he would need to be more sensitive to that possibility during his nonworking hours, but then, what was there to hide?

Stevie Tramonto came forward in his thoughts. Stevie had helped him clarify and organize the scattered ideas that had been floating in his cluttered mind. He could articulate three questions that seemed important. *Why Candy?* Stevie pointed out that Candy's routine was as predictable as his own. He wanted to know more about her. He wanted to talk to Alex, and perhaps Candy's brother Caleb, as well.

If he was a target, why Candy, and not him? Harjo seemed convinced that Candy's death was somehow aimed at him. If that were true, how so? It affected him, to be sure, but if that unnecessary death was aimed at him, it hadn't worked. What should he look out for, be careful or cautious of? Maybe Gamble wasn't staking out the lounge, not watching him as a suspect, but perhaps guarding him at the place he could predictably be found.

Adam determined to pass by the Creekstone after the AA meeting to see if Gamble was there. That would answer at least his second question. Was Gamble observing Adam or the lounge?

The third was the most obscure. What possible connection between Candy's murder and New Orleans was Harjo considering?

A flash of lightning strobed through his room, followed so quickly by a clap of thunder that the strike had been close. It interrupted his thoughts and broke the spell of concentration. He got up to see if the rain was coming in through his window. It continued to fall steadily, soaking the ground and coursing along the curbs of the parking lot toward storm drains.

He checked the windows in Elf and Tom's room as well, but the screens showed no signs of water droplets.

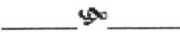

With Riley due back Monday and Gamble finishing his last desk shift, Harjo and Lake decided to meet in the Creekstone lobby. The seats were comfortable, private enough and, importantly, Alba wouldn't be at work.

"Don't you think Gamble's persistent interest in this case is a little… *unusual?*" Lake asked.

"You mean like a perp who wants to be close to the investigation?" Harjo mused. "I thought of that, but unless he's a psychopath, and I don't rule that out, I can't see a motive."

"It seems excessive to me," Lake added. "Think about it." His eyes glanced toward the smoky glass room in the corner.

"I *am* thinking about it. As long as he isn't misrepresenting the department, he's a free citizen. If he were in uniform, or flashing his badge, or running his own investigation, we would have something to address with him. According to Alba, all he does is sit there nursing a beer."

Lake recognized a losing battle and accepted that at least Harjo had the thought on a back burner of his mind. All Lake knew was that he would never dream of doing what Alba said Gamble had done, even as a rookie.

Harjo changed the subject. "I think this missing guy, Christian Rhome, the one Alba called the Butterfly, is an important lead in the case. There was a direct connection between Rhome and Alba. According to Alba, Rhome was also connected to the private area in the Balustrade."

"It could be just a coincidence," Lake said. "He was here for his sister's wedding. It just so happened that the bachelor party was held in the Creekstone lounge. I don't discount your theory, but I don't see any connection between Yates and Rhome." Lake tossed the objection out like a roll of the dice.

"Right. No obvious connection—yet. There's not much else to go on. Two things I can't let go of, and so far, they are casual connections: Alba and the Creekstone lounge."

"There's a third," Lake said flatly. "They were both part of the LGBTQ world."

Harjo looked away. "I did think of that Lake. One is dead; the other is missing. If we had a string of LGBTQ questionable deaths, that factor would seem more relevant than it does."

"You're going to bring up the planning again, aren't you?" Lake settled in.

"It's unavoidable. Premeditation is obvious. And let's face it. It's the only practical evidence we have."

"It's true but… " Lake hesitated, afraid to go too far in arguing with Harjo.

"Speak up. But what?" Harjo insisted.

Lake couldn't tell whether Harjo honored his hunch or was patronizing him. "Okay. I know I have a lot to learn, but it just feels like we're too focused on Alba as the common denominator when Alba had no connection to Candy Yates except giving her a glass of water. Hell, he didn't even know the Butterfly's real name."

Harjo softened his voice and looked Lake in the eyes. "Lake, keep fighting me on this. You may not realize it, but you are the other voice in my head. You are not doubting me or my hunch any more than I myself am. I appreciate it."

Lake nodded and felt like he had just climbed to the next rung toward being a detective. "Alright. I've got some information on Christian Rhome."

Harjo seemed to lighten and even glow. "Please."

Lake half-narrated, half-read from his notes. "Rhome was the only groomsman on the bride's side. He disappeared sometime before the bridal dance. He was supposed to dance with his sister after she danced with their father. That was when most people noticed he was missing. No one, not his family, not his roommates in New Orleans, has seen or heard from him since."

Harjo spoke up. "You interviewed wedding guests. Anyone surprised by the fact that Rhome was missing?"

Lake thought it was an interesting question but didn't know why. He hardly noticed it when it came up. "Yes, a couple guests left the reception early, before the bridal dance. They hadn't heard about him going missing."

Harjo raised a brow. "So, he disappeared sometime between when they left the party and the bridal dance. That narrows it down a bit. Did anyone indicate if he left alone or with someone?"

"I asked that question. No one admitted to seeing him leave, so no one knows."

Harjo continued. "I have more questions we might consider. Why did he go? Did he leave because he was bored, enticed, coerced, or frightened. Did he act strangely or react suspiciously to another guest?"

Lake shook his head. "I did ask questions along those lines. I've got the transcripts. I've gone over them a couple of times. Nothing stands out as relevant to any of those questions. No one saw him leave. No one had even the slightest guess as to why."

"The groom's side?" Harjo asked.

Looking at his notes, Lake filled Harjo in. "McFadden, the best man, nice guy, didn't give me much more than Alba, except he added that he felt sorry for Derek having to spend Christmas with his wife's family. He called them wankers. Do I need to translate that for you?"

"No, I think I get it," Harjo said.

"The consensus among the other groomsmen was about the same. One said if he hadn't been at the wedding of his friend, he might have given Rhome a good hiding. I haven't heard that one since I was a kid."

"The groom's family didn't think much of the bride's brother, but thought the parents were nice enough. I have transcripts if you want them. I had to translate some of it from Scottish vernacular. Translations are in brackets." He began to shuffle through the files in his lap.

At that moment, a speaker went off in Lake's ear. The volume was high enough for Harjo to hear and recognize Terry Gamble's voice. "Did he say a body was discovered in a dumpster?"

"*Behind* the dumpster," Lake said as he stood up.

A Mona Lisa smile formed under Terry Gamble's new mustache. He wondered if Alba had an alibi.

Seventeen

"I was wheeling out the dumpster when I noticed her." The trash collector was recounting the event. "I just froze." His head shook slightly—nerves.

"Did you empty the dumpster into the truck?"

"No." The head shaking was more emphatic. "The area is too tight to just back up and grab the dumpster," he rambled. "This one, we have to pull out. Otherwise, I might never have even seen her."

"Did you go inside?"

"Only to pull out the dumpster."

After radioing for the ME and a CSU, the senior officer interviewed the truck driver while his junior taped off the area. "Len stopped pulling the dumpster. I thought it was too heavy for him. I got out to give him a hand. She was just lying there, not moving."

"Did you enter the dumpster area?"

"Only when I called 911 and the lady asked if she was breathing. I got close enough to see she was dead—and it wasn't a woman; it was a man in a plaid skirt."

"Did you touch the body?"

"Oh hell, no. I could see he was dead."

Harjo and Lake pulled in behind the squad car, its light bar flashing. From that distance, they could see the dumpster sitting at an angle outside a cement block enclosure.

Harjo joined the officer interviewing the driver and listened.

"Did you empty it?"

"No."

"You're sure?"

The driver looked at the officer impatiently. "Of course, I'm sure. Listen, can we go? We got a route to run."

Harjo spoke up. "Excuse me. I'm Detective Joe Harjo, and I have a few questions for you. How many dumpsters do you service in this strip mall?"

"All of 'em," the driver said. "But this is the only one that has that cement block surrounding."

"How many of them have you emptied already?" Harjo asked.

"You mean all together or just from this mall?"

"Just this mall," Harjo said.

"Two."

"I'm afraid you're stuck for a while."

"Fuck," the driver complained. "I knew you were going to say that."

Harjo smiled. "Watch a lot of TV, do ya? Sorry for the inconvenience, sir."

Lake called to Harjo. "Looks like we found our missing groomsman, Joe. Not many men wearing kilts go missing in Broken Arrow."

Harjo approached the dumpster. The body of a man wearing a kilt lay propped against the back corner of the enclosure, legs spread. Harjo nodded, unsurprised.

Lake raised a hand to his ear. "Gamble says the ME and a CSU are on the way."

Together they walked around, giving the immediate scene a wide berth. Harjo's eyes scanned the area while Lake, who knew he should be doing the same thing, preferred to follow Harjo's gaze. There was so much potential for contamination, debris everywhere, who knew what objects might or might not be evidence.

The enclosure backed onto a small section of the strip mall, and a much battered and splattered metal back door to a restaurant called Fit to be Thai'd.

"My wife likes this restaurant," Harjo commented. "Nice family place. They're closed for a couple of weeks, visiting family in Thailand."

Each business in the strip mall had its own dumpster, and each had a surveillance camera mounted near the roof.

"Joe, did you notice that the camera from this business has been shot out?"

Harjo nodded slowly. Backing further away from the police tape, he said, "I want to get closer, but let's wait for the crime scene manager to call the shots. I don't like all the coincidences."

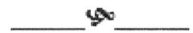

Elf knocked on Professor Herzog's door at exactly three o'clock.

"Wait," Herzog barked.

He waited. Hands clasped behind his back, he scanned the empty, silent hallway. Chairs stood neatly between office doors. At either end, tall, latticed windows filled the hall with the afternoon light. After one o'clock on Fridays, the whole campus was a ghost town, a vacuum of space.

Elf fought off the urge to pace. If he moved too far, he might not hear Herzog's call. His thoughts drifted to Frank at the Moonstone, on his feet covering Elf's shift. Frank, who'd trained him when no one else would even look at an ex-con on probation. If it hadn't been for Frank… And now he was doing Elf yet another favor, giving him the whole day off.

The Moonstone grill was Frank's life. He chatted with regulars, bundled silverware, and washed a few dishes. At busy times, he'd man the register to help the staff keep up.

"Lord, please send angels to help Frank and open Professor Herzog's heart to making this counseling fit into my work and school schedule." Elf muttered these words under his breath and winced as the quiet words echoed through the empty hallway.

He hadn't told Frank that the schedule change would likely be permanent. He didn't want Frank to hire someone else; he didn't want to lose the shift. But he might have to, and then Frank would hire someone to take over, but no one would want to work just one day a week, so he might lose even more work hours. Elf couldn't afford that.

A voice spoke from behind him. "Mr. Flemming."

Startled, Elf spun on his heels, trying to offer a sincere smile. "Oh, sir. Sorry. I didn't hear you open the door." He stepped toward his teacher and offered his hand.

Herzog ignored his extended hand. Instead, he gestured for Elf to enter the room. He closed and locked the door behind him.

As he sidled past Herzog, Elf felt once again the shrinking sensation that emotionally worsened his ingrained feeling of being tiny when near a much larger man, either in height or girth. Herzog had the advantage in both.

Herzog offered an unspoken command to sit by gesturing toward the two chairs that faced his desk.

The large windows behind Herzog's desk faced southwest, and the sun had dropped just enough to spotlight Elf in his chair and to turn Herzog into a looming, black silhouette.

After a short prayer, Herzog said, "Mr. Flemming, I thought we'd begin today with 2 Corinthians 12:7-10."

"Paul's thorn," Elf said, reaching for his knapsack and his Bible. "Shall I read it?"

Herzog nodded.

Elf read the passage.

"How do you interpret that passage, Mr. Flemming?"

Elf cleared his throat. "There are several leading interpretations. The most literal, exactly what Paul said, a thorn in his flesh, might be a physical affliction of some sort. Though he doesn't specify what it is. And it's obvious that he wasn't speaking of an actual thorn." He ended there, knowing that Herzog was a literalist.

"Interesting," Herzog said. "But I asked you about *your* interpretation."

"In referencing the thorn, some suggest it is a person, perhaps from his past, who is pestering him. Others suggest the thorn is the persecution he suffered at the hands of either the Jews or the Romans. Of course, he could have been speaking figuratively. If by 'flesh,' he means sinful nature, he might be talking about internal conflict between his old self and the new creature in Christ. The figurative interpretation might be supported by Romans 7:19, where Paul says he still struggles with everyday challenges and failures as a Christian."

"Again," Herzog pressed. "Which do *you* think is right?"

"Sir, in pastoral care, they all could be right. It depends on the person's problem. The scripture can help people through difficult times. That is one way that the Bible is described as living and active in Hebrews 4:12."

The silhouette sat back in his chair. "And how do *you* apply this scripture to *your* life?"

Elf felt Herzog trying to push him into a corner. "Professor, you know my history and my testimony. I was in prison for possessing and selling narcotics."

The silhouette leaned forward again.

"But Jesus stepped into my life and saved me. I detoxed and got clean. When I got out. I couldn't find a job. I had no money. I did odd jobs just to feed myself. Sometimes, the thought to use drugs to escape or sell to get some money crossed my mind. Back then, my past was my thorn. It took effort to stay the course."

"And now?"

"Now, my thorn is less about my old nature. It's practical. Financial. I'm on my own in the world. I have to work, and as an ex-con, my options are limited. I barely make ends meet. My thorn now is having to accommodate both the practical and spiritual aspects of my life. I guess I'm a tent maker of sorts. No one is paying my way." Elf forged on. "I'm grateful for this one-on-one counseling, truly. But I usually work Fridays, one to eleven. I need that job."

Herzog crossed his arms. "This is the only time I have available." He paused. "Perhaps... you need a different job."

"I like my job. I'm good at it. And most places wouldn't take a chance on someone like me."

Herzog regarded him for a long moment. "Sometimes, Mr. Flemming, the job we *need* isn't the one we *want*."

An uncomfortable thought flashed through Elf's mind. *What is he going to ask me to do?* As soon as he thought it, he dismissed it.

Adam saw Elf's car parked in front of Rizzoli's Pizza. He checked his watch to make sure he wasn't late. Elf was early. The anchor store of the strip mall housed an independent gym, and Adam took advantage of their bike rack.

The smell of yeast, oregano, and a hint of charred crust enveloped Adam when he walked through the restaurant door. Suddenly, he was a little boy again, at his grandmother's church on Friday afternoons, where the ladies of the church sold pizza to raise money. He breathed it in and felt himself melt into the room.

The sound of powerful fans back in the kitchen barely muffled the sounds of the three men who were engaged in a lively conversation in Italian. Adam watched them for a minute. One was spreading dough, another was placing toppings, and the third was manning the ovens.

To his right was a counter and register for takeout orders. Above the counter hung a menu indicating pizza sizes, prices, and toppings. A high school-age girl leaned against the register, thumbs dancing on the screen of her cell phone.

Adam spotted Elf sitting in a booth along the back wall. An array of six large ceiling fans filled the dining room with a gentle breeze, slightly warmed by the ovens.

Adam walked over to the table and asked if they needed to order at the counter.

"No, that girl is the server."

Adam slid into the booth opposite Elf. He noticed the table was a collage of business cards and small advertisements for local businesses, all covered with a thick layer of clear resin. "Hope you weren't waiting long."

"No, not at all. Do you like pepperoni and mushrooms?" Elf asked.

"You must be as hungry as I am. Sure. Have you eaten here before?"

"Lots of times," Elf said.

"Hi, I'm Angelina. I'll be your server."

To Elf's surprise and to hers, Adam spoke to her in Italian.

She smirked and rolled her eyes. Quietly, she said, "I don't talk Italian." Then, with a volume no one would expect her to have, she shouted, "Enzo! A guy out here wants to talk to you!"

The dough spreader, a short man with dark receding hair, a thick five-o'clock shadow, and a full belly dusted with flour, came out from behind the counter.

Elf watched wide-eyed as Adam and Enzo carried on a brief conversation. Angelina waited, expecting Enzo to translate. Enzo shook Adam's hand animatedly and then went back to the kitchen. Adam told her, "A medium with mushrooms and pepperoni. And a medium Margherita."

"We don't serve margaritas. No alcohol," Angelina said emphatically.

"It's a kind of pizza. I know it's not on the menu. Enzo will tell you what to charge."

Elf spoke up. "Two medium pizzas? That's too much."

"Too much what? Pizza? You can never have too much good pizza. Money? It's on me. You don't know how happy you've made me by bringing me to this place. These guys are from Naples. They know what they are doing. My guess is that even their American pizza is better than other places in town. But I also ordered a real Italian pizza, so relax and enjoy."

Elf wasn't sure what American pizza was, but didn't bother asking. "I didn't know you spoke Italian."

"Growing up, my sister and I spent a lot of time with our grandparents. They came from Italy. Our Italian is a little different, but we understood each other."

Elf was grinning. "Dude, when you and that guy were talking, your hands were all over the place."

Angelina brought them plates and silverware.

"What are these for?" Elf was confused.

"You don't have to use them. They know I'm Italian. I didn't eat pizza with my hands until I was in high school with my friends."

When Angelina brought the pizzas, Elf stared at the unknown pie. "Adam, it has leaves on it."

"It's basil. Tomato, mozzarella, and basil. It's like the Italian flag: red, white, and green."

Adam noticed three Italian men leaning out of the kitchen to watch him take his first bite. The flavor was perfect. The best pizza he ever had outside his grandmother's house. They watched his facial expression. He drew his hand across his chest, pinching his thumb and forefinger together. They cheered.

"What does that sign language thing you did mean?"

"I told them that it was perfection itself. They already knew that, of course, but they wanted to make sure I knew it, too."

For a while, they ate in companionable silence. Adam served Elf a slice of the Margherita.

He tasted it. "It's alright, but I prefer the other," Elf said.

"No worries," Adam said. "More for me. How did it go with the professor?"

Elf stopped chewing and swallowed. He pared down the details as much as he could.

"Did he actually ask you if you were gay?" Adam asked, finishing the Margherita pizza.

"No, not directly. He did that before, but not again today. He's punishing me, making me pay for having the temerity to ask a question during one of his lectures. He says he is 'counseling' me." Elf gestured quotation marks. "He even asked me about Grace and why we broke up."

"Did you tell him?" Adam felt his heart sink.

"No. If I went into those kinds of details, who knows what crazy ideas he'd come up with? I just told him that since Grace wasn't there, I didn't feel comfortable betraying her confidence."

"Smart move. Why don't you just tell him you're not gay and to leave you alone?"

Elf stared at Adam. "That is exactly what a student who struggles with same sex attraction *would* say. It's a power trip. I can handle him. I'm not gay, and I'm not breaking any school rules. The real problem is it's going to cost me a day of work and maybe more."

Adam furrowed his brow. "How so?"

Elf explained. "I'm scheduled to work one to eleven on Fridays. My professor wants to meet at three every Friday. That is the middle of my shift."

"Can't he change it?" Adam asked.

"He won't. I asked. I get the feeling he just wants to intimidate me. The campus is creepy on Friday afternoons. The place is deserted."

"Maybe he thinks it's private enough for you to be honest with him."

Elf appeared to consider it. "Maybe, but it doesn't feel like that. He waffles between being harsh and *almost* nice. It's like he's playing good cop, bad cop, but it's only him."

"You think he has it in for you, like it's personal or something?"

Elf finished his water and crunched a piece of ice. It took him a moment to form his response. "It feels like that. He reminds me of people I'd prefer to forget. Of course, if he really thinks I'm secretly gay... "

"You can't be a good Christian and gay?"

"Not at my school. The Bible says a few things, but the Bible says a lot of things we no longer pay attention to. On a personal level, I don't care if someone is gay or not, but I haven't worked out what I think about it in theological terms."

"Can you just refuse to be counseled?"

Elf deflated. "He could have me tossed out of school. He has me over a barrel, and he knows it. He also seems to enjoy it, but that could just be me."

Adam leaned back, his belly full. He remembered covering for Henry back in Ur. A few extra hours a week. Why not? "Hey, you're scheduled to work at one, right?"

Elf nodded.

"What if I covered for you until after your session with your teacher? I've seen the menu at the Moonstone; I can handle it. If your boss will go for it... "

"Would you really do that?"

"I don't work on Fridays. If your boss agrees... "

"It would be almost every Friday until I graduate in June."

Adam shrugged. "So what? But maybe not. It sounds like if this guy gets convinced you like girls, he might think he cured you."

"Adam, I could kiss you."

"Don't. Your professor might be watching."

Their hearty laughter filled the dining room.

Adam recognized the entrance to the church basement by the crowd vaping outside before the meeting. He smiled at them as he passed. Inside, it could have been any church basement anywhere in America, built with flexibility in mind. A cart of folding tables and another with a rack of folding chairs lined the back wall.

It was an open meeting. Anyone could attend. The center of the room had a circle of chairs, nicely spaced in the event they needed to add a chair here or there for additional attendees.

There was a table that held a large urn of hot water, a stack of foam cups, and the fixings for tea or instant coffee. A quarter of the table held bottles of water carefully arranged in rows and columns.

Seeing the bottles lined up like that reminded Adam of playing toy soldiers with his cousin Ralphy. They would set up little green plastic soldiers in rows. Then they took turns shooting marbles—cannon balls—at each other's army. The last soldier standing won the war.

He hadn't thought of playing with Ralphy in years. The game was fun at the time, but the memory unsettled him. He couldn't say what it was. It wasn't the nostalgia he would have expected. It felt more like an embarrassing secret.

Outside the circle of chairs along a wall, a boy with sandy blond hair bent over his phone. Adam guessed him to be about twelve or thirteen years old. On the floor, next to his feet, sat a sweating Big Gulp. His shoes were untied, and Adam wondered if they were too tight or small. At that age, boys grow fast.

It was possible that he was a participant, but Adam thought it more likely he came with someone who didn't want to leave him at home unattended.

Adam felt triumph when Alex backed through a kitchen door carrying a tray of pastries. He noticed Adam almost at once and acknowledged him with a nod.

Alex's setting down the pastries on the refreshments table seemed to signal that the meeting would soon begin. People gathered around the refreshments. Adam recognized a few of the vapers. Having just eaten, he wasn't interested in refreshments.

Alex came up and shook Adam's hand. "I meant to call or text you. Thanks for your help. I don't know how long we would have waited without that little push from you."

"I trust Harjo is doing all he can."

Alex shrugged. "He called me today and asked if Candy had ever gone to New Orleans. I didn't know. I asked Caleb." He gestured toward the teen sipping the Big Gulp. "He didn't know either.

"Come. Let me introduce you to Caleb. I've told him about you, but I haven't told him what Candy was doing at the Creekstone. So don't let that out. That'll come later when he's prepared to understand. He still thinks she was a hostess at a restaurant." Attendees began occupying the circle of chairs. "There's a celebration of life tomorrow, if you can make it. I'll text you the details."

Adam had only a minute with Caleb. He seemed like a good kid. Earnest. A little scared and not fully processing what happened and what was still happening. Adam promised to talk with him again after the meeting. Caleb welcomed the idea. "I'll have to wait for Alex anyway."

It was a regular meeting, but Adam felt a separation where he should have felt comfortable. He hadn't been at a meeting in a few years, and there was an awkwardness when he introduced himself.

"Hi. I'm Adam, and I am an alcoholic."

He realized for the first time that he didn't often use that word, alcoholic. Most of the time, he said nothing at all. Just refused a drink when it was offered. If pushed, he'd say he was sober. They meant the same thing, of course.

After the meeting, he rejoined Caleb. "I'm on a quest. It's almost finished." His whole body tensed as his fingers feverishly attacked the screen."

Adam watched him play the game over his shoulder. It was the same multiplayer game that Elf played with Tom's brother Ben.

"I know that game," Adam said.

"Do you play?" Caleb quickly glanced at him.

"Only once. I wasn't good at it."

"No one is at first. You should try again. It's fun."

"Have you ever run into a player called Ben the Bold?"

Caleb paused the game. "Ben the Bold. I think he hangs around with a level three elf. I see them sometimes."

"What's your name in the game?" Adam asked.

"WolfRyder" with a Y, not an I." Caleb wanted to be clear.

"That's a cool name. I like the way you spelled it."

"Somebody else already had the name with an I."

Adam watched Caleb play for a few minutes until Alex came to get him.

"Nice to meet you, Adam," he said politely, standing up and grabbing his Big Gulp.

"It was very nice to meet you, too, Caleb. I'll see you tomorrow."

Caleb paused for a moment. Then, remembering Candy's celebration of life, he stiffened. A tear ran down his cheek. It embarrassed him, so he turned and walked away.

Eighteen

"Were you ever a scout, Adam?" Stevie asked.

They were in the Ray Harral Nature Park looking at a statue of an early twentieth-century Boy Scout.

The day promised to be glorious. The sun was warm, gently caressing the day. Clouds chased across the sky, casting fleeting shadows on the ground. Leaves danced in the wind, like an elegant ballet.

"For a few years, until high school," Adam said. "We never had uniforms like that, though."

"Did you enjoy it?" Stevie said.

"I did," Adam said with a smile.

"Why did you stop?"

"My family moved to a new school district with a better reputation. My old district was pretty rough. The move was only a couple of miles, but coordinating everything was a little more difficult. Wrestling and scouts conflicted, and I had to make a choice."

"I'll bet it was a hard one," Stevie said.

"More practical than anything else. I had a better chance at a scholarship with wrestling than scouts. I still saw my old friends. Sometimes there'd be four or five of us altar boys hanging out in the sacristy before or after Mass."

Stevie insisted on taking Adam's picture standing next to the statue, making the Boy Scout salute. He recognized the feeling he had when his parents would make him and Cathy pose on family vacations.

Stevie slipped her hand into Adam's elbow as they turned toward the trailhead.

"How about you? Did they have Girl Scouts in Brooklyn?" Adam asked.

"They did, but I wasn't really interested. My father passed away from cancer when I was twelve. Being the oldest, I had to be a latchkey babysitter for my brother and sister, twins, five years younger than me."

"Latchkey?" Adam had heard the phrase but wasn't sure what it meant.

"I got out of school early to pick them up. I had to watch them until our mother got home around six-thirty. She worked in Manhattan."

"That sounds tough," he said.

"It wasn't. It made me feel grown-up, and I became a hell of a good cook. Our neighbor, Mrs. Santini, taught me a lot. She'd check in on us and help me cook dinner."

For a Saturday, it felt like they had the whole park to themselves.

"You sound like my sister Cathy. Our grandmother technically took care of us, but my sister still feels responsible for me."

"It's natural. The twins are closer to each other than they are to me. They are about to turn sixty, and I still check on them at least once a week. My sister is happily married and living in New Jersey. My brother married a whore and was miserable until she left him. I tried to warn him about her, but he wouldn't listen. He lives alone in Brooklyn in our old apartment. He bought it when the building went co-op." She laughed. "If he would just sublet it, he'd have enough money to retire completely. He works for the MTA, the subway. He sold tokens until a few years ago. Now he just answers questions."

Birds chirped and tiny invisible creatures, probably squirrels, scuttled along under dry leaves. An occasional patch of sunlight warmed their walk, and then they were back into shade.

Stevie stopped before stepping on a wooden plank bridge. "Let's just wait a minute until those children move along."

Three children, all around six or seven, were jumping on the suspension bridge trying to make it bounce. Their mother stood at the other end of the bridge waiting.

"I'm sure it's strong enough." Adam thought she was afraid the bridge would collapse.

"Oh, I'm sure it is. It's not that. They're having fun. I don't want to interrupt them. In a minute or two, they'll move on."

The mother noticed Adam and Stevie waiting before crossing the bridge and sent them a sheepish smile. She herded the three children off the bridge, and they continued.

"It's normal for kids to want to play like that. But there are more suitable playgrounds for rambunctious children," Stevie said.

"You're not fond of children?" Adam asked.

"Love them as long as they are well-behaved and go home with someone else."

215

The bridge didn't sway or move more than a tiny bit under their combined weight. The trail was easy, the visit companionable, and the conversation flowed naturally. The more they strolled and talked, the closer they became.

"How's work? You said they hired a new bartender… "

"He's terrific. I haven't had to restock the bar at the beginning of my shift since he started. The old guy, Hector, used his downtime to study. Elliot uses his to keep things in order. The only thing Elliot doesn't do is take out the trash."

"Do you think he knows about… " Stevie didn't bother finishing the statement.

"It's possible. The hotel staff are still buzzing about it." Adam considered. "I'm just weird about trash. It's never full when I start my shift. I just like it to be empty before I get too busy."

"I don't miss work at all, but sometimes I think it would be nice to have something to do. I'm not really bored, and I always find something to occupy my time. But retirement is a little too free."

"If you were a good short-order cook, you could take up half of one of Elf's shifts. I'll be doing that on Fridays."

She stopped and looked at Adam, her hand on his arm, turning him to look straight at her. "Why? I thought things were tight for him. Wasn't that why he and Tom moved in with you?"

Adam sighed. "I don't think he has much of a choice." Adam went on to explain Elf's situation. As he told her the story, he sensed her hardening, a stern scowl forming on her face.

"Who the hell does that guy think he is?"

Adam was surprised by her fury. She only knew Elf through him and as a cook at the Moonstone.

"Adam, that is religious abuse, and it must be traumatic for him. Poor thing."

"Elf says he can handle him, but the professor refused to change their meeting time. I'm just going to cover for him for a few hours."

She looked like she was ready to stomp, like a bull getting ready to charge. "That's not the point. Christians are supposed to be loving, caring, and supportive. I absolutely despise hypocrisy. Why is it that those people are ready to move their religion into schools—the Ten Commandments in the classroom—but fall back on the separation of church and state when it's convenient for them? It pisses me off."

She pointed at Adam, but he didn't feel accused; she was making a point. "People with religious authority shouldn't be immune to the law. There was a priest in Brooklyn…" She stopped herself. "If that happened in a secular school, Elf could complain to the dean, the school president, and the press, and he could sue them."

"He can't do that. He says this guy could get him kicked out of the school."

"Red flags! Red flags! Red Flags! What's that guy's name? I'll just bet there is a string of complaints about him." She rummaged in her purse for her cell phone.

"It's something like Hog. I don't remember. I'll find out for you."

She closed her purse. "You do that, honey." Her ire gradually abated. It took her a little while to walk off the excess steam. "Of all the unmitigated gall!"

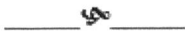

After identifying the body of their son, the Rhomes had been understandably inconsolable. Harjo had waited as long as decency allowed. Some questions couldn't wait until tomorrow.

When she saw the body, Mrs. Rhome froze. "I knew it," she whispered. "I just knew it." Then came the tears.

Mr. Rhome, on the other hand, had reddened with fury. He didn't comfort his wife. He didn't collapse. He raged at everyone and everything.

Every time Harjo or Lake tried to ask a question, he only voiced angry thoughts. He was angry at his son for leaving the wedding, for being self-centered, for being a pain-in-the-ass embarrassment, and for ruining Christina's special day.

Instead of consoling his wife, he turned on her. "You coddled him. Never let him grow into a real man."

And then he turned on himself. "I should've sent him to that military school. Or one of those camps—the kind that *fix* kids like him."

He pitched his voice high, mocking. "*Give him time, Ernest. He'll grow out of it. You should spend more time with him, Ernest. Don't be so hard on the boy, Ernest.*"

Witnessing the display, Harjo and Lake postponed formal questioning. The plan was to return the next day, Sunday afternoon.

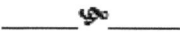

"Hell of a way to spend a Sunday afternoon," Lake muttered as they parked in front of the Rhome house.

"Welcome to detective work," Harjo replied, undoing his seatbelt and buttoning his jacket.

Inside, Mr. and Mrs. Ernest Rhome sat at opposite ends of the same sofa, as far apart as it allowed. She stared at her clasped hands wedged between her knees. He angled his body away from her, one leg crossed tightly over the other.

Their daughter Christina, sat in a nearby chair, red-eyed, dabbing at tears with a crumpled tissue. Her new husband, Derek, stood behind her, one hand resting awkwardly on her shoulder.

Harjo nodded to them. "Thank you for seeing us today. I know this isn't easy. Officer Lake and I want you to know that our best way of expressing sympathy is by finding the person or persons responsible for what happened. We'd like to ask you a few questions to help us do that."

"If you'd done your job when we first called," Mr. Rhome muttered, "we wouldn't be here now."

Lake felt the sting, but Harjo ignored it completely.

They began. Question after question met minimal response.

"Is there anyone who might have wished your son harm?" Harjo asked.

"No," they all replied, nearly in unison.

Harjo suppressed the intrusive thought that *Mr. Rhome* himself might have wished Christian didn't exist. But skipping his daughter's wedding to commit murder seemed too much of a stretch.

"We'd like to speak to any local friends," Harjo continued. "Anyone he stayed in touch with?"

"None," Mrs. Rhome said. "He left home at sixteen… at sixteen! If he had any friends, they were in New Orleans."

Christina frowned. "There was Madeline. They were close in high school. Maybe they kept in touch."

Mr. Rhome snorted. "She of the false hope."

"Only you, Ernest, thought Madeline was a girlfriend," his wife said. "I told you at the time."

Lake stepped in, calm and clinical. "Sixteen's pretty young to leave home. What happened?"

"Go figure," Mrs. Rhome said, shooting a look like daggers at the back of her husband's head.

"I never said anything about you sending him money," Mr. Rhome shot back. "Even though we could barely afford it."

Christina rolled her eyes. Clearly it wasn't the first time she'd heard this argument.

"He wouldn't even let his own son stay here for the wedding," Mrs. Rhome snapped. "Made him stay in the hotel with the out-of-town guests."

"He *was* an out-of-town guest," Mr. Rhome said. "Good enough for the other groomsmen."

Mrs. Rhome stood abruptly. "You're going to be the next one staying in a hotel. Starting tonight!"

Harjo raised a hand. "It's clear we need to speak with each of you individually. Lake, do we have contact information for everyone?"

"Yes, sir."

Harjo stood. "We'll be in touch. I trust we'll have your full cooperation moving forward."

Outside, Harjo climbed into the passenger seat of Lake's car. Before Lake could circle around, raised voices erupted behind them. Lake paused and turned. Derek was jogging toward them.

"Alright?" Derek said, lifting a hand. "Just before you go, I have a wee thing to mention. Might not mean much, but before anyone noticed that Chris was gone, I saw him chatting with some bloke like they knew each other. When we heard about Chris, I asked Christina about it. She hadn't seen them talking. I tried to describe them, but she didn't recognize them. That guy and his family shot off early."

"Thanks," Lake said. "And just out of curiosity, what did you think of your brother-in-law?"

Derek scratched his neck. "I didn't really know the lad. Christina said he was gay—fair enough, who cares? But aye, he could have toned it down a bit."

Lake made a note. "Look forward to speaking with you again soon."

After their walk, they sat on a shaded bench near the Nature Center. Stevie had packed a lunch of hand-held pies that she called crostini, but Adam knew as falagone. "One is sausage, the other is potato and hot peppers." She handed him two pies wrapped in paper towels. "You get your meat and potatoes without all the mess."

Adam bit into a pie. The crust was flaky, and the potato and hot pepper filling brought tears of nostalgia to his eyes."

"This is amazing," he said to her.

"Mangia," she said. "Mrs. Santini taught me how to make them."

They ate in brief, companionable silence. Then Stevie spoke, her tone shifting.

"I was at the coffee shop a few days ago. Two men were talking about what happened at the Creekstone. I would've mentioned it earlier, but I wasn't sure it mattered. I'm still not sure. But... here goes."

She described the men to Adam.

"Sounds like Harjo and Lake. They're detectives." Adam said. "Did they say anything worth remembering?"

"I wasn't paying much attention until I heard your name. Want the good news or the bad news first?"

"The good."

"I don't think you're at the top of their list of suspects. They're focused on someone who's vanished. They were talking like he's the missing link to all this. I don't fully know what they meant. Honestly, most of it would've gone over my head if I didn't have your version in the back of my mind."

Adam polished off his second pie. "And the bad?"

"I don't think the list of suspects is very long."

Adam winced, but then his laughter, despite being muffled by the trees, seemed to echo through the park. It wasn't anything he didn't already know or suspect.

Nineteen

Harjo and Lake sat behind closed doors. Indirect morning light diffused throughout the office. Fresh air, cool from the early morning, puffed through the window, making the room exceptionally comfortable.

Each had a cup of coffee in a BAPD mug. Lake was unraveling and eating a cinnamon roll bit by bit. Harjo tried not to watch. He mindlessly fingered the collection of carrots and celery sticks in a plastic zip bag in front of him.

Lake said, "That was some shit show yesterday, huh? Glad I'm not a marriage counselor."

Harjo sighed. "I didn't expect the daughter and her husband. I'm glad they were there, though. Did you see the daughter's reaction to the argument? She's heard it a thousand times. At least we know they were being themselves."

Lake scowled. "I guess it takes all kinds."

"No wonder people lose weight on this stuff," Harjo complained. "Who in the hell wants to eat this?"

"Rabbits, Joe, rabbits. You want a hunk of my cinnamon roll?"

"Bribery is a crime, Lake."

"How'd you get your wife to go with you to that celebration of life? That was a brilliant move. Wish I had thought of it," Lake said.

"It wasn't hard. Unless she's around, she thinks I'm going to do something embarrassing. A few comments here and there, a bad choice of a tie, and she starts getting dressed and putting on makeup."

"So, you lied to her."

"Oh no," Harjo confessed. "I'm sure I *would* have done something that she'd call embarrassing."

"I noticed that Alba monopolized the kid. I hoped to have a few minutes with him to set up rapport. I barely got a chance to express my sympathy," Lake said.

"Alba was protecting him or at least supporting him. When are you going to talk with him?" Harjo asked.

"Tomorrow at seven-thirty. Alex, as de facto guardian, will be present."

"I've got Alba coming in at nine-thirty. Baxter, the sergeant from Ur will get here about nine."

"That's interesting. Something I should know?"

"They're friends of a sort. Baxter knows Alba pretty well and Alba might feel more comfortable with him around."

"You think Alba is holding back?"

"Not intentionally. I think he's already said what he's sure of. I want to press him. Baxter in the room will get us further than just you and me."

Lake nodded. "Is that the ME's report?"

"Yep, let's go over it."

Harjo got down to business scanning the report. "The body spent some time in cold storage postmortem. ME says either a short time in a freezer or a long time in an unreliable fridge. Some parts of the body show signs of having been frozen," he said, making a face. "It explains the location of the body." He rifled through papers on the desk. "The owner of Fit to be Thai'd reported a break-in last night. According to this, he went to check on the restaurant when he got back from his trip. The cooler door was open, food was spoiled, and the compressor irreparable. The officer who took the report found a purse under a rack in the cooler. She bagged it as evidence. Turns out it was a thing called a… " he read from the report "… sporran, part of the kilt getup."

"Break-in? There were no signs of forced entry. I checked." Lake was surprised but was sure he hadn't missed any signs of a break-in.

"I figured that was what you were doing when you walked around to the front of the strip mall. Good thinking."

Lake secretly basked in the compliment. It felt good to brag a little. "What about fingerprints?" Lake asked.

"Only yours on the front door. Everything else was wiped clean. The only person who had keys was the owner's brother-in-law, that is, the husband of his sister. He says he never entered the place but checked it out front and back every day. Nothing was ever amiss." Harjo said.

"So, it was either a skilled locksmith or someone with keys. I'll check with the management company. I jotted the number down from a sign on the side of the building." Lake offered.

Harjo nodded approvingly, then said, "Listen, Lake. I'm still bothered by the coincidences. Two bodies disposed of behind dumpsters. Both died of ligature strangulation with evidence of blunt force trauma. Both seem to have been killed elsewhere some length of time before disposition of the body. A few hours at least for Yates and what seems to be a few days for Rhome. And the only obvious link between them?" Harjo let Lake fill in the blank.

"Adam Alba. He's strong enough to move a body, and by his own account, he had the opportunity for both," Lake offered. "But questionable means and no obvious motive."

"And absolutely no evidence," Harjo finished the thought.

Adam sat cross-legged on the grass with his eyes closed and his sweat-soaked T-shirt clinging to his torso. He had pushed himself extra hard this morning, going a bit further on his neck-strengthening exercises. Now his concentration was on relaxing the muscles in his shoulders and neck.

He nearly jumped out of his skin when something brushed against his knee. Startled, the cat whose habit was to observe Adam's unusual behavior every morning, backed away. Eyes open, Adam smiled at the tabby.

"Getting friendly now, are ya?"

The creature hesitated momentarily before approaching him again with a loud purr. Adam reached a hand toward it. It sniffed his fingers before letting Adam stroke the fur behind its ears.

"That's some purr you have there."

To Adam's surprise, the cat crawled into his lap and nestled in his crossed legs. He wore a silicone collar with the name Bert and a phone number printed on it. "Well, Bert, this is a pleasant surprise, but I don't have much time to hang with you. There's a detective expecting to see me." He gave the cat one last scratch behind the ears before jogging back inside to clean up and change. By nine-fifteen, he was chaining his bike in front of the police station.

At the front desk, he was greeted by a middle-aged, wash-and-wear woman. She had short, mousey brown hair and wore little, if any, makeup.

He introduced himself. "Adam Alba. Detective Harjo is expecting me.'

Behind her polite smile, her eyes traced his face and what she could see of him from behind the desk. Adam couldn't decide if she was checking him out or if she was memorizing him for an accurate description should it be necessary."

She stood up. "Yes. This way." She led him down the hallway to the same office where Harjo had interviewed him for the first time. Harjo wasn't alone but it wasn't Lake or Terry Gamble with him. It was Sergeant Baxter.

Adam's face brightened. "Bax... Sergeant Baxter. What a surprise!"

"It's okay, Adam. He knows we go back."

They shared more than a handshake but still less than an embrace. Adam also offered his hand to Harjo.

"Would you like a cup of coffee? If I remember, you take your coffee black," Harjo asked. "How about you, Baxter?"

They both declined.

The three sat down in an amiable group.

"I called the sergeant yesterday and invited him to join us."

"I'm glad to see him, but why?" Adam ran his hands along the arms of the chair.

"Sergeant Baxter is insightful. I've asked him to consult on an informal basis," Harjo said.

"I agreed, Adam, because it's you. I'm naturally interested. Besides, there's not much happening in Ur right now."

Adam nodded. "Glad to help if I can."

"Do you like Thai food, Mr. Alba?" Having found the body of Christian Rhome behind a Thai restaurant, Harjo wanted to see how Adam would react to the question.

Adam was nonplused, visibly confused. "What?" He looked at Baxter as if to say, *What the fuck?*

Baxter shrugged and smiled.

Adam answered, "I don't often have Thai food. The first time I tried it, it tasted like soap. It's not my favorite."

Harjo chuckled. "Like soap? I have to tell my wife that. She loves Thai food."

"Okay, what's the point? I mean, what does my liking Thai food have to do with anything?" Adam felt like he was a rat in a maze trying to find his way out. His shadow feeling was awakened but remained in the distance.

Baxter interjected. "The man you call the Butterfly. Do you know his real name?"

"No, I never even spoke to him until he ordered a drink at that bachelor party. I assume you know about that."

Baxter nodded.

Harjo sat back in his chair and picked up a piece of paper. "We found him." He waited for Adam to react.

Adam shrugged and opened his hands in a helpless gesture. "Okay."

Harjo went on. "Christian Rhome, known to you as the Butterfly, was found dead behind a dumpster in much the same position as you found Candy Yates. The dumpster belonged to a Thai restaurant called Fit to be Thai'd. Have you been there?"

Adam's mind spun. He didn't know what to make of the statement. "No. That is really creepy."

"Mr. Alba. Two people are dead, most likely by the same hand, and you are the only person we are aware of who knew both victims."

Adam looked at Baxter. "What exactly is going on here?" Adam's hands on the arm of the chair tightened. He wouldn't panic, and he consciously controlled his voice. "I didn't *know* either of them. Not really." His eyes flickered to Baxter, then back to Harjo. "And I had no reason to harm either of them."

Harjo appeared to relax. "Mr. Alba, these two deaths are connected somehow, and you are the only connection we see."

It wasn't a question. It was elicitation. Baxter recognized it and waited. Harjo was no rookie. After a prolonged silence in which he watched Adam's baffled reaction, he said, "Adam, being one connection yourself, you may be able to help them find or recognize another."

"If it's not more than that, pick my brains, but what you said, Detective Harjo, sounded like an accusation. So, I have a question of my own. Why do you have Officer Gamble undercover in plain clothes in my lounge?"

It was the first time Baxter had heard about it, and it unsettled him. It was clear he didn't have the full story.

Harjo's brow furrowed. "Again?"

"Still! Every night I work, he's there. And on nights I'm not there, neither is he."

Harjo preferred to keep his reactions under control, but the news clearly bothered him. He puffed out a sigh. "Did he tell you that we sent him there?"

"No. He just buys a beer and sits there for hours."

Baxter looked at Harjo. Harjo saw his gaze but didn't react. A moment of silence passed before Harjo spoke again. "Mr. Alba, I haven't sent Officer Gamble to the Creekstone lounge. I don't know what he's doing there. Of course, he's free to spend his free time as he likes. What makes you think he's undercover?"

"For one, he keeps taking pictures. It may not be obvious to guests, but it is to me."

"Pictures of what?" Harjo wasn't showing emotion, but Baxter guessed he was either suspicious or annoyed.

"People, guests, especially interactions with me. If I talk to someone more than give them a drink, he finds some way of aiming his phone in our direction. He tries to be slick, but it's obvious. I tested it."

"How so, Adam?" Bax was both curious and proud.

"Keeping one eye on him, I simply engage random customers in small talk. Every time I do that, he picks up his phone. It's annoying. That booth is perfect for observing the entire lounge. Alex Duke sat there hoping to see Candy. Tell you the truth, until I confronted Duke, I thought he might be the one who killed Candy. He was there the day I found the body. I thought he could just be there for the show."

Harjo puffed out an exasperated breath. Was that what Terry Gamble was doing? First on the scene, itching to get in on the case. He said, "Mr. Alba, do me a favor, the next time he comes in, just text me."

Adam nodded. "Sure… okay."

The conversation grew more collaborative as Adam relaxed. He understood that Baxter had agreed to come for a reason of his own. Whether that was to support Adam in this meeting or to make sure Adam wasn't railroaded the way he had been in New Orleans.

The three of them explored the possible connections between Candy or Andy Yates and Christian Rhome. Harjo showed him photos of Andy as a male.

"The transformation is remarkable," Adam commented. "I wouldn't match the two. But to my recollection, I never saw him as a man. But then, I might not have noticed."

"Please think back to your time in New Orleans. Do you recall seeing Candy or Andy there?"

"I never saw Candy. Women in the Balustrade are rare. I don't recall Andy ever being there or here, for that matter. It's remarkable how different they look," Adam said.

Baxter asked, "How long did you work at that bar in New Orleans?"

"Nearly two years. A lot of people came and went during that time. I'd recognize regular customers but not casual visitors. Neither Andy nor Candy were regulars."

"How about the back rooms?" Harjo asked.

The question caught Baxter's attention. He didn't know anything about backrooms at the Balustrade.

Adam shook his head. "I think I made it clear that I don't know much about the private area at the Balustrade. Once in a while, someone went back there through the bar, but that was very unusual. That door exists mostly for fire regulations. It's also the emergency exit. Most backroom patrons enter through the rear door in the alleyway."

"Do you know how long the Balustrade keeps its surveillance footage? We may need to pull footage from the Balustrade. Just to verify movement, timestamps, that sort of thing." Harjo hated the thought of reviewing it, but doing so was one way of getting at the information in an evidence-based way.

Adam raised a single eyebrow wondering how Harjo knew about surveillance at the Balustrade.

Baxter was fully engaged.

Harjo answered Adam's unspoken question. "I noticed the cameras in that molded ceiling."

Adam raised his opinion of Harjo. Those cameras were almost impossible to see, even if you were looking for them. "I don't know," Adam admitted. "But you'd need a warrant, a raid, and probably a forensic computer specialist to get at them. I don't know if there are cameras in the back. If there are, they are even better hidden, and the recordings would be kept for 'insurance purposes.'" Adam air quoted the phrase.

"You think they'd be reluctant to provide the recordings?" Baxter asked.

"I think they'd be reluctant to admit they even had them. It wouldn't be good for business, especially if there were cameras in the back rooms. You might not get those recordings even with a warrant."

Baxter's interest increased. He asked, "Exactly what do you mean by insurance purposes?"

"I mean, the owners of the Balustrade aren't going to take the fall for anything. If the shit were to ever hit the fan, such recordings could come in handy," Adam said. "Imagine how incriminating recordings might be for a staunch conservative politician. There are different kinds of insurance, and if the Balustrade were to go down, it wouldn't go alone. Surely, you are smart enough to know *that*."

Harjo pressed his lips together, seemed to deliberate about what to say next. "Mr. Alba, perhaps you *are* a target because someone *thinks* you know more than you do."

Baxter sat up straight. "Blackmail?"

"You've got to admit it fits the profile," Harjo said.

"I don't know enough about anything to blackmail anybody," Adam spoke in his own defense.

"But someone might think you do." Baxter said slowly, softly as if speaking to himself.

"If anyone knew too much and they tried to use it, no doubt they could end up..." Adam stopped mid-sentence.

"Precisely." Harjo said.

Baxter wore a sick and painful expression.

Exasperated, Adam answered him. "No. I'd be dead."

"I've got two deaths with you appearing near the center of both. That's a pattern I can't ignore, even if I want to. If I were like your pal DuPuis in New Orleans, it would be easier to convict you than it would be to protect you. I'm trying to do the latter. I'm not suggesting you are a blackmailer, but it is possible that someone is being blackmailed and *thinks* you are involved in it. Candy could have been a warning, and as for Rhome, you said he went into that back room."

Just then a knock on the door. "Who is it?" Harjo called.

"It's me, Lake."

"Come in."

Lake entered, and Harjo introduced him to Baxter. "We were just discussing the blackmail angle," he said, filling Lake in.

Lake nodded. "My vote is for the owners of the bar. Just think of the intelligence they could have gathered over the years."

"It's a possibility," Baxter conceded. "But would they frame Adam?"

"I don't believe it," Adam interjected. "I know them. They have a good thing going and are well paid for it. They wouldn't want to fuck it up. They wouldn't blackmail anyone, though they could." His chest sank in thought.

"What is it, Adam?" Baxter asked.

Adam hesitated. "It's just a thought, an idea. We don't know that blackmail is really in the mix. If a patron were being blackmailed, and they brought it up to the owners of the Balustrade, the owners would know it wasn't me. But they just might have a good idea who the blackmailer was. Their business would also then be at risk."

Lake turned to Adam. "Are they capable of setting you up?"

Adam shrugged. "I wouldn't exactly call them friends. They seemed to genuinely like me and were appreciative of what I did for the community. I don't think they'd do that unless the alternative was much worse."

After a brief silence while everyone in the room thought through what Adam said, he said, "If all you want to know is if Candy or Andy has anything to do with the Balustrade, send those photos to DuPuis. There are other people to ask, and DuPuis can get the information without too much disruption."

"The owners trust DuPuis?" Baxter said.

"Trust isn't the right word. They know him, of course. He is more likely to get the information you want than any stranger would, with or without a warrant, as long as it doesn't put their business in danger. DuPuis knows how to ask questions without crossing lines, but more importantly, he knows *who* to ask. I don't think confronting or even questioning the owners of the Balustrade would work."

Harjo said, "So, DuPuis knows about the back rooms?"

"I don't know what he knows. Lots of people know that those rooms exist. They're not a secret, just discreet, and everyone knows that. They cater to prominent citizens, politicians, and wealthy people who prefer to keep their private lives private."

Lake's expression looked serious. He leaned into Alba and said in a low tone, "You seem to know a lot."

The atmosphere in the room thickened. It was a rookie mistake. Baxter would hate to eavesdrop the next time Harjo and Lake were alone.

Adam felt defensive. "I'm trying to help, but there is a real difference between knowing something like a fact and recognizing when there are things that you simply don't want to know. I've been clear about those back rooms."

Baxter could see the new trajectory of the interview, and he suspected Harjo did as well. More importantly, he could see Adam's patience thinning. How much longer would it be before Adam said something he'd regret? Harjo, though being direct, didn't come off as aggressive. He painted an accurate picture hoping that it would jar something in Adam's mind. And it worked. He at least confirmed one of their avenues of investigation.

Even in Ur, Adam had skirted any real talk about New Orleans. In this interview, he had given Harjo and Lake more than they bargained for, and Adam was getting close to shutting down.

Baxter made an elaborate gesture, looking at his watch. "Gentlemen, I've got to head back to Ur soon. How long until we wrap things up?"

Lake gasped, and Harjo had a look of understanding.

Adam may be able to contribute more, but not now. Tightening the screws might get a perp to unwittingly incriminate himself, but it wouldn't help Adam to remember more.

Whether Harjo fully understood or not, he could see that the momentum of the interview was broken, and it might take hours to get it back on track, if ever at all. Adam was already less prone to collaboration, not with Lake, in any case.

Harjo stood up and shook Baxter's hands. "Sergeant, it was kind of you to come all this way. Your perspective has helped immensely. Perhaps we can speak later today." He didn't wait for confirmation from Baxter. He turned to Adam. "Mr. Alba, you've given us something to consider, and I thank you for your cooperation. Remember, if Officer Gamble comes back to your workplace, let me know."

Baxter and Adam left the office. Outside the station, as Adam unlocked his bike, he thanked Baxter for breaking up the meeting. "It was getting stuffy in there."

Baxter asked, "Adam, do you want to get lunch before I go back to Ur? Do you have time? I'm hungry."

Adam smiled. "I'd like that. I know just the place. You can find out what real pizza tastes like."

Twenty

S tevie couldn't stop thinking about Elf. Every time she started some little project or picked up her book, her thoughts would drift back to Elf being bullied by his professor. Adam said Elf could handle the guy. He was a grown man after all. But no one should have to endure religious abuse.

The thought of Elf enduring that kind of treatment gnawed at her, the same way she'd felt when the diocese quietly reassigned that priest instead of handing him over to the authorities. They were protecting the bastard. Priest or no priest, if he'd stayed in the neighborhood, someone would've strung him up like Mussolini. And he deserved it.

Adam still hadn't given her the professor's name.

She blinked and realized she'd wandered through every aisle of the supermarket without placing anything in her cart except a box of discounted chocolate cookies. She was tense and feeling a headache coming on. Her shoulders had stiffened and tugged at her neck. She rolled her head, first in one direction and then the other, in an attempt to relax.

"I don't even like these," she muttered, staring at the offending box of cookies. She didn't remember picking it up. "Unconscious self-sabotage!" she said aloud. Cookies weren't on her list, and even if they had been, she wouldn't waste carbs on that kind of junk.

With a renewed sense of resolve, she set the box down on an endcap and steered her cart back toward the produce section. While selecting a bulb of fennel, hidden spray nozzles sprang into life, creating a mist around the fresh vegetables. She pulled out her phone and sent a text to Adam to remind him she still wanted to research that professor.

Adam's bicycle chain clanged at the bike rack in front of the gym a few doors down from Rizzoli's. As he snapped the lock closed, his phone vibrated in his pocket. He swiped at the screen, got Stevie's text, and saw the unsent message above it. He hit send and then followed with an apology and an explanation.

Because he could weave through traffic and ride on sidewalks, he had beaten Baxter to the strip mall by several minutes.

When he stepped into the restaurant, the sound of the bell that hung above the door announced his presence. The familiar, intoxicating scent hit him again. For a split second, he was ten years old. Nonno had sent him in to get his grandmother. He could hear all the ladies in the pizza kitchen embarrassing him with comments about how big he was getting or how handsome he was.

"Do you have a girlfriend?" Mrs. Conte asked.

"No," he answered, turning red.

"Why not?" she asked.

"I'm ten," he answered. For some reason, it made all the ladies laugh and coo.

Angelina, still behind the counter, barely looked up from her phone to send him a meek smile of recognition. He approached the counter, and when her thumbs stopped tapping, she slipped the phone into her back pocket.

"Don't try talking Italian again. I know you speak English." It was only half a tease. "What do you want to eat?"

Remembering the pizzas Baxter used to bring to him in Ur, he ordered one with the same toppings and another Margherita."

"Because of you, Enzo added it to the menu," she said, pointing up at the sign. "Margherita" was written on the sign in permanent marker. Adam felt a certain satisfaction in that. He glanced back to the kitchen. All three cooks were grinning at him. Enzo waved.

When Baxter glided into the booth opposite Adam, he pulled the table toward himself to make more room for Bax. Taller and more muscular than Adam, Baxter outweighed him by at least thirty pounds and had an appetite to match.

"Halito," Adam said in Choctaw. Baxter's family was part of a small Choctaw minority in Ur.

"Halito," Baxter said. "You're not studying Choctaw, are you?"

Adam shook his head. "It's all I managed to learn back in Ur. That and something that sounded like *Attack Ohio*. Rosie used it when Halona brought the fry bread."

Baxter laughed. "Was it *Hatak Ohoyo*? That's only for women. You're safe with *Halito*."

"I ordered a couple of pizzas. One I'm sure you will like, the other I want you to at least taste."

"I take it that this is better than Pizza Hut," Baxter said.

Adam stopped and stared at him. "Are you not breathing? It's a world away."

Angelina interrupted them with glasses of water. "I'll also have a coke," Baxter said.

"Coke coke or some other kind?"

"Coke coke."

"Diet or regular?"

"Regular."

"Is Harjo Choctaw?" Adam asked.

"Creek." Baxter corrected him. "Don't *Halito* him unless you want a lecture on the tribes of Oklahoma. I think it's *Hesci* in Muscogee. You can try that."

"Why does he have it in for me?"

"Not Harjo. Lake. To Lake, you are still a suspect until evidence excludes you. I think Harjo has ruled you out in his own mind."

"You think or you know?"

"I think, sorry. For what it's worth, I feel sorry for them. I'm not even sure they know where else to look. It's one thing to investigate a murder without a body. They have two bodies with the same MO and the only connection they can find is, unfortunately, you."

"Do I need a lawyer?"

"Lawyering up has the same effect as claiming the fifth. If they arrest you, lawyer up. Have they informed you of your rights?"

"No, not yet."

"Well, that's a sign that Harjo doesn't seriously think you are a suspect. If he had any inclination in that direction, he would have informed you of your rights. That makes anything you say admissible in court against you.

"He thinks you know more than you think you know, and he wants the information. That's what today was all about. Apart from wanting to see how you are doing, I was there to help you feel comfortable. When Lake came in, I didn't know what might happen next. And I didn't like the way it was going."

"But I told them everything I know," Adam shrugged.

A loud conversation in Italian erupted in the kitchen. Baxter straightened up as if a cop might come in handy. "You speak Italian, don't you? What are they fighting about?"

Adam spoke through a chortle. "You'll never know how many times I've had to answer that question." Adam smiled. "They aren't fighting. Call it passion. They are talking about a sport. Rugby, I think. It's not soccer. The terms aren't familiar to me."

"How's your neck, my friend?" Baxter once again relaxed in his seat. "Are you ready to walk around your own head yet?" He was referring to one of Adam's wrestling exercises he never got the chance to see.

"Maybe soon. Not yet."

Bax returned to the meeting. "They need something. Maybe sending those pictures to DuPuis will produce something they can move on. Right now, they have a lot of forensic items, but they don't yet know if they are evidence or not. I know they are waiting on DNA."

"Candy or the Butterfly?"

"Both. If they match, it's good strong evidence against the perp. But Candy was a prostitute. That complicates things. It could exonerate you as long as you weren't the one who—"

"I wasn't… in either case," Adam interjected.

"Then let them swab you, if they ask," Baxter said. "My best advice to you is this. Until they Mirandize you, cooperate as much as you can. Stay calm. Stick to the facts. Respond to their questions and try not to react. Don't let them get under your skin. The second someone Mirandizes you, lawyer up. Even if they ask why you think you need a lawyer. Especially if they say they have evidence against you. Say nothing after that. You'll be in custody but say nothing without your lawyer."

Angelina, the server, was bringing them plates and cutlery. "Pizzas will be out in a minute. Can I get you something more to drink?"

They both shook their heads.

"But I've done nothing," Adam continued.

"I believe you. They are looking for evidence. It all comes down to what evidence they are looking for. Harjo wants a direction; Lake wants something to hand off to the DA."

"Is that why you ended the meeting? They didn't seem to like you doing that."

Baxter nodded. "My time really is tight. I don't have much, and I wanted to spend a little time with you. When I saw them getting to you..."

"Yep, I was getting pretty pissed off."

"I knew it and so did they. If it were an interrogation, you might have been there for hours and hours until you cracked. This was just an interview, but if Lake had his way, it might have turned into an interrogation."

"Then why did they let me go?"

Baxter tilted his head to the side. "Because I ruined it. Actually, Lake ruined it, but I got you out of there. I think Harjo is hoping that I can get more out of you because we're friends."

"Is that what we're doing?"

Baxter's sigh was short and heavy. "No. But if there's something you need to say, I want to hear it. I can pass it on in a way that won't count as evidence. That's why I'm sure Harjo doesn't truly suspect you. If he did, you wouldn't be sitting here, and the two of them would be working on you."

He paused, studying Adam. "They trust me to a point, but they know our history. They don't have enough to arrest you. They also don't have enough to clear you. You're still in the picture."

Adam sighed. "I don't see any connection between the Butterfly and Candy other than they were both LGBTQ. I never saw Candy as Candy at the Balustrade. And I never saw the Butterfly in the Creekstone lounge until the bachelor party. I'm sure about that. I don't remember seeing Andy at the Balustrade. He wasn't a regular twink. He may have come once or twice, but not enough for me to remember him."

"Twink?" Baxter wasn't sure of the term.

"One of the young guys playing for a sugar daddy."

"How did Rhome make himself known to you?"

"He didn't say a word to me until he approached me for a drink. He mentioned the Balustrade and it came to me. He normally drank a Negroni."

Angelina brought the two pizzas and positioned the trays on the table so that they could both share.

Baxter said, "You ordered a Margherita!"

"How do you know about that?" Adam was shocked.

"YouTube. I looked up real Italian pizza one day because you said I didn't know what real pizza was. Can't wait to try it." He paddled a slice onto his plate. "So, what was so unforgettable about Rhome?"

"He was a regular. There was a small group of three, sometimes four guys, that he hung out with. They bought him drinks, and he entertained them. The way he talked, the way he acted. He put a lot of energy into his performance. He stood out. At the bachelor party, he looked the same except for the kilt. He wasn't as loud but then he didn't have to entertain anyone. He never spoke a word to me at the Balustrade."

"Why do you think that was?"

"Someone else always bought his drinks for him. It was always a Negroni."

"Interesting," Baxter said thoughtfully. "Rhome drank Negronis and Yates didn't drink at all."

"She drank, just no alcohol. She drank seltzer with a twist of lime," Adam corrected him.

"Okay, they both had a signature drink," Baxter continued, giving the Margherita pizza a thumbs-up. "Rhome was flamboyant and attracted attention. Yates was quiet and discreet."

Adam nodded. "What's this about?"

Baxter shook his head slightly. "Just a little victimology. Yates was a hooker, but Rhome was not."

Adam straightened up. "I never said that, Bax. There were plenty of times I saw the Butterfly's friends give him cash, sometimes quite a lot of it. I don't know why or for what, but I know what I saw."

Baxter's expression shifted, like clouds parting before his eyes. "Adam, I could kiss you."

"Why do men want to kiss me in this restaurant? First Elf and now you."

"I don't know about Elf, but you just revealed another avenue of investigation. Can you identify the people who gave him money?"

"By sight, not by name. People at the Balustrade didn't often tell me their names unless they were trying to pick me up, and even then, they lied. I can describe them well enough. Three, sometimes four older guys. The three were regular regulars, the fourth maybe once or twice a month."

"I need to give this to Harjo. He'll want to talk with you about the descriptions. At least it's something to go on." He had to partially stand to fish his phone out of his pocket. "Why did Elf want to kiss you?"

"I'll explain, but first, why do you?"

"Don't you see? I don't know if Rhome was a hooker or not, but if he entertained older men and they tipped him, there isn't much difference, is there? What if that money wasn't for services but silence. I'd want to talk to those people who gave him money. I might also want to talk with other regulars of the Balustrade."

Adam squared his shoulders. "I guess it's worth a try, but I don't know how much you'll get from them. Discretion is what the Balustrade is all about."

"Murder has a way of loosening some tongues."

"Not in my experience," Adam mumbled.

"In any case, it's a start. Either Harjo goes back to New Orleans or DuPuis cooperates. Do you mind if I call Harjo with this now?' Baxter held up his phone.

Adam shrugged.

Baxter held up a finger to get Adam's attention. "Harjo wants to stop by your place in the morning around seven-thirty. Okay with you? He says he'll come alone."

"Tell him to bring donuts. I'll make coffee." Adam was joking, but Baxter passed along the message and gave a thumbs-up to Adam.

Twenty-One

After driving down the alleyway and checking that the surveillance cameras were still intact, he turned into the west parking lot of the Creekstone Hotel. He backed his car into a parking space in the farthest corner of the lot. It was the perfect space. It was the least convenient for hotel guests. It also had a perfect view of the area behind the hotel. He looked at his watch and waited.

Like clockwork, tall, handsome Adam Alba came out carrying a half-empty bag of trash. He looked at his watch. He was consistent within a few minutes. He watched Alba tug at the enclosure door. The creak of the metal hinges was audible even at this distance. The lid of the dumpster rose and fell. Then Alba emerged from the enclosure and pushed the metal door closed. A second later, he watched Alba go back into the hotel through the back door.

Some jobs were almost too easy. He drew a long sip through the straw of his large, icy, sweet tea, almost losing his grip on the sweating plastic cup. He felt around under the seat for his notebook. Without the engine running and the air-conditioning in the car, he had started to sweat, even with the windows down.

He opened it to the first blank page. He wrote the date and time in the upper right-hand corner of the page. He documented his observations.

When Adam walked back into the lounge, Jenna was poised behind the POS. "Oh, Adam, I've decided to stock that Scottish import. You sold the whole case in a single day. That is amazing."

Adam waved his hands. "No, no. Don't do that."

"Why not? It's a top seller." She was surprised at his reaction.

"I sold them *to me*. I saw Hamish and his buddies in the restaurant the night they left. I invited them for a drink to thank Hamish for that tip. They drank the whole case. I paid for it in cash. Have the receipt if you want to see it."

Jenna looked crestfallen. Adam imagined the words she might have used if there weren't patrons in the lounge. All she said was, "Oh, I see. Well, push them and we'll see how they do."

As Adam expected, Gamble showed up within half an hour of his beginning his shift. Adam slipped into the back to text Harjo.

Lake arrived first.

As he drew Lake's draft beer, he noticed Gamble slide deeper into his booth and take special interest in the photo on the wall.

Draft in hand, Lake pretended to notice Gamble and invited himself to sit in his booth. Gamble was clearly uncomfortable. He was acting polite, but he wasn't a good actor. He kept glancing at Adam with a look that was part embarrassment, part frustration, and part pleading.

All the while, Lake appeared to be chatting away.

Harjo walked in. Glanced around and joined them. He sat next to Gamble, causing Gamble to slide deeper into the booth.

Adam had no idea what they were talking about, and he didn't think he wanted to know. From a distance, the conversation looked friendly, but Gamble's glances at Adam caused him to feel a little pity for the guy.

He hadn't really done anything bad or even distracting. He had just caused Adam to feel annoyed. When they left together, all three of them nodded at Adam, serving other customers. Adam guessed Terry Gamble wouldn't be back. He felt a twinge of guilt for having tattled on him.

"I've completed the paperwork to be a foster parent," Alex told Caleb as he dished out a plate of mac and cheese and placed two plain hot dogs on the plate. "If they approve me, I'll need to learn how to cook healthier food."

Alex didn't say anything about all the other steps in the approval process. There were several, and they could take months. It was likely that Caleb would be with someone else until then, if they approved him.

"I can make spaghetti and meatballs. Meatballs come frozen. You just put them in the sauce when you heat it up," Caleb offered helpfully.

Alex smiled. "I can do that too. Not sure that's the kind of cooking they are interested in. If I get approved, they offer a cooking class. Maybe we should both go together."

"Okay," Caleb said. He was eating quickly, almost wolfing down his food.

"What's the hurry?" Alex asked.

"I don't want to miss Cagney and Lacey."

"You like that old show?" Alex had seen it a couple of times and hadn't thought much of it. It was already in syndicated reruns when he was still a little girl.

"What show?" Caleb asked through a mouthful of mac and cheese.

"*Cagney & Lacey.*"

"It's a TV show?"

"Yeah. It was on TV before I was born."

"Wow, that's old." Caleb was unaware of the tacit insult. "Cagney and Lacey are dogs. They belong to Jason and Will."

"Huh! And where do you meet these dogs?"

"In the park. Jason or Will walks them every day." He forked a piece of hot dog and used it to scoop up some mac and cheese."

Alex felt uneasy. "Mind if I come with you?" He wanted to get a good look at Jason or Will.

"Do you like dogs?" Caleb asked.

"Sure, I do."

Once the dishes were soaking in the sink, they went together to the park and sat on Caleb's usual bench.

"There they are," he said. "It's Jason. He's nice."

The two dogs were straining at their leashes, pulling Jason toward Caleb. Caleb ran to meet them, and Jason handed him the leashes. The two dogs bounced and sniffed at Caleb. "They've been looking forward to seeing you," he said with a smile.

Alex stood up when they approached the bench. Jason thought he sensed Alex's protective instinct when Caleb introduced them, and they shook hands. Jason sat down next to Alex. "Is it alright if Caleb takes the dogs for a walk around the park? I'm pooped."

"Can I really?" Caleb was excited.

"How could I object?" Alex said.

"Now Caleb, it comes with a real important responsibility," Jason said, holding up a roll of doggy poo bags.

"No problem." Caleb took the bags and packed them into his back pocket.

They watched Caleb walk Cagney and Lacey down the path. The dogs seemed to buddy up to Caleb instead of tugging at their leashes.

Jason spoke kindly. "Before the interrogation starts, and I expect it will, I have federal government security clearances, and my husband Will is an embedded counselor at OKEQ. Caleb is a great kid."

Alex sighed deeply.

"I hope that was a sigh of relief," Jason said quietly.

"Yeah, it was, and he is. He's had a rough time. When he told me about meeting you and your husband, I don't want to tell you what I thought."

"I know what you thought," Jason said with a mix of humor and resignation. "May I ask your preferred pronouns? Your name doesn't give me a clue."

"Does it matter?" Alex asked.

"No, not really, not to me, but if we become friends..." Jason was being sincere.

"He/Him," Alex said. The simple suggestion of their becoming friends erased some of the remaining distance between them. While they talked, Alex kept looking around to glimpse Caleb.

Jason said, "Don't worry, Alex. Cagney and Lacy have adopted him. They're quite playful, but they won't let anyone hurt him. I assure you."

Alex looked at him out of the corner of his eye. The word adopted caught his attention,

"Jason, how much has Caleb told you and your husband?"

Stevie grabbed her purse and car keys. She had to see Adam. This Herzog was a real prick and proud of it. She had found him all over the internet. She found his picture in the list of esteemed faculty members on the school's website.

One reference led to another. There were a number of church websites that promoted him as a featured guest speaker on various topics, most of which dealt directly with same-sex attraction and the gay agenda. These churches spanned the United States and included a few other countries—Australia, Paraguay, and Uganda, among them.

Herzog was listed as a member of the board of directors for two conversion therapy camps. One in the state of Indiana; the other in the Australian outback. Each had pictures of him visiting the camps with groups of campers. Though they were all smiling, Stevie thought that half of the campers looked like they desperately needed a bathroom.

Apart from on their own websites, the camps both had earned scathing reviews.

She had listened to several podcasts on which he was a guest authority on the Bible and homosexuality. Those were hard to listen to.

Even more difficult to endure was the litany of podcasts that featured people who left the church because of the religious trauma they experienced. More than one former student accused him of sexually pressuring them. When one of them complained to the school, Herzog claimed he was just testing the student. The school sided with Herzog, and the student was expelled. There were several ex-campers who suggested that he made improper gestures toward them,

On a website where students rate their professors, he had glowing, inspired reviews while others labeled him a bigot, a racist, and a hypocrite.

The sooner she intervened, the better it would be for Elf.

By the time she reached the Creekstone Hotel, Stevie was at full steam. Adam watched her plunge through the glass doors, a look of determination on her face.

Ignoring the customers waiting at the bar, she just started talking. "You got to hear this! This guy is a piece of work. Better said, a total piece of shit."

"Excuse me a moment," he said to his customers, leading Stevie to the back where he would eat his dinner. "Sit here and I'll come back as soon as I can. Take deep breaths."

In between customers, he ducked into the back. Stevie, when she had the chance, tossed him facts the way some people feed bread to ducks. With each crust of bread, his desire to protect Elf increased.

"Elf says that Herzog thinks he's gay," Adam said.

"If you ask me, he wants Elf's ass in more ways than one," Stevie confided, telling Adam about the students and campers who claimed Herzog had sexually pressured them. "Isn't that a knee in the balls? What crust! And the school just backs him up. It pisses me off." She handed him her phone displaying a picture of the man named Herzog, champion against the corruption of same-sex attraction. "That's him. That's the prick."

Adam stared at the face. His stomach churned. His anger burned. He connected one piece of the puzzle to another. He thought about what he *should* do. He knew what he *wanted* to do. The two weren't the same.

Twenty-Two

Adam stood stiffly near the walk-in cooler, fists clenched, jaw tight, his breath hissing through flared nostrils. He looked like a man seconds from charging into a fight. "I should go down to that damn school right now," he growled. "Find him. Tell him I know exactly what kind of game he's playing, and that it ends—tonight!"

Stevie took a step back and planted her feet, steady and firm. "No, Adam." Her voice cut clean and low. "If you blow up on him now, he wins, and Elf loses. It's an old story. I've seen the patterns. Guys like this? They know how to twist things. If you go at him swinging, he plays the victim and throws Elf under the bus, and maybe presses assault charges."

Adam trembled with rage. "I can prove it. He's not just some random monster. He's one of the Butterfly's people. I've seen him at the Balustrade at least twenty times." He slammed his palm against a beer crate. "Hell, I saw Elf's face when he talked about Herzog. It was the same face he made when he told me about what happened to him in prison. He tried to play it down, but I saw it. I can't ignore that."

Stevie exhaled slowly, trying to control her emotions. "Listen to me. I didn't grow up in Pittsburgh. But if you grew up in Brooklyn, you would have learned two things real fast. One, never let your mouth get ahead of your brain. That gets you jumped, arrested, or worse."

Adam's eyes narrowed. "And the second?"

"You learn how to play the long game. You learn who to tell and how to tell them, so you don't end up owing favors or taking the fall when it all blows up. You keep your hands clean."

Adam rubbed his eyes, his shoulders shaking from the effort of holding back. "I just can't sit this one out, Stevie."

"You don't have to," she said softly. "But standing with Elf means not torching his life to vent your fury. We fight smart, not loud."

Adam nodded slowly, though his fists hadn't unclenched. He pressed his back to the cooler, trying to think.

Stevie glanced over to the bar. "Hang tight. I'll be right back."

He watched her approach the bar and greet a customer. She drew a perfect glass of beer and handed it over with a bright smile. "System's updating. This one's on the house." The customer chuckled and thanked her, and Stevie made her way back to Adam.

"How does someone like Herzog live with himself?" Adam asked. His voice had quieted, but his rage still simmered just beneath the surface.

"I've never understood it," she muttered, swiping through her phone. A moment later, Adam's phone buzzed with an alert. She didn't wait for him to check it. "I just emailed you everything I found— forums, articles, podcasts, everything."

Adam opened the email, scrolling through the links. His brows drew together. "Jesus. This is a lot."

"It's enough for your detective to start digging," Stevie said. "And it's enough to warn Elf."

Adam nodded again, slower this time, like a man shifting gears. "I'll talk to Harjo in the morning."

Stevie was scrolling through her email. She hadn't checked it for several days. "Hey, what's this picture you sent me?"

Adam thought back. "The one with my new address?"

"No. Oh, it's the picture of you here at the bar, the one out front." She stared at the unedited photo. She pulled it closer to see it better.

"Jenna sent it to me. I thought it was a good photo."

"It is. Better than you think."

Adam looked up at her.

"Look at this. Look closely at the customers behind you."

A chill ran down Adam's spine. He hadn't recognized him. Sitting down with Candy was Herzog. He whispered to himself, "That son of a bitch."

"You bought donuts, Joe?" Lake eyed the three survivors on the edge of Harjo's desk.

"Leftovers," Harjo said. "Baxter said that Alba wanted donuts. He ate one. I had two. Your mission is to eliminate the temptation."

Lake picked one up and bit into it. "Noted. For future missions, I prefer eclairs over glazed."

"Man's gotta do what a man's gotta do. I appreciate your sacrifice," Harjo quipped.

"Anything in the cause of justice," Lake mumbled, swallowing. "What'd you get out of Alba?"

Harjo's face lit with quiet satisfaction. His eyes said, *I told you so.* "Looks like we finally have a new direction. Alba described three guys who regularly kept company with Christian Rhome. He didn't know their names, but he gave me a fourth: Helmut Herzog."

"Herzog?" Lake straightened. "The guy from the wedding? Left early with his wife."

Harjo nodded. "I noticed that too. Called the wife this morning. Gave her a story about needing to speak to Herzog about one of his Bible school students on parole. She gave me his office line and his cell."

"Did you just make that up, or is there a real student on parole?"

"Real enough. Elvin Flemming. Goes by the nickname Elf. He's one of Ridgway's cases."

Lake whistled. "Poor guy. Ridgway's a damn steamroller."

Harjo nodded. "According to Alba, Herzog's just as bad, maybe even worse. And Flemming told him so himself."

Lake leaned back, wiping glaze from his fingers. "You believe him?"

Harjo shrugged. "I don't think he's lying. I've seen Adam watch people like a hawk. He remembers what he sees. He says Herzog was at the Balustrade at least twenty times over the last two years. One of Rhome's regulars. DuPuis is looking into the other three for us. They should be able to corroborate Alba's testimony—if they will, that is."

"Why wouldn't they?"

"Maybe they wouldn't want to go public. But DuPuis knows what he's doing—he's used to dealing with citizens with discretion."

Harjo opened a folder and laid out the color copy of the photo. "This was taken by Jenna Klingensmith on Adam's first day at the Creekstone. She provided the original file. Forensics has it. This is just

258

for reference. That's Alba. That's Candy in the background. And that… " he tapped the corner of the printout, "… is Herzog sitting at her table."

Lake studied the image. "They're both looking at Alba. Do you think Herzog recognized him?"

"My guess is yes. Remember, I've been to the Balustrade. The best lit person in the room is the bartender, and Alba's a good-looking guy."

"And Alba says he didn't recognize Herzog? I find that a little hard to believe, don't you?"

"Says it was the setting. Different context, different haircut, and he was starting a new job. But a defense attorney's going to ask the same question."

Lake frowned. "So where do we go from here?"

"I want to talk to both of them, Flemming and Herzog. You still want to talk to the brother, Caleb?"

"Tonight at seven-thirty."

"Take a uniform with you. Female is better. I'll be at the Herzog's at the same time. Unless we call each other, we meet back here tomorrow. Same time."

Lake stood and dusted off his hands. "And next time, Joe? Eclairs."

Harjo smirked. "You solve this case, and I'll buy you a dozen."

Alex tried not to appear nervous while the social worker reviewed Caleb's file. "You'll need a larger apartment, two bedrooms. And I'm afraid your income isn't sufficient to cover Caleb's needs."

Alex wanted to ask if that wasn't what the subsidy was for, but he dared not sound like he wanted or needed the money, so he didn't ask.

"Andy's apartment was the same as mine. Why is it now unacceptable?" Calling Candy Andy felt like betrayal, but it had to be done.

The social worker had a ready response. "Andy was a blood relative, his brother. They could legitimately share space."

Oh, if she only knew, Alex thought, but it wasn't good to bring up the topic of Candy. "Well, I can ask about a two-bedroom apartment in my complex. I may be able to find something affordable without moving to a problem neighborhood."

"That would help, but the income issue is also a factor."

"But Caleb knows me, is comfortable with me, and he wants to stay with me. That should count for something. Of course, I can look for a second job then..."

The social worker looked up from the paperwork. "Then the supervision time will be limited. In any case, these two things would need to change before we could move forward with your application."

"And what does that mean for Caleb?"

"We'll place him with another foster family."

"And if I'm eventually approved? I mean, I find a higher-paying job and a bigger apartment?"

"We'd have to reevaluate the situation then."

Alex's heart sank. He thought that he could read in her voice the undercurrent of prejudice that got in his way again and again. "Can you consider keeping him in the same school?" Alex asked. "Change is hard. At least give him that." He hoped to be able to keep in contact with Caleb, but he wouldn't reveal that.

The social worker made a noncommittal sound. "We'll note the request."

Alex nodded, lips pressed into a line. He didn't trust her neutrality, but he knew better than to challenge it.

The social worker closed the file. "We'll be in touch when placement is confirmed."

Alex stood, unsure if this was the end or just the beginning of a different kind of fight.

Twenty-Three

The Herzog home was a very large house on a sizeable property with nearly a tenth of a mile of driveway that led to a four-car garage. A paved walkway wound around the house to the stately front door.

Dierdre Herzog greeted Detective Harjo at her front door, opening it only wide enough to frame her large, formidable stature. It was as if she wanted to decide whether or not he was worthy of entering her home.

As he introduced himself, Harjo noticed her glance at his shoes and wouldn't have been surprised if she asked him to remove them before walking on her floors. He must have passed inspection because she led him into a large room with a ceiling that vaulted at least twenty-five feet above them. Her voice echoed as she invited him to sit. "Helmut will be with you shortly."

Herzog was impressive in his size. Tall, solid, husky, with a commanding voice that seemed to fill the great room. Harjo stood up to greet him and offered him a hand. "Thank you for agreeing to see me on such short notice, sir."

"Always support the boys in blue," Herzog said, gesturing for Harjo to sit again. They sat on two separate sofas where they were closest, a coffee table between them. "Actually, you caught me at a good time. In a week or so, I'll be traveling to several congregations to speak, just a little mini tour, but I'll be gone a week between summer and fall semesters."

Mrs. Herzog carried a silver coffee service. She set it down on the table and poured coffee for Harjo. "How do you take it, Detective?"

"Just black," he said, accepting the dainty painted porcelain cup and saucer.

She smiled, fixed a cup for her husband and handed it to him. "I'll excuse myself if you don't mind. I've got some work to do. She pointed at a large, elevated dining area in the far corner where a laptop sat open. Harjo noticed that if she sat facing the computer, she'd have a view of the entire room. "That is, if you don't need me for anything."

Professor Herzog smiled. "I'm sure we can handle refills if we need them, dear." Then to Harjo. "I don't talk about my students much at home. My wife wouldn't be much help in a conversation about them. Now, which student are you interested in?"

Harjo opened his notebook, uncapped his pen, and flipped through the pages. "Elvin Flemming. I assume you knew he was on parole."

"Yes, all the faculty at the school are aware of Brother Flemming's testimony, quite an impressive one, I might add."

"I understand that you have begun working with him one-on-one." Out of the corner of his eye, he could have sworn that statement had caught Mrs. Herzog's attention.

"You've spoken with him?" he asked.

"No, actually, not yet. I've conferred with his parole officer and his employer. Apparently, the employer had to rearrange his work schedule to accommodate Mr. Flemming's meetings with you."

Herzog nodded. "It's the only time I have available for office hours. What would you like to know, Detective? How can I help you?"

Here, Harjo started winging it. "His parole is up for review in a few months. Since you are meeting privately with him, we thought you might have insight into his rehabilitation."

Herzog furrowed his brow. "I'm not sure what you mean, Detective."

Harjo observed his body language. He thought Herzog was becoming uncomfortable and yet, for some reason, seemed to enjoy it.

"If you could verify the information he's giving to his parole officer," Harjo said.

Herzog pulled a distasteful face. "I have no idea what he's telling his parole officer."

Harjo noticed that he had Mrs. Herzog's attention again. Her fingers had stopped tapping at the keyboard. The laptop screen reflected in her glasses, but her head turned slightly in their direction.

"Well, Professor," Harjo said, matching Herzog's body language. "We are simply interested in whether or not he is breaking the terms of his parole, particularly the use of drugs. As you are working with him one-on-one, he might be confiding in you."

Herzog gave a superficial smile. "Using illegal drugs is forbidden for students. I dare say, Mr. Flemming would not confide drug use to any faculty member. If he did, he'd be out on his ear."

"I assume the same policy goes for faculty members." His words weren't a question, just a soft push across the line. Harjo tilted his head slightly. "We just want to make sure he's getting the support he needs." He paused briefly.

A moment of awkward silence passed as Herzog and Harjo stared one another down. Harjo kept a soft expression while Herzog's face shifted from confident to curious to cautious. Herzog took a deep breath, expanding his chest and squaring his shoulders, still offering the same shallow smile. "Of course," he said. "Detective," he said with emphasis, "I find it unusual that the Broken Arrow police department thinks checking up on a parolee is a practical use of a detective's time."

Harjo noticed a slight smile on the distant face of Mrs. Herzog. He, too, took a deep breath of his own and reached for the coffeepot. He said in a cordial, disarming voice, "This coffee is delicious. I hope you don't mind if I help myself. Would you like a warm-up, Professor? As he refilled his own cup. "I investigate a lot of different things on behalf of the people of Broken Arrow, Professor. I trust you understand that your school is in my jurisdiction. I'm just doing my job."

"Detective, is there anything else I can do for you? I'm a busy man," Herzog said.

"Just one more thing. I'm sure the students who gain your personal attention appreciate it. I'm just wondering what you get in return."

Herzog pressed his lips together and answered. "Satisfaction, Detective." Then he added, "I too am just doing my job." He stood up, indicating that the interview was at an end.

Harjo rose but didn't move to leave just yet. "Before I go, I'll need your travel itinerary, in case we need to follow up."

Herzog's smile thinned. "Dierdre can get that for you." And he turned and walked out.

As the door clicked behind him, Harjo let the silence settle. One-on-one time with students. Travel on the horizon. A wife who didn't ask questions but didn't leave the room either. Harjo wondered who really held the reins in that family.

After getting a call from a detective named Harjo, Elf's heart pounded in his chest, and he felt a little short of breath. He wasn't sure what to do. The detective had asked him about his professors and seemed to focus on Herzog. *This can really mess things up for me,* he thought, trying to control his breathing. He took out his wallet and pried out a business card from behind his driver's license and called the cell phone number.

"Sergeant Baxter here."

"Hi, this is Elf. You gave me your card a while back... "

Baxter interrupted him. "I remember you well, Elf. What's up?"

Twenty-Four

There were two eclairs on Harjo's desk in the morning when Lake arrived carrying a cup of coffee. "I didn't know if you wanted cream or custard, so I got both," Harjo said. "Take your pick. I like them both."

Lake smiled and said, "I'll take the custard." He held up his cup. "I thought you might have gotten coffee already. Can I get you a cup?"

"No. Thank you. I've had three cups already," Harjo said, taking a bite of the cream-filled eclair, a little lump of cream oozing out of the other end. "Shit." He wiped the cream from his desk with a tissue.

Lake chuckled. "Always start on the end with the hole. Learned that from my dad."

"How'd it go with the kid last night?" Harjo was anxious to get down to business.

"He seems like an intelligent boy. He couldn't add much to what we know. He knew his sister was his brother, of course, and that Candy had to become Andy and get a job as Andy to get custody."

"Did you tell him his sister was a hooker?" Harjo glanced up from the papers on his desk.

"No. Figured when the case goes to trial, he'll find out. Alex Duke said he'd break it to him gently if he wanted to attend the trial. No benefit now; you were right about that."

"Anything at all then?"

"No, but I recorded it and have the transcript in case I missed something. After the interview, Alex walked me to my car. He didn't get approved as a foster parent. Apparently, money and the size of the apartment are the reasons they gave. That's too bad. He really cares about the kid." Lake paused, considering. "Listen, Joe, I didn't tell you because I thought it was a waste of time. I talked to that kid's last foster family. They were awful. Elderly couple who talked too much about discipline and didn't notice the social isolation Caleb experienced while he lived with them. I just hope he doesn't go back there."

"You're getting soft, Lake. I'm proud of you. There are times when detectives need to be hard or tough, but that bit of hoping for the best keeps us human. If I were you, I'd find out who the kid's caseworker is and butt in. The worst that can happen is they tell you to fuck off, but I doubt that would happen. Anything else?"

Lake nodded. "I checked the wedding photos. The Herzog family looked like they'd been buffed with shoe polish—two kids, one pair of shoes between them. And the wife... built like a barn."

"You don't have to tell me. Met her yesterday. Served coffee on a silver tray like it was royal protocol. I nearly dislocated a shoulder lifting the pot. But she floated it around like it was a feather duster. Send a copy of that picture to forensics. Once we get a warrant, we'll have to get the clothes Herzog wore. If he was with Rhome after leaving the wedding, there may be trace evidence."

"Already done, Joe," Lake said reassuringly. He wanted to add that he knew what he was doing, but too often Harjo had pointed out things that he hadn't noticed. At least Harjo knew he was on the ball. "So, tell me about your meeting with the Herzogs."

Harjo described his encounter with Helmut Herzog and the hovering Dierdre.

"When I sensed him getting defensive, I leaned in a bit. He was sharp enough to shut it down. Next time I speak to that man, I want it to be here at the station and Mirandized. I kept the conversation focused on Flemming. Didn't mention the wedding or Rhome, so I don't think he's onto me yet."

"It's kind of obvious that it was him," Lake said.

"Maybe a little too obvious. The case is still too circumstantial, Lake. We need forensics—fibers, hairs, something to connect Herzog to the bodies of Yates and Rhome. Without that, we'll never get it past the DA, let alone a grand jury. Herzog is too high-profile to expect people to believe circumstantial evidence. You looked at those websites Alba gave us, right?"

"Disgusting."

'Damned disgusting. But you see what we're up against." Harjo's eyes flickered right and left conspiratorially. "Would be great to get a DNA sample without asking for it."

Lake had been thinking the same thing.

Stevie learned that classes at Elf's school began at eight, so at six-thirty she parked a block away and walked onto campus. The parking spaces closest to the buildings were reserved for faculty. She found the one with the sign that read, "Reserved H. Herzog." She found a bench in sight of the space, sat down, and waited.

It was a beautiful morning, warm but fresh. There had been nighttime rain that washed the dust from the air. A gentle breeze lowered the *feels-like* temperature down enough that she regretted leaving her sweater in the car. *No matter*, she thought, *things will heat up soon.*

She wasn't sure what she would do if or when she caught a glimpse of the man. She considered several alternatives, from doing nothing to outright confronting him. She had rehearsed several strategies: a feigned prayer request, a question about Bible interpretation, or pretending to be a student's concerned aunt. She didn't need to convince him, just unsettle him. She wanted to make him sweat.

She could almost hear Adam cautioning her against doing anything at all, even spying on the man. After all, at least in their minds, the man was a menace, a predator who had killed at least two people already. How many more would he kill to keep that closet door locked shut? Seeing him sweat would make it worth a little risk.

The previous evening, she had successfully stopped Adam from doing anything other than advising the police. That was the best way to proceed, and she had done her part with the list of websites for them to examine. Herzog railed against gay and trans people from inside his own fucking closet. Herzog might have recognized Adam from that bar in New Orleans, *but Herzog doesn't know me from Adam.* She chuckled to herself at the turn of phrase.

If anyone could get away with putting the fear of God into that guy, it would be someone he didn't know. If she did anything at all, she had to make sure that he couldn't tie it back to Adam or Elf.

By quarter to seven, the parking lot began to fill up. Many came in cars, a few on bikes, and even fewer on foot. Most of the students and a few of the faculty walked into a modern chapel-like building that reminded Stevie of the Crystal Cathedral she had visited in California way back before it became Catholic. She knew from the school's website that there was a worship service every morning at seven.

She lost herself in a memory. She was in junior high. A friend was telling Stevie about a confusing event that happened after a Catholic

Youth Association meeting. Janet always told her about CYA meetings. Stevie couldn't go because she was taking care of the twins.

Stevie could still remember the look of confusion on Janet's face when she said, "Oh, Janet, I'm sure he didn't mean it *that* way. He's a *priest!*" And in hindsight, she still felt the shame over the pain her flippant remark must have caused in Janet.

If Herzog hadn't slammed his door, she would have missed him. She looked up to see him walking with a tall, sturdily built woman who reached for and took his hand. *Must be his wife*, she thought. Without thinking, she stood up, picked up her purse, and followed them. They passed the chapel and followed a cement path to an administration building.

"Yoo hoo, excuse me, Professor?" Stevie called, waving, her bracelets jingling on her arm.

He stopped and turned around. Not recognizing her, he looked around. Perhaps she was addressing someone else.

Her eyes were steady, looking directly at him. He waited in some confusion. He was more annoyed than interested.

As she approached, she rephrased one of the things she planned to say to mimic a Pentecostal woman she knew from her old job. "I'm so sorry to bother you. You *are* Professor Hizog, correct?" She intentionally mispronounced his name.

"Herzog." He nodded skeptically.

"Yes, that's it. Oh lord, I'm so nervous. I never do anything like this." Acting out of breath, she pressed her ringed fingers to her chest. "You see, I was praying this morning for the students and faculty of this school. I do that every morning."

"Thank you, ma'am."

She hated being called ma'am. He had to be close to her age. The anger gave her courage. "The Lord gave me a word for you. He said I should tell you to read Luke 12:2-3. The time is at hand. I hope you find it encouraging."

His wife's eyes snapped to their corners to look at her husband. Letting go of his hand, she pretended to look for something in her purse. Stevie kept an eye on her. She might pull out a gun, a knife, or a can of mace.

"Luke 12:2-3?" Professor Herzog said.

"Yes," she nodded. She began to rummage in her purse. Unfortunately, the only Bible I have is a Catholic one. I can read it to you if you'd like."

"No need, madam. I have a Bible of my own," Herzog said coldly.

"Good then. Phew. That's over. Bless you, brother. And you too, sister." Stevie snapped her purse closed. She smiled at the woman. Had Mrs. Herzog squinted or had her gaze grown in intensity? Stevie could feel the tension between them. She smiled once again, making sure the smile reached her eyes. She turned and walked away. *That went well*, she thought as a genuine Mona Lisa smile teased at her lips.

Herzog didn't move. He didn't take his wife's hand. He didn't even look at her. He just watched that strange woman wend her way through the parking lot.

Twenty-Five

Adam stood up and stretched. His mornings were going more slowly, more relaxed now. He was spending more time with Bert, the curious cat who watched him do his workout and now routinely climbed into his lap during his cooldown.

He'd been working on his puzzle for the last hour and had reached the point where it was more than half-finished, and all the pieces were on the table; none left in the box. If he had the whole day free, he could have finished the puzzle, but he didn't have the whole day and finishing it was never quite the point. The comfort was in the sorting, the slow emergence of order from chaos.

Three people hovered in his thoughts while doing his puzzle. The first was Stevie. She had become a kind of partner in crime. At least, he didn't feel like he was alone.

The second was Elf. When he first met Elf back in Ur, their casual talk led to deeper topics, and they became fast friends.

The third person made his phone ring.

"Hey, Bax. How ya doin'?" Adam's voice was bright.

"I'm okay. Listen, I wanted to ask you how much you told Elf about what's going on."

Adam didn't have to think about it. "Nothing. The only person who knows is Stevie. I told you about her."

"Yeah. Um, I think you need to have a talk with Elf. He called me. Harjo called him to get a lead on this guy, Herzog, but Elf thinks he's in trouble and is afraid his parole is in danger. He's confused about how Harjo knows about Herzog."

Adam felt like he had betrayed Elf's confidence telling Harjo about what Herzog was doing to Elf, but it was part of the story. He sighed, the lightness of the morning leaving him with the breath. "How much do you think I should tell him?"

"Give it all to him, as much as you know. Just let him know, it has nothing to do with him, his parole or anything. I'm surprised you haven't told him already."

"All of it?"

Baxter hesitated. "As much as he needs to know to feel safe. Harjo used Elf as a pretext to interview Herzog. If it somehow gets back to his parole officer, it could get complicated for him. It wouldn't happen on Harjo's end, but it might on Herzog's. Harjo didn't explain to Elf why he was calling. He doesn't know Elf like we do. Elf called me scared shitless. If he can keep a secret, tell him everything. It won't hurt anything. He just needs to know that he shouldn't jeopardize the investigation."

"Okay, I can talk to him tomorrow."

"Do it today. Now—if you can."

"So, it really was Herzog?"

"Looks that way."

Lake silently promised himself that if he were ever working on another case that required this kind of surveillance, he'd be high enough in rank to assign it to someone else. He had shadowed Herzog from the time he and his wife arrived on campus.

Three tedious hours outside Herzog's classroom, students coming and going, felt like an eternity. He kept his distance, changed positions, paced, listened outside the door, and discovered the best place to wait was outside the ladies' restroom, where people would think he was just waiting for his girlfriend.

At eleven-thirty, he followed Herzog to his office and a few minutes later, watched him leave with his wife. Had she been there the entire time, or had she gone and returned?

His heart raced as he followed them in his car to Fit to Be Thai'd. He shot a picture of them leaving their car and going into the restaurant. *Another link in the chain*, Lake thought.

Lake waited.

Forty-five minutes later, Herzog and his wife came out of the restaurant with large takeaway glasses of Thai iced tea.

Back on campus, Lake watched Herzog get out of the car, carrying both cups now empty. Herzog watched his wife drive away, then tossed the empty cups into a trash bin.

Bingo. Lake made a fist of victory. He might not know which cup was whose, but one of them was Herzog's.

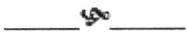

At the usual time, he eased through the alley and checked the cameras. Still intact. Not today. Broken lenses would be the signal.

He parked in his usual spot, rolled down the windows, and slouched low, eyes half-lidded like a man napping. At four twenty-five, right on cue, Alba came out, tossed a trash bag, and vanished back inside.

277

One more night, and Alba should be off for the weekend. He'd be back anyway. If the bike was there, he'd wait. If not, he'd watch for the Black kid when the shifts changed. If the Black kid left, it meant Alba was covering.

Satisfied, he jotted his notes, slid the notebook under the seat, and drove away.

Elf sat at the little table where Adam would normally eat his dinner. The T-bone steak and baked potato in front of him were untouched. He had lost his color halfway through the story. He had lost his appetite back when Harjo called.

Adam leaned against the doorframe keeping his eye on the lounge. It took the rest of the story to restore Elf's ability to speak.

"When did this happen?" he asked through a dry mouth.

Adam went out to the fountain and poured a ginger ale for himself.

"The day before I moved into our apartment," he said, setting the glass down in front of Elf.

"Why didn't you say anything? I mean, what are friends for?" Elf didn't mean it to be a cutting remark, but Adam felt the sting.

Adam shook his head slowly. "Everything was so good. Getting the place, seeing you and Tom, you guys wanting to move in with me—I didn't want to think about it. I had no idea it would work out this way. It had nothing to do with me."

"Well, it did, didn't it?"

"Only indirectly. I mean, Stevie and I just put it together by chance. It still has nothing to do with me, personally."

"So, Harjo wasn't really checking up on me, and you told him about Herzog being a prick."

Adam hung his head. "Elf, I thought you might be in danger. Two people are dead and after seeing those websites, God knows what he might have pressured you into." He pursed his lips and frowned. "How did Stevie put it? Herzog would have your ass, one way or the other—something like that."

"It's all so hard to believe. How do you know this stuff isn't just disgruntled students complaining?"

"Elf, pull yourself together. What do you think he was doing in the Balustrade? I recognize him."

Elf seemed to shrink before Adam's eyes. "I don't know what to do."

Adam snorted. "Act normally and keep your mouth shut. Tell no one, not even Tom. Baxter said if you wanted, he would come in uniform to the class you have with Herzog on Friday and pull you out of class. That way you wouldn't have to go to the meeting with Herzog."

"No," Elf said forcefully. "If the school thinks I did something wrong, I'd be out."

"Okay, okay." Adam held up his hands. "Then listen to a piece of advice from me. You might not like it, but do it."

Elf aimed his chin at Adam. "Tell me."

"Actually, it also comes from Stevie. Try your best not to be alone."

"What? Why?" Elf was suspicious. "What are you going to do?"

Adam smiled meekly. "Bro, nothing. Just don't give him the chance to catch you alone."

Elf swallowed hard.

Adam said nothing.

Twenty-Six

At quarter to five on Thursday morning, Adam walked Elf to his car. The soft clicking of Adam's bike gears echoed in the cool silence of the early morning. He was going to work with Elf to train to cover his shift the next day.

"Dude, there's nothing I can do." Elf insisted on keeping his meeting with Herzog on Friday.

"Don't go to school at all on Friday. You won't be in class, and you can tell the secretary to give him your apologies. Tell him you're sick or something."

"First of all, I don't want to miss school. Second, I don't want to lie." Elf was emphatic. "I'm telling you, Adam, I can handle him."

Adam threw a verbal sucker punch. "Not physically, Elf. According to Stevie, he is a big guy. Damn, I wish I could just be standing outside that door if you needed me."

"And what are you going to do? Burst in like Superman to save the day?"

Adam's face reddened. "Something like that," admitting it embarrassed him. He had already broken confidence by telling Harjo about Elf's predicament. Would Harjo be willing to have someone stand outside that door?

Elf stopped. He had to tilt his head up to look him in the eye. "I appreciate it, Adam. I really do. But even if all that stuff about Herzog is true, I still need his class and his endorsement to graduate."

Adam's face hardened. "And what if he pressures you like he did those others? What will you do then?"

Elf took a breath to control himself. "I'm not going to let him fuck me, Adam."

"He's a big guy, Elf. What if—"

Elf interrupted. "Tell you what, Adam. Would you feel better if I just left my phone recording on Do Not Disturb Mode? That AI notetaker app picks up everything. It's technically not a wire but—"

"Elf," Adam cut in. "He's killed twice!"

Elf stopped short. His face twitched like he had been slapped.

"I heard everything you've said. Anyway, you don't know that for sure." Elf's head shook. Adam couldn't tell if it was anxiety or denial.

"Come on, Elf. Wake up." He straddled his bike.

Elf sighed deeply, then paused, his hand on the door. "I've got this, Adam," he said, but his voice didn't sound convinced. "See you at the Moonstone." Then he slid behind the wheel.

A gentle rain began to fall.

The morning cloudburst of rain resolved into a constant drizzle that wasn't strong enough for an umbrella and not fine enough to go without one. The wipers on Lake's car had trouble getting the timing right. The day before, he pushed himself to finish his reports. He left them on Harjo's desk along with updated forensics.

After all that, he still had more to report to Harjo. They were getting close. Herzog was their perp. It was his turn, so he stopped off at the coffee shop, got himself a heated cinnamon roll and for Harjo, the croissant sandwich he liked.

As he stood in line, he noticed an odd woman he was sure he had seen before. Colorful dress, bracelets jingling like wind chimes. He remembered. He had thought her an odd person to be waiting at the Bible school. She was the woman who stopped Herzog on his way to his office the day before.

Coffee in hand and waiting for his name to be called for his order, he sat at the table next to her. He intended to find out who she was and why she had been so obviously waiting for Herzog and his wife. She, of course, had recognized him as one of the detectives upon whom she had eavesdropped before. When he sat down at the next table, she put her book down.

She smiled at him as he watched her cut her cinnamon roll in half. "Would you like half? I can only eat half. Actually, being diabetic, I shouldn't eat any, but they are so good."

"No thank you, ma'am. I've ordered one of my own."

His calling her ma'am triggered her, but he was young enough to get away with it. After all, she was old enough to be a ma'am to him. "Well, if you change your mind, it's here. I am just going to throw it away."

She's friendly, Lake thought. *It won't take much to get her talking. I just need to figure out my approach.*

Stevie didn't give him the chance. "Of course, you know my friend, Adam. Adam Alba? I believe he's helping you on a current case."

Lake froze and began to blush.

"Oh, I didn't mean to startle you." She laid her fingertips on his forearm consolingly. "I'm helping you, too. My name is Stevie Tramonto. I'm the one who made that list of websites Adam gave you."

The barista called his name. "I'll be right back, and I *will* take half that cinnamon roll. I hope you have a few minutes to talk."

She sent him a motherly smile as if she were proud of him in some way. He went, recovered his order, and sat with her again.

"I really only have about fifteen minutes. I have a salon appointment. But it's just at the other end of this little mall. So I have time."

"Thanks for the list. It was helpful." With raised eyebrows, he pointed at the uneaten half of her cinnamon roll. She pushed the plate toward him, looking around to make sure no one was listening to their conversation.

"I wish I could say it was my pleasure. Reviewing those sites was revolting. He's a vile man," Stevie said quietly.

"Well, thanks again." He paused to decide that the direct approach was best. "Why did you do it in the first place?" He wanted to take out his notebook, but decided against it. This chat would be off the record unless they needed to repeat it.

"Well," she said, tilting her head. "I don't know Mr. Flemming as well as Adam does." She didn't want to call him Elf. It would sound like she knew him better than she was admitting. "Adam told me about the *special attention* Mr. Flemming was getting from his professor. Frankly, it sounded abusive, so I looked him up. Finding what I did, I thought Adam might want to warn his friend."

Lake smiled. "That was truly kind of you. May I ask how long have you known Adam Alba?"

The question surprised her. She thought about it, mentally counted the days, and realized that it would sound absurd to admit the truth. She would if she had to, of course, but... "Not long."

Lake didn't press. "How did you meet him?"

She snorted. "The same way I just met you." She laughed. "I gave him half of my cinnamon roll. You have no idea how many new friends you can make with a generous offer like that."

Lake laughed with her. She looked at her watch and slipped her book into her purse. "Really, I do have to go. They open early for me because with hair and nails, I'm there forever." She started to stand up.

Lake took a deep breath. His next question might be giving too much away. "I'm curious. What did you say to Professor Herzog and his wife yesterday?"

"Ah, so you are taking it seriously, I see." She told him what she said and why she did it. "That's Luke 12:2-3. Look it up if you'd like. I know it was a risky thing to do. I tell you, the look on both their faces was worth the risk."

He watched her leave. It was only after the door closed behind her that he realized that one key question was unanswered. How did she recognize *him*?

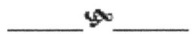

Harjo waited in his office for Lake. He had arrived early to plow through the reports and updates Lake had left on his desk. He was looking forward to catching up with Lake and had news of his own to report.

Lake was ten minutes late. "Sorry, Joe, couldn't be helped," he said, setting down the bag with Harjo's croissant sandwich.

"Thanks. Long line at the coffee shop?" Harjo said, opening the package.

"No, but you'll never guess who I met there."

"If you say you met Elvis and that he really is still alive, your career is over," Harjo joked.

"Stella Vera Tramonto, the lady who put together that list of internet sites about Herzog."

"How the hell did that happen?" Harjo bit into his sandwich.

"If you read my report about tailing Herzog yesterday, she was the woman who approached Herzog and his wife."

Harjo's face showed no amusement. "She could have really messed things up for us if that little episode tipped him off that we were onto him. Besides, it was a stupidly dangerous thing to do."

Lake hadn't thought of that, but knew Harjo was right.

Harjo continued. "That moves things forward at a pace I'm not comfortable with. If the search warrants I've requested come through today, we pick him up today."

"Do you think they will?"

"No telling," Harjo said, shaking his head. "The evidence is all circumstantial now. Thankfully, it was boosted last night by DuPuis. He must have known who those characters were because he had results in a day. Two refused to talk at all. One identified Herzog from a photo lineup and is willing to testify. Seems he had special feelings for Christian Rhome."

"That's great news."

"Let's just hope that Herzog doesn't connect that woman's feigned prophecy as a hint that we're on to him." Harjo sighed.

"Joe, we have enough probable cause, don't we?"

"As far as I'm concerned, yes. If we had a DNA match, it would be a done deal. Unfortunately, things can go really wrong when we move too quickly without hard evidence. Hunches are a cop's best friend and his worst enemy. We don't want tunnel vision, and rushing in can make the case difficult to prosecute. I don't want to fuck this one up." Harjo shook his head. "Damn it. If we had the DNA and there was a match to the blood stain under Rhome's armpit... "

Lake's face grew confused. "Armpit?"

"Did you read the latest forensic report or not?"

"Skimmed it," he admitted.

"They taped the clothing of both victims. Similar human hair on both, different fibers collected, both had been dragged along the ground—scuff marks on the backs of their shoes. There was a tiny blood stain under Rhome's armpit. Unless he cut himself and wiped the blood off under his arm, the blood isn't his. Chances are, it belongs to the perp."

"The bitch of it is that we don't know where either of them was murdered," Lake said.

"It certainly would make life easier if he had just left them where he killed them," Harjo agreed.

Just then, there was a strong knock on Harjo's office door. Lake had to unlock it to let in the front desk clerk. "Joe." She spoke directly to Harjo. "There's been another murder. Riley and Gamble were first on the scene, and Riley says you'd want to know right away. ME and CSU are on the way."

"Where?" He expected to be led to another dumpster.

"Bible school. Professor's office. Reverend Helmut Herzog."

Both men sprang to their feet, and if they admitted it, their hearts sank. He was their main suspect but...

Harjo said, "Tell Riley we're on our way." Then to Lake, "You know where to go, right?"

Twenty-Seven

The only available space in the parking lot was Herzog's. "Should I, Joe?"

"Why not? He won't need it. Wonder where his car is?"

Lake shrugged. "His wife brought him and picked him up yesterday. Maybe one of their cars is in the shop."

"He has a four-car garage," Harjo said.

Lake shrugged again and unlatched his seatbelt. He led Harjo through the campus to the administration building.

"Harjo's office is on the third floor." Lake led him to a stairwell. "There's also an elevator, if you prefer."

Harjo shook his head, his eyes laser scanning the scene, taking it all in.

They emerged from the stairwell to see Gamble standing guard outside Herzog's office. White-suited crime scene techs could be seen moving inside the office. Riley was talking to the medical examiner on the other side of the hall. When they saw Harjo and Lake, they turned toward them and waited.

Harjo greeted them with a nod. "Riley... Ernie, What do we got here? Run it down for us." Harjo's eyes were still scanning.

"You go first, Officer Riley. Not much more to tell on my end yet," said the medical examiner.

"The secretary from the first floor says she saw Herzog check his mailbox about seven-fifteen this morning. That's it until the professor didn't show up for his eight o'clock class. She tried ringing him, but he didn't pick up. When he didn't show up for his ten o'clock class, she came up to check on him. Needed to use her passkey to get in, found him, and reported the death."

Harjo nodded.

Lake asked, "Time of death?" He instantly realized that it was a stupid question. The timeline made it obvious.

Ernie spoke up. "Between seven-fifteen and ten a.m. When I got here, there were early signs of rigor mortis, so I'd say closer to eight a.m., but I can't be more precise than the timeline suggests." His tone was indulgent if a little patronizing of the upcoming detective.

To Riley Harjo asked, "Any other witnesses? This floor has a bunch of offices. Surely?"

Riley shook his head. "I've spoken to everyone who has come up on this floor and taken preliminaries. Mostly faculty, a couple of students. None of them noticed anyone coming or going."

Lake closed his eyes, feeling fatigued. "Our main suspect gone. It's like starting all over again," he whispered to himself, but Harjo heard it.

"Not quite, Lake. I want to get a look inside.

Frank, the owner of the Moonstone grill, watched appraisingly and appreciatively how well Elf and Adam worked together. The breakfast service went more smoothly than he could have hoped for. Elf was clearly in charge, and that made him proud.

Adam noticed the tension between them had disappeared with their collaboration. He thought then of his grandmother, who always insisted they all have the same dinner together at the same time, no matter how confused or chaotic their schedules seemed.

He, too, felt proud of Elf and realized that he was becoming more than just a friend. The two could hardly be more different, but Elf was becoming a brother—at least it felt that way.

Elf knew that Adam had the best of intentions, but he just didn't understand the stakes that were involved. Every break in the service, his mind went back to the same thought. If Herzog propositioned him, he'd only say he was testing him. It sickened him every time, so he kept busy and he kept Adam busy as well. No time for conversation, not now. Not until after his meeting with Herzog the next day.

Stevie sat, her fingernails resting in a bowl of soapy water, her hair wrapped in pieces of foil. She glanced at herself in the mirror and chuckled.

"Okay, what's so funny?" the woman working on her other hand asked.

"Oh, have a look at that mirror. If I were a kid, I'd go trick-or-treating dressed just like this."

The manicurist said, "My brother makes my daughter's costumes every year. Last year, he had my daughter go as a bride—the dress made entirely of bubble wrap with little LED lights running through it. This year, she wants to be a Christmas tree. If anyone can pull it off, he can."

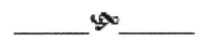

291

The crime scene manager supplied Harjo and Lake with head coverings, masks, gloves, and booties to cover their shoes. Inside Herzog's office, three crime scene techs and a photographer were intently busy. A number of evidence markers had already been placed around the room.

One of the chairs in front of Herzog's large desk was overturned. One of the techs was dusting the wooden arms for prints. A separate evidence marker was next to a picture frame, face down on the floor, and bits of glass glinted in the light through the picture window behind the desk.

"It looks like a heavy chair," Harjo said, reaching a gloved finger under the seat of its twin, gently trying to lift it.

He walked around the desk, and Lake approached Herzog from the opposite side. Herzog sat leaning forward, his forehead resting on crossed forearms like a kid putting his head down at school. Herzog's suit jacket pulled at the sleeves and bunched at the shoulders.

"If I were going to take a nap," Lake said in a soft voice, "I'd have taken off the jacket. It looks uncomfortable, a little too small for him."

"I don't think his nap was voluntary," Harjo replied in an equally calm tone. "I know this looks bleak, Lake. But this gets us closer to the truth."

Lake looked at him. "Closer?"

"Yep, closer. You'll see."

Herzog's necktie had been pulled around so that the knot was in the back and the tie hung like a leash. It still looked tight, cutting into Herzog's fleshy neck.

"Unless the perp wore gloves, there's got to be DNA on that tie. They'd have to have pulled it tight and held it for five minutes or so," Lake muttered, crouching down to glimpse Herzog's face and hands.

"The perp has had practice, and so far, he hasn't missed the mark," Harjo said.

"Looks like he has something in his mouth." Herzog's mouth was slightly open, and something protruded slightly.

Harjo bent down to look. He had to fish for a tiny pocket flashlight to see better under the hunching professor. Squinting, he said, "Could be his tongue."

"He must have had a big breakfast. His belt is undone," Lake observed.

Harjo nodded. "Maybe so." An evidence marker under the chair caught his attention. "Lake, notice the pencil wedged under the wheel of the chair." It was short, stubby, and without an eraser end, like the kind you get at IKEA.

"Maybe it fell off his desk."

"That's one explanation. It also might stop the chair from moving."

"Do you think this was staged?" Lake stood up straight.

"I don't know, but I'd be curious about what might happen if the pencil were removed."

The crime scene manager, a woman whose red hair filled the covering on her head, had a serious but pleasant face. She said, "We noticed that, too, Joe. We'll take the chair and test it out. I mean, who uses pencils these days, anyway?"

"Depends on when. If rigor is advanced, the muscle contractions might hold it in place."

Ernie's voice startled them. The ME had followed them into the room. "Transport is here. As soon as Bonnie gives the go-ahead, I'll be able to do more in the lab."

293

Harjo scanned the room again. "Bonnie, please include the pictures in your report, and I'd appreciate daily updates, if you don't mind.

Hand on hips, she smirked. "Aw, Joe. That hurts," she teased him. "When have I ever done anything else?"

"Sorry, Bonnie. Just a habit."

On the way out of the room, Harjo started talking to Lake. "We need fingerprints of everyone who has access to this office, including the students he sees in here, if we can get them. I want to talk to those three guys in New Orleans, the friends of Rhome. I'll call DuPuis to bring them in, and we'll conduct preliminaries on Zoom.

"DuPuis said two wouldn't talk."

"They'll talk. Obstruction of justice."

He leaned back and made eye contact with Bonnie. "Don't forget the computer and any external storage or drives."

"I ain't no rookie, Joe." She was smiling and shaking her head.

He held up a hand. "Sorry, again sorry. Saying it out loud just keeps things straight in my head."

She gave him a thumbs-up.

Then to Lake again. "I want to see every professor who has an office on this floor and any staff or students they've seen here. Also, add in the secretary from the first floor and any student workers. We don't go home until these interviews are scheduled. Oh, and go through that website list; I want to talk to every person who made public statements about the alleged misconduct of Professor Herzog.

Standing between Harjo and the stairs was a man in a crisp tailored suit, expensive-looking shoes, and a forcefully determined expression. He extended his hand. "Detective, I'm Alonzo Jones, the president of this institution. I want to assure you that you will have our full cooperation. I am glad you used the word 'alleged' in referring to any misconduct. I'm counting on your discretion. The reputation of our school and consequently that of our students is paramount."

Harjo looked him in the eye. "Sir, I am discretion itself, but discretion will not stand between me and solving three murders. I'm sure you will want to join your other staff in meeting with me to get to the bottom of this heinous crime."

Lake surprised himself, the old verse tumbling out of his mouth before he knew he was speaking: "Let justice roll down like waters and righteousness like an everlasting stream."

The president raised an eyebrow. "I'm impressed. Amos 5:24. But you had it a little wrong." His smile was thin, as correcting Lake was more about his authority than getting the verse correct. "It's an ever-*flowing* stream. You see, the phrase in Hebrew is—"

Harjo cut him off. "Sorry, sir, I hate to interrupt this Bible study, but Officer Lake and I have the unfortunate duty of informing Mrs. Dierdre Herzog that she is now a widow."

Twenty-Eight

Dierdre Herzog stood closely framed in the open door, the way she had the first time Harjo had summoned her with a doorbell ring. Despite the steady rain, she did not invite them in. Harjo and Lake brought along Deputy Laura Stacks, a uniformed officer who knew the Herzogs from church. Lake figured a familiar face might soften the blow for Mrs. Herzog, but Laura looked like she'd rather be anywhere else.

"I'm afraid my husband isn't here, Detective. He's at work."

"Yes, ma'am. It's you we'd like to speak with," Harjo said.

She hesitated a second, then said, "Me? I don't know anything about that student."

"It's a different matter, ma'am. It's sensitive. Perhaps we could come inside?" Laura Stacks said softly.

Dierdre squinted at Deputy Stacks. "Little Laura Stacks, is that you? I didn't know you joined the force. Keeping it in the family, I see."

"Yes, Ms. Dierdre." She smiled meekly. "It would be better if we could come in."

Stiffening, Dierdre Herzog nodded curtly with a slight grimace. "I don't have much time. I need to pick up my husband from work. His car is being detailed. It should have been done yesterday."

As they followed Mrs. Herzog into the great room, Laura whispered to Lake. "That's CJ's. My brother works there. Maybe they haven't started on it yet."

Lake got the message, lagged behind, and quietly called the auto detailer.

Laura sat next to Mrs. Herzog. Harjo took the same seat he had when he spoke to her husband. Harjo began as he had many times before: "I'm afraid I have some bad news... " He delivered the news as gently as he could and watched her reaction.

Lake wasn't sure what to expect: hysterics, denial, or anger. Harjo, having met her, knew exactly what to expect and was not disappointed.

Dierdre Herzog froze. Rain tapped on the large windows of the great room. Her backbone could have been made of steel, her shoulders squared, her face sharp, and her lips pressed together. Her lips parted slightly, but no sound came. Harjo wasn't sure she was even breathing.

The silence lasted only a moment but felt like an eternity waiting for a response.

Lake spoke up. "Ma'am, is there someone we can call to be with you? We can remain here until they arrive."

Dierdre Herzog didn't move. She didn't even look at Lake.

Harjo had learned that there was no such thing as a natural response. There was often a visceral, emotional response that might be panic, fear, anger, or gut-wrenching grief. Only rarely was there a response as stoic as Dierdre Herzog's. No tears, no loss of control.

He watched her carefully and continued. "However, we have reason to believe that his death was not natural."

Her eyes met Harjo's, but still, she did not speak. She flinched and pulled away when Deputy Stacks tried to comfort her with a touch.

Lake watched her as well. He struggled to reconcile the image of her reaching for her husband's hand as they walked across campus the day before, with her seeming lack of emotion now. She seemed stunned, in shock, as if her worst fears had come to pass. He wanted Harjo to prompt her to get some sort of reaction. *Other sins merely speak, but murder shrieks out.* He flashed on a quote from one of those thee-and-thou plays back in college that he found so intriguing.

Harjo wasn't poking, and he couldn't wait any longer. "Ma'am, I realize this is a difficult time, but we need to get to the bottom of this, and time is of the essence. Is there anyone you can think of that might want to do your husband harm?"

Her eyes moved slowly toward Lake, then back to Harjo. "Only the whole woke world. Especially those gender benders," she spat out. Pulling herself together, she calmly asked Harjo, "When will they release his body? There's a lot to arrange. My husband is... was... " she swallowed, "... a widely loved and respected man in the *Christian* world."

Harjo jumped in. "That depends on the coroner, Mrs. Herzog. You will be notified." He paused and then pushed through. "Mrs. Herzog, can you possibly narrow down the field?"

"Not really." Hands on her knees, she decisively stood up, signaling the end of the discussion. "I can't think of anyone other than that ex-con you were discussing with my husband. If I were you, I'd start there. If you don't mind, I'd like to be alone with the Lord just now." She led the way to the foyer. "I'll just see you out."

Lake and Stacks followed suit, but Harjo hesitated. "Mrs. Herzog, I'm sure you want us to find the person or persons who have caused your husband's death. I understand this is a difficult time for you, but we will need to speak with you in greater depth. I'll be in touch." He stood up slowly, straightened his jacket, and followed them out of the room.

"Pull into that gas station," Harjo said softly.

"We don't need gas, Joe," Lake said, making the turn.

"Just park near the convenience store. I'd like us to talk a little before heading back to the station."

The rain had stopped. Coffee and cellophane-wrapped pastries in hand—Harjo's treat—they went toward a picnic table under a small gazebo next to the store. Deputy Stacks felt both privileged and intimidated by being included in this detective meeting.

"Deputy, I'm interested in your impressions of Mrs. Herzog's reactions," Harjo began.

Stacks thought for a moment. "She didn't like it when I touched her. I should have known better. She's not a huggy person."

"Yes, that was an interesting reaction, but really I want to know if you think the way she reacted to her husband's death was in character."

The deputy pursed her lips. "She wouldn't want to show emotion in front of anyone. In that way, she was herself. She'd hide her feelings, whatever they were."

"Whatever they were," Lake whispered under his breath.

Harjo turned to him in appreciation. "Lake?"

"If you told me my wife was dead, I'd have a thousand questions, and I wouldn't stop asking until I got some answers. To me, she seemed more put out than upset."

Harjo nodded slowly.

Deputy Stacks snorted. Both Harjo and Lake turned toward her. She flushed. "Uh... nothing. Just a stray thought."

"What is it?"

"It's nothing, really."

"Come on, Laura," Lake said. "Out with it."

"When you said that, my first thought was, who would she be angrier with? The killer or her husband?" She raised her eyebrows and grimaced. "From what people say, she'd be more concerned about the scandal than anything else."

Harjo looked at Lake to see if he reacted to her statement. To Harjo, it was in line with his own impression of Dierdre Herzog. *If there were any truth to those websites about her husband...*

They sat in silence for a moment, sipping coffee.

"I don't want to read too much into this. It was traumatic news, after all," Harjo admitted. "Lake, we should check on the whereabouts of Flemming, Alba, and Tramonto."

The clouds parted, and a bright patch of blue sky sent a beam of sunshine across the table. Just then, his phone alerted. Harjo looked at the screen. "We got the search warrants. Let's get back. I want to brief the team."

"Hey, Joe That's her." Lake pointed to the road as the Herzog car passed by.

Elf sat at the counter, his half-eaten lunch set aside. He wasn't all that hungry. He watched Adam through the service window. Adam was smooth, unruffled, and organized. Adam would have no trouble covering for him while he met with Herzog.

His phone vibrated in his pocket. He pulled it out. Looking at the screen, the color drained from his face. He looked up at Adam behind the service window. He slid off the stool and, gathering his plate, went back into the kitchen.

"Tom says Herzog didn't show up for classes today, and his classes for tomorrow are cancelled."

"Does that mean you're meeting with him is also cancelled?" Adam asked.

Elf didn't respond at first. He seemed to be stunned, disorientated, pale.

"What's up, dude? What happened?" Adam turned to him.

"Tom says they carried him out on a stretcher. His face was covered. He's dead." He looked Adam in the eye. Shaking his head, he said, "I-I don't know how I feel about it."

Ben had been squirmy all day at school, having difficulty concentrating and watching the clock. When the final bell rang, he bolted out the door and ran the whole way home. He didn't wait for the bus. Too much energy and too little patience. His brother Tom would be home tomorrow. There'd be breakfast at the Pioneer's Rest on Saturday and ice cream after church on Sunday. But the best part of all was that he'd get to be a little brother again instead of the man of the house.

When he got home, it was still too early to meet Elf to play his favorite game online. He booted up and logged in anyway.

He spawned at Druid's Clearing, a quiet forest zone where players sometimes camped between quests. It was almost empty.

Perched under a tree was WolfRyder, a player Ben had noticed before, always solo, always watching, rarely part of a team. His armor was basic but patched together like someone who knew how to survive. BenTheBold jogged over.

Using his mic, "Hey, WolfRyder. Are you here?"

There was a pause. Then WolfRyder's avatar turned and gave a slow nod. "Yeah, you usually run with that Elf, right?"

Ben blinked. "Yeah! He's my friend. He's not on yet, though. You wanna run a quest with me while we wait?"

"You asking me to team up?"

"Yeah, dude. Why not? The Hollow is spawning rares right now. We could hit it before the crowd shows up."

Another pause. Then WolfRyder stood up and unsheathed a glowing short sword. "I've never really... like teamed up from the start. I just get pulled into groups sometimes. Nobody really asks."

Ben's voice softened. "Well, I'm asking. Wanna party up?"

A ping appeared on WolfRyder's screen: BenTheBold has sent you a party invite. He clicked *Accept*.

"Cool. Just, uh... I might have to bounce kinda quick. Real-world stuff."

"No worries, dude. If you gotta log off, I'll save your share of the loot."

"Thanks. That's cool of you."

As they jogged off toward the grove's edge, a message popped up on WolfRyder's screen: "You are now in a party."

And for the first time in a long time, he wasn't playing alone.

The quest was done, treasure and weapons earned. Caleb felt like he was part of the team. Then he heard the real-world doorbell ring. He gave Ben a wave and logged off.

Alex was already opening the door when he walked out of the room. He recognized the woman from social services, and behind her stood Jason and Will, without Cagney and Lacey.

Caleb stopped short, not believing his eyes. "You?"

"Hey, kiddo. Yep. Us," Jason said with a broad grin. Will, a little more reserved, couldn't hide his delight at the surprise.

Seeing Caleb's reaction, Alex glowed and had to fight off a tear.

"Really? I mean, for real?"

Jason laughed. "For real. This time, however, we brought paperwork instead of poop bags. That is, if you want to live with us. You can stay in the same school. Alex is close by. And Cagney and Lacey can't wait."

Caleb looked at Alex, who nodded approvingly.

Harjo sat alone in his office, a look of satisfaction on his face. His main suspect dead—killed by the same hand that had taken Candy Yates and Christian Rhome. Tramonto, Flemming, and Alba had all alibied out completely.

He leaned back, elbows on the arms of his chair, fingers tenting in front of him. His thoughts ran through the possibilities, like a chess player planning three moves ahead. Only two possibilities remained. It would come down to testimony, confession, or forensics.

Twenty-Nine

I t had been a long and tedious day. Usually, days went by quickly, always moving, always alert. As of late, it was the evenings that had been restfully uneventful. The day had certainly been eventful, but his range of movement and attention were purposefully restricted. He had found it difficult not to daydream, even harder not to involve himself either by watching or taking part. He was more tired than he had ever been.

He told himself, only another hour or so and he'd be on his way home. He looked forward to stopping at Reasor's, picking up one of their frozen pizzas and eating the whole thing for dinner while watching the news. Hell, he'd probably fall asleep in the middle of it all, but it would be a good sleep.

Driving down the alleyway behind the Creekstone Hotel, his eyes scanned all the key points. The door to the dumpster enclosure was slightly open. A homeless man with a bushy mustache, wearing a baseball cap and a long raincoat, sidled out of the opening, carrying what looked like a handful of discarded rolls. The man nodded at him as he slowed down.

He nodded back and smiled. His eyes flashed at the cameras on the back of the building. One hung awkwardly on the hinges; the other was shot out. His heart began to beat harder in his chest, and he could feel sweat under his hands on the steering wheel. His first thought was to ask the homeless man if he had seen anything, but the homeless man was already gone.

He kept driving so as not to attract attention. Tonight will be the night. It was going down. There was more adrenaline running through his veins than blood. He could hear the palpitations of his heart, even feel them in his ears.

He pulled into the hotel parking lot. His usual space was empty. He parked. The dumpster enclosure was in full view. All he had to do now was wait for Alba.

It was just before four in the afternoon. Alba's bike was chained to a tree on one of the islands dividing the parking lot. He unlatched his door and left it slightly open. The warning bell would stop in a few seconds. He slunk down in his seat. He fixed his eyes on the hotel's back door.

Alba would be out in less than half an hour. He'd use the right-hand metal door to the enclosure. Alba habitually used the left dumpster. The window of opportunity was narrow. To happen out of sight, it had to happen when Alba was inside the dumpster enclosure.

He used all his training to stay out of sight, alert, and wait.

Adam didn't know what to make of the news that Herzog was dead. All Tom had said was that there were lots of police around. *Of course,* he thought, *it could be natural causes. Any unattended death would attract the police. But what if it wasn't? Which one of Herzog's victims might take their revenge? Did it really have something to do with the Balustrade? One of the twinks, perhaps? But then why go after Candy or even the Butterfly?*

Maybe it was one of those clandestine patrons who didn't want to be discovered. Someone like that would never do it themselves; they'd pay someone.

306

Adam tried not to think about it but couldn't help it. His job, at least at the beginning of his shift, was routine. He could do it without thinking at all, so his mind was free to roam, and it roamed to Elf and his feelings about Herzog. *Did Elf really believe that Herzog was a man of good and honorable intentions? Could he be that blind?*

He gathered the half-empty trash liner, tying the top with the built-in drawstring. It gave a subtle sucking sound as he pulled it from the bin. New liner in place, he headed out to the dumpster with the day's trash.

The day had an amber tone. The rain had cooled off the pavement, but humidity hung in the air like a blanket. Each time Adam took out the trash, he thought the same thing. How long would it be before he wouldn't think of Candy? Perhaps it would linger forever like his shadow, nipping at his heels.

He noticed that one of the huge metal doors to the enclosure was open enough to just sneak through. He opened it a little more and entered. As he reached for the lid of the dumpster, he heard what sounded like a piece of windblown cardboard skitter along the pavement.

The mallet felt like the punch of a prizefighter to his temple. The pain was instantaneous. He felt it reverberate down his neck and spine. Then everything went black, and he was far away from Broken Arrow. Ken Griffin, his last wrestling opponent, was bent over him, trying to wrap a silk scarf around his neck. He wanted to tell Ken he'd be alright. Blackness again.

Finally, he saw Adam exit the hotel carrying the trash bag. Eyes fixed, he watched him push the metal door open and step inside the dumpster enclosure.

From the shadows, movement. The homeless man in the long raincoat and cap slipped through the opening behind Adam.

In an instant, the watcher was out of his car and closing in, quiet as a cat and lightning fast. If the killer kept his pattern, it would take several minutes. Plenty of time to get the advantage, but the faster, the better.

He reached the open door, pressed his back to the warm metal, and peered through the gap between the hinges. The raincoat figure was kneeling beside Adam's limp body, looping a silk scarf beneath his neck.

The watcher moved. In one smooth motion, he had the muzzle of his pistol pressed hard against the back of the figure's neck.

"Do not move," he said in a low, sharp voice.

The figure froze.

"Listen carefully, the slightest wrong move and I will blow your brains all over this alley. Do you understand me?"

A stiff nod.

"Hands behind your back. Now!" Pushing the figure down, metal cuffs flashing in the amber light. Practice made the work quick, efficient, and clean. He rolled the suspect onto their back, then stopped, staring at the face.

The bushy false mustache was peeling away. He tugged it free. The suspect gasped. A woman's eyes wide, unblinking, and furious.

"Dierdre Herzog," he said, keeping his voice steady. "You are under arrest for the assault and attempted murder of Adam Alba. You have the right to remain silent. Anything you say can and will be used against you in a court of law.

He pressed the radio on his shoulder. "Officer Terrance Gamble requesting immediate backup and an ambulance to the rear of the Creekstone Hotel."

Thirty

"I was off duty, on my own time, doing nothing illegal." Terry Gamble was in Harjo's office, and it felt like he was sitting in the hot seat, trying to defend himself for saving Adam Alba's life.

"We both read your report, Officer Gamble. Stalking is a crime. And weren't you disobeying orders by going back to the Creekstone?" Harjo pressed.

"With all due respect, sirs," his eyes shifted from one to the other, "I wasn't stalking Adam Alba. I never followed him home. I never parked outside his house. I never sent him any messages. He didn't even know I was there."

Lake nodded. "You were told to stop going to the Creekstone."

Gamble puffed out a sigh. Despite the heroic outcome, he wondered if he would be leaving his badge and gun behind. Gathering his strength, he said, "I was told to stop going to the Creekstone *lounge*. Whether that was a valid order or not, I followed it." He sucked in a long breath and spoke carefully. "I admit I was playing detective. I wanted to see what it would feel like to be undercover, to see what I

311

would notice. My notebook makes that obvious. It was for no one but me, but I gave it to you. And, well, now, it is evidence, isn't it?"

Lake asked, "Why didn't you tell us this when we talked in the lounge?"

Gamble looked from side to side as if he were searching for something that was missing. "Look, I was embarrassed. I was a rookie playing a childish game." Then to Harjo, "What would you have said to me, or what would you have thought about me if I told you?"

Harjo suppressed a smile. "I would have told you to leave it alone and just do your job."

Resolute, Gamble looked Harjo in the eye and said, "And Adam Alba would be dead. All I did was follow your hunch that Alba was somehow in the center of the case. I heard what you said about his being a possible victim. I was there when you questioned him. Remember? I figured if Alba was somehow in the center of things, he would still be a target."

Lake looked at Harjo in recognition of the times Harjo insisted on his hunch. Harjo saw the glance and got the message.

Gamble continued. "When you and Lake pulled me out of the Creekstone lounge, I followed orders. I never went back inside. Of course, as it turns out, it worked out for the best."

Harjo looked at Lake and smiled. "Terry, you know you'll have to testify and that means cross-examination by one of the best defense attorneys in Oklahoma. Dierdre Herzog comes from a wealthy and well-connected family."

Gamble nodded. "Is that really what this is all about?"

They didn't answer, but Terry Gamble felt better. For the first time in weeks, it felt like they were on his side.

312

Harjo said, "I want you to meet with the city attorney. Have you testified in court before?"

Gamble shook his head. "No, sir."

"Someone will work with you. And thanks."

They stood up and shook hands, and Gamble left the office, closing the door behind him.

Harjo said, "It'll be up to forensics to tie Dierdre Herzog to the Yates and Rhome murders."

"We have the rubber mallet and the scarf," Lake said.

Harjo nodded, "Now we need science to tell us what Dierdre Herzog won't."

Stevie Tramonto opened the door to find Officer Lake on her front porch. She recognized him from the coffee shop. "What can I do for you, Officer? I hope you're not here to tell me someone else is dead."

"No, Ms. Tramonto, but I'd like to talk to you. Perhaps we could sit down."

Stevie didn't like the sound of that. She would have preferred him to get right to the point, but this was the South after all. "Certainly, come in. I was just making a cup of tea. Have a seat at the table… I'll get you one, too."

"Ms. Tramonto." Lake's face was serious. "Dierdre Herzog was released on bail after her arraignment this morning."

The news surprised her, but she didn't need to be seated to hear it. She shook her head. "Isn't that something," Stevie said sarcastically. "A woman murders three people and tries to kill a fourth, and she walks out on bail!"

"I'm afraid she was arraigned only on the crime witnessed by Officer Gamble," Lake conceded.

"Why are you telling me this?" Stevie asked, setting a cup of tea in front of the Lake. She sat down and stirred some allulose into her own cup.

"We had to hand over to her lawyers the evidence we had. We're relying on forensics to give us enough evidence for two of the three murders."

Stevie held up a ringed hand; her bracelets sounded like chimes. "Let me guess. The kind of evidence that links that woman to the first two murders wouldn't mean much when her husband was the victim."

Lake's eyebrows rose appreciably.

She continued. "That list of websites about her husband and my confronting them on the Bible school campus is going to be used to establish a motive, isn't it?"

"You are absolutely right. Things like fibers or DNA would be expected between a husband and wife. Your evidence and testimony are all we have right now on that case."

"That and the modus operandi."

"There are differences that her attorney will certainly exploit," he admitted.

"So, I'll likely have to testify in court." She exhaled as if she had been holding her breath.

"That is up to the prosecutor, but it's a reasonable assumption. We're looking for other evidence, emails, letters, text messages, anything to show that she knew about her husband's activities and objected to them."

"And now she's out on bail, and you think she might come after me?" She set her teacup down. It was as if it had suddenly gone cold and unappealing.

Lake nodded. "It's a possibility, ma'am."

After a pause, Stevie said, "No, she wouldn't be stupid enough to do it herself. She'd get someone else." She thought of Adam. *That means Adam isn't out of the woods either.* She felt a little relief knowing that he preferred to keep his back to the wall.

Lake thoughtfully tried to find the right words. He didn't want to frighten this woman, but frightened is better than dead. "Ms. Stevie, Dierdre Herzog comes from a very respected and influential family." He hoped that was enough to get his message across.

"She's well-connected," Stevie said crinkling her nose.

She smiled, pushing her cup to one side. She leaned toward him. "Detective, I grew up in Brooklyn. I have been watching my own back my entire life. It's a habit."

Lake looked down at the floor for a moment. "Glad to hear that, Ms. Tramonto. I'd like to ask you for a sworn deposition. Mr. Alba is in the process of doing so as we speak."

"You mean, in case something happens to me," she said resignedly.

Lake shrugged and nodded at the same time.

Elf sat in the last pew of the chapel. The final week of hermeneutics class had been cancelled since Herzog's death, and Elf hadn't been able to stop obsessing about the last thing the professor might have written in his grade book. Every time he thought of it, every time the angst built up in his gut, he prayed for forgiveness. Forgiveness for being selfish, for thinking first of himself, for being relieved that he didn't have to face Herzog again. Were those the sins that had turned the heavens to brass? Had God looked away, closed His ears, and left Elf to figure it all out on his own?

Tom had already left. Without classes, he would spend the next week with his family back in Ur. Elf thought of his ex-girlfriend, Grace, and reprimanded himself for not having been better at helping her through her own journey through the shadow of death. Death really did cast shadows, dark ones that never left. No matter which direction you looked, they were there.

His Bible in his lap was opened to the book of Psalms. He had tried to read Psalm 22 any number of times. He had had to Google the verse he was looking for and felt embarrassed about that. He just couldn't concentrate. His eyes passed over words that meant nothing. He wanted—needed—someone to talk to.

Staring at the shapes through the tall, frosted glass windows behind the pulpit, he disappeared into them, a world of vague images in the blinding glow of the sun through the frosted glass.

He wasn't alone in the chapel. There were two other students also seeking some quiet and solitude. They were far enough apart that they didn't have to be aware of one another. Elf could feel them, though. He felt transparent, vulnerable, and profane.

He was so annoyed that someone was entering the pew he occupied that he closed his eyes to avoid any conversation whatsoever. He thought it might be Mrs. Herzog. Adam had told him she was released on bail. He wouldn't know what to say to her. More to the point, what might she say to him?

As the woman sat down next to him, he thought he heard chimes. Then, a gentle touch on his wrist as she said, "I thought I might find you here."

He steeled himself and opened his eyes. He looked into the compassionate eyes of Adam's friend, Stevie Tramonto. Inside, he melted. He didn't know why, but he felt like crying.

"This is a beautiful place, but not a place for talking. Let's just go out to the lobby. I want to tell you a story."

He nodded and followed her.

They sat together on a leather sofa. She began. "I think I might know how you feel. When I was a little girl, there was this priest... "

As he listened to her story, he knew that she really did understand. She also helped him understand how Tom might feel if and when the truth about Herzog was revealed.

He silently thanked God for seeing the desire of his heart and giving him what he needed before he even asked.

Epilogue

"Enzo! Your friend is back!" Angelina called out as Adam and the others came in and took a booth in the back. Baxter slid in next to Adam, and Elf sat beside Stevie. Angelina brought water and took their orders before retreating to the counter.

"I still can't get over the jury getting hung up on the third count," Stevie said, stirring her water with a straw. "We all know that bitch killed her husband."

Baxter leaned back. "It's called reasonable doubt."

"Unreasonable doubt, if you ask me," Stevie huffed. "It's obvious. Anyone who knew her husband wasn't who he pretended to be had to go."

Adam said, "Do you think they'll retry the case?"

Baxter shrugged. "Not without new evidence. I hear her family wants this whole thing to fade away. From what I hear, the prosecutor's reading the wind."

"The school does too," Elf said. "Students have been told not to talk to reporters about Professor Herzog."

Baxter nodded. "Funny thing—in Choctaw culture, you can grow up good or turn out bad, you're still Choctaw. Family doesn't stop being family."

Adam smiled, thinking of Henry and Halona back in Ur. "Same for Italians. Your family will call you an ass to your face but defend you to everyone else."

Stevie waved her hand. The chiming of her bracelets made Elf smile. The sound reminded him that he wasn't alone in the world.

"My family would use stronger language," she said, "but it works out to the same thing."

Thoughtfully, Elf's voice softened. "Sentencing in two weeks. I remember my time waiting for sentencing. It was hell on earth."

Stevie squeezed his hand under the table.

"Think she'll get the death penalty?" Stevie asked, glancing at Baxter.

He considered for a moment. "Depends on what the judge sees as mitigating circumstances. I doubt it, though—not because she doesn't deserve it. By Oklahoma standards, she does. More likely because it would mean years of appeals. Her family will want this to go away quietly. No doubt there'll be people talking to the judge, framing it as what is best for Oklahoma."

Angelina arrived with two steaming pizzas, filling the air with the aroma of oregano, tomato sauce, and cheese. Conversation paused. Plates were passed around and napkins unfolded.

Adam caught Stevie scraping the toppings off her slice, setting the crust aside. "What the hell are you doing?" he asked, making a pleading gesture with his hands.

She returned a sheepish smile. "Cutting carbs."

Adam laughed, shaking his head. "After everything we've been through... "

Stevie smiled, shrugged, and bit into a forkful of pizza toppings.

He leaned back, savoring the warmth of being with friends—real friends. For the first time in a very long while, the shadows felt like they belonged to someone else.

About the Author

Joseph Onesta is a board-certified clinical hypnotist, author, and speaker based in Pittsburgh, Pennsylvania. Known for blending science, storytelling, and humor, he helps clients and readers explore the mind's role in healing and transformation.

In his acclaimed Adam Alba Mystery series—beginning with Long Shadows and continuing with Shifting Shadows, Onesta weaves psychological insight and emotional depth into stories of suspense, redemption, and self-discovery.

When not writing or working with clients, he enjoys good coffee, good company, and tending his vegetable garden, where new stories often take shape.

P.S. Book Three in the Adam Alba Mystery series is coming soon!

Adam returns home to Pittsburgh for Christmas, expecting a quiet family visit—but the holidays bring a reckoning with a past that threatens his future.

Visit www.AdamAlbaMysteries.com to sign up and be the first to know when the next mystery is released!